DEVIL'S PAWN

THE DEVIL'S PAWN DUET
BOOK 1

NATASHA KNIGHT

NOTE FROM THE AUTHOR

IVI

Imperium Valens Invictum

The story you are about to enjoy is set in the world of *The Society* created by A. Zavarelli and Natasha Knight. Although you do not need to read any other books to follow this story, here is a brief description of what IVI is and how it operates.

Imperium Valens Invictum, or IVI for short, is Latin for Strong Unconquered Power. The organization is frequently referred to by its members as The Society.

We are a well-established organization rooted in

powerful dynasties around the world. Some call us thieves in the night. A criminal syndicate. Mafia. The truth is much more intricate than of those simplistic terms.

Our ancestors learned long ago there was power in secrecy. The legacy handed down to us was much more evolved than that of the criminals waging war on each other in the streets. We have money. We have power. And we are much more sophisticated than your average knee-breaking Italian mob boss.

IVI holds its members in the highest regard. With that power comes expectation. Education. Professionalism. And above all, discretion. By day, we appear as any other well-bred member of society. They don't and never will know the way our organization operates.

Thirteen families founded the ancient society. These families are held in the highest regard and referred to as the Upper Echelon. These are the Sovereign Sons and Daughters of The Society.

The Society has its own judicial branch, The Tribunal, that operates outside the norms of what is acceptable in the world today. Its laws are the final law for Society members.

The Society will go to great lengths to protect its members from the outside world but their expectations are often higher and sentences handed down from The Tribunal often harsher if even, at times, Medieval.

Welcome to The Society...

1

ISABELLE

A masquerade ball. What can be more beautiful? More perfect? Especially one put on by The Society.

Bouquets of flowers spill over tables set with the best china. Waiters serve champagne in crystal flutes and an eight-piece orchestra plays a waltz beneath the dazzling glow of a dozen chandeliers.

It's every girl's fantasy.

Every girl but me.

I stand in the shadows and watch the dancers. Men and women move together as if they've practiced this all their lives. I wonder if they are guests or professional dancers hired by The Society to add to the ambiance. I wouldn't be surprised if it was the latter because I'm pretty sure I didn't look like they do when I danced with the stream of men my brother, Carlton, arranged for me.

I shudder at the thought of my last dance partner. A man old enough to be my grandfather.

A breeze blows into the grand Baroque ballroom as someone opens a window a few feet from me. The rain has slowed to a drizzle and the room is muggy even with the air conditioning running on high.

After a quick glance to confirm Carlton isn't watching, I drink the last of my champagne and set the empty flute on a nearby table. I slip quietly toward the exit and out the double French doors that stand open, in spite of the damp night.

In the courtyard, small tents have been erected to protect guests from the rain. They're decorated with warmly glowing lanterns and too many flowers to count. Men and women collect beneath the tents drinking, smoking their cigarettes and laughing too loudly.

Everyone turns to look at me as I pass. It's the dress. It's ridiculous with its feather skirt that barely reaches mid-thigh and the cinched waist of the corset top which is seriously limiting my oxygen supply. Carlton's choice. It showed all my best attributes apparently. At least the mask, which I liken to chainmail, leaves only my eyes on display.

The mask is pretty with it's delicate gold chains and coins brushing my shoulders with each step. And it offers some protection from curious eyes. The too-revealing dress I could do without.

Deciding to risk the drizzle that will likely make

the feathers of my dress wilt, I hurry to the small chapel on the other side of the courtyard. No one will be there. I know that for sure. Society members may profess to be religious but from what I've seen, they're going through the motions. Showing up in their Sunday best, each outdoing the other, at least where fashion is concerned.

The wooden door is heavy. It creaks open just far enough to let me slip inside. I close it behind me and breathe a sigh of relief at the familiar sight, familiar scent. I miss incense when I'm away too long and Carlton isn't the church-going type.

I like this particular chapel especially. I have since I was little and my mom brought me with her when she cleaned the compound. I still remember sitting in the front pew, my legs too short for my feet to touch the floor. I remember how at home I felt when she sat me here to wait for her while she did her work.

I walk to that pew now, taking in the usual shadows of the place. The only light comes from candles lit along alcoves in the walls and those on the altar. When I get to the center of the aisle, I bow my head, make the sign of the cross, then take a seat. I slip off my shoes. The heels are too high and the fit too narrow. I touch the familiar carving in the pew. Two initials. *CY*.

It's the same seat I always take when I can get here. Right in the front row as if God could see me

better for it. It's not that I ask for anything. I know
better than that. It's not even that I pray. I just close
my eyes and feel the silence here. The absolute
absence of sound.

It's better than any masquerade ball. Better than
dances with a hundred men as Carlton brokers a
union that will benefit the family. I don't think it's
crossed his mind what I want. Don't think he's
considered the fact that while it may benefit his—
our—family, it has already taken me off the course
I'd set for myself years ago.

But I can't dwell. Not now. I need a reprieve and
this chapel, these stolen moments, are it.

And so, I open my eyes and lift my gaze to the
altar. One of the candles that is usually lit has blown
out. I wonder if I did that when I walked in. I get up
to relight it.

A creak along the back of the chapel startles me.
I gasp, spin around. It's darkest there, just before the
baptismal font. Almost pitch black. I peer into the
shadows but see no movement, hear no other sound.

"Is someone there?" I ask, feeling silly when no
one answers.

It's old wood creaking. That's all.

I turn back around, trying to ward off the chill
that's clung to me all night. But I remind myself it's
always cooler in the chapel and resume my walk to
the altar. There, I find the book of matches and

strike one. The flame glows bright and I have to stand on tiptoe to reach the wick of the tall candle.

Soon it's lit and I'm blowing out the match when the sound of laughter from just beyond the door disrupts the peace of this place. Before I know it, the chapel door slams against the wall.

I jump.

Two men stumble in, laughing as they do, and one rushes to shove the door closed behind him. With them they bring the stench of alcohol and weed. The moment I see their faces, I'm sure they're both high. I can see it in their red eyes, in the flush of their skin, hear it in their strange, giddy laughter.

I'd guess them to be twenty, twenty-one maybe. Just a year or two older than me. And I recognize one of them. I danced with him not one hour ago. Although I can't recall his name. Only that I didn't like him. Didn't like the way his fingers caressed the exposed skin of my back as he spun me around the dance floor.

"There she is," he says, as if recognizing me, too. His mask is pushed to the top of his head and he licks his lips, allowing his gaze to linger at the swell of my breasts above the bodice of the dress. "That's the girl," he tells his companion with a nudge of his elbow.

The other ones eyes are locked on me, mouth hard, set in an ugly line.

"The Bishop girl," he says. Both come closer, one stopping behind me. "Half-Bishop," he clarifies.

"The right half," the other one says, and they both laugh although I don't get the joke. "Let's get that thing off your head so we can get a proper look at you," he says, reaching for the clip holding my mask in place.

"I don't think so," I tell him, stepping out of his reach but in doing so cornering myself against the altar.

"Why not? I wouldn't make a deal with your brother sight unseen. You never know, am I right?"

"I think Manson is the one making the deal, bro," his friend says and makes a face.

He reaches again and this time when he gets his fingers in my hair I shove at him with both hands, managing to push him backward. He's off balance because he's both high and drunk. I realize how much more dangerous that makes him when his eyes narrow to angry slits as his friend laughs.

"Excuse me, I need to get back," I say, turning to slip away, managing to take a step before he catches my arm.

I stop, look at his hand then up at him. I paste a smile on my face and step closer. My heart thuds against my chest. I'm not sure if I'm more angry or afraid but I know two things.

First, I need to get away from these two or it's not going to bode well for me. And second, I cannot show my fear no matter what. Some men get a high from that alone.

"My brother is on his way. He won't like you putting your hands on me," I say.

"I wouldn't call this putting my hands on you," he says, then turns to his friend. "Would you?"

His friend shakes his head. "Nope."

"Now this I'd call putting my hands on you," the one who has hold of me says, turning me slightly and slapping my ass so hard that I stumble forward. It makes both men erupt in laughter as his grip around my arm tightens.

But that's when I hear that same sound I heard before. Coming from the same shadowy corner. Except this time, it's not creaking wood.

Something moves when I look to the spot.

Dust motes dance in candlelight, but the two who barged into the chapel don't notice the shift in the air until we hear the footfalls. They turn and we all watch as the darkness takes form and begins to move toward us.

My heart pounds against my chest and for a moment, I'm not sure if it's man or beast for the shadow it casts. But then I recognize the long black cloak of the Sovereign Sons. It billows around the man making that darkness following him even bigger, more frightening.

He's too tall. Too broad-shouldered. Everything about him too dark, from the black-on-black beneath the traditional cloak, to the horned mask hiding his face, to the fury directed at the men who've cornered me.

He doesn't bother with words. He simply steps toward us, the two looking like boys as he looms closer, towering over them in build and height and sheer presence. He glances only momentarily at me before his eyes hone in on the one grasping my arm. It seems to take no effort at all for him to pry the man's hand off me. My tormentor's face contorts in pain as the masked stranger twists his arm behind his back. His friend backs away one step, two before running for the door.

"What the fuck, man?" cries the one who can't run. "Let go!"

The stranger twists a little more.

"She's not yours to break," he whispers, voice low and hard.

I process the words, shudder at the strange sense of foreshadowing.

I realize I've backed up against the altar. I'm staring, mouth gaping, heart racing. And I see what the mask he's wearing portrays. Some sort of horned beast. A devil.

But it's when he pins me with his gaze that something drops to my stomach, possibly my heart, because I stop thinking. Stop breathing.

I stare back into the darkest eyes I've ever seen.

Danger.

It's the only thought I have. The single word my mind can muster.

One of his eyes is midnight blue, the other a steely gray. And his gaze is full of something so malevolent, I feel it like fire burning my flesh.

It's an eternity before he releases me from his gaze and simultaneously shoves the drunk man toward the door. A moment later I'm alone with the masked stranger.

He'd been here all along. Sitting in the shadows silently watching me.

All night I'd felt it. Eyes on me. All night I'd felt that chill. I shudder now because it was him. This masked man. I recognize the sensation, the unease. That sense of being exposed. Alone in a room full of people.

My mouth goes dry. I press my back to the altar, hands clutching the edge of it.

His gaze roams over me leaving goose bumps in its wake. I shudder. He must see it. Must realize I'm terrified. And only when he takes a step back are my lungs able to work again. Am I able to draw breath again.

"You shouldn't be in here alone," he says. "It's not safe for a woman alone when there's alcohol and idiots about."

I stare up at him, stupefied.

"Your shoes," he says.

"What?" I ask, my voice a whisper.

He gestures down and I look at my bare feet, then up at him. I point to where I'd left them. He gets my shoes and carries them back to me. He stands just a little too close, too much in my space like it's his, like it belongs to him and I'm the invader.

I still can't seem to move.

"I won't eat you," he says in that low, rumbling voice.

My chest shudders with a deep breath. I tell myself to relax. It's nothing. He just saved me. What I felt, that chill, it's just my imagination.

"Not yet anyway," he says, and I know he's grinning beneath his mask.

I swallow. I'm shaking.

He bends to set my shoes on the floor. I take in the sheer size of him. He's easily twice as big as me. He straightens and holds out his hand, palm up. Along his wrist I see the creeping of a tattoo. A serpent's tail.

I'm staring. It takes all I have to drag my gaze up to his.

"Put your shoes on," he says.

My throat is too dry to speak, to form words or make sound, so I slip my hand into his and gasp at the sudden shock.

He closes his fingers around mine and I feel the sheer power in the palm of his hand as he holds me steady. He studies me for a long, long moment before I blink, lowering my gaze and slipping on my shoes.

"Good," he says, and I just keep standing there, my hand trapped inside his.

The gong announcing dinner rings. I look up at him.

He lets his gaze drop to my lips, then lower, to the swell of my breasts. Sweat slides down the back of my neck. He releases my hand and cups the gold chains hanging from my mask as if weighing them, his eyebrows furrowing.

"Isabelle Bishop," he says, looking at me again.

He knows my name. How does he know my name?

The gong sounds a second time. And, after long moments of silence, a third.

He steps backward.

"Go back to the party, Isabelle Bishop, and remember to keep out of dark rooms. You never know who's lying in wait."

2

JERICHO

I turn my back on the girl and walk out of the chapel. I should have known not to come here. Known I wouldn't find solace even in the chapel. Not while any Bishop lives and breathes.

Half-Bishop, my brain clarifies.

Bishop all the same, I tell it.

I adjust my mask as I step into the courtyard. The drizzle has turned to rain. Her ridiculous feather dress will be ruined. Carlton Bishop will be pissed. I turn in the direction of the darker building. Set apart from the main part of the compound, it's unlit except for one window. But before I've taken half a dozen steps, the phone in my pocket vibrates with a message.

I dig it out, glance at the screen. Open the message because it's my mother.

Come home.

Something twists inside me at the words, and I pause. She knows not to message me unless it's important. And I know it is when her next text comes through.

She needs you.

I don't hesitate. I change direction, heading back toward the courtyard as I type out my reply.

On my way.

Then, to Councilor Hildebrand, the man sitting inside that single lit room in the Tribunal building, I type another.

Change of plans. Meeting is at my house.

I hit send then do something I hadn't planned. I type out a second message to Hildebrand.

Bring the girl. I will take possession tonight.

I switch off the phone before Hildebrand can reply, not quite sure why I sent that last part. It will upend the plans set in place. Plans I have been working on for too long.

Voices quiet as I pass through the courtyard, my cloak billowing in my wake. I don't care. I stand tall, walk through the center, the sea of people parting at my approach. They're afraid of me. Intrigued too, but more afraid.

They should be. Because the rumors are true. Jericho St. James is back. Returned home from self-imposed exile.

Let them know.

Let word get to Carlton Bishop if it hasn't already.

I want him trembling.

For five years he's lived his life while I've been in hiding. Not for myself. No. If it was only me, I'd have returned. Taken my revenge. Killed him. Even if I died doing it.

No, my disappearance from life was to keep something—someone—much more precious safe. My daughter.

But it's not her I'm thinking about now. It's the woman I left behind in that chapel. Her small hand in mine. The strange feel of it.

What would she have done if I'd not been there? What would those men have done?

Men. No, not men. Boys. Entitled idiots. The future of The Society, for fuck's sake. But what would she have done? How would she have defended herself? She's small. Half my size. How will she defend herself against me?

As soon as I set foot out of the gates of the compound, the valet rounds the corner with my Lamborghini. He comes to a stop inches from me. I rip off my mask and toss it to the ground as the kid steps out of the vehicle looking awestruck as if I'm some god. Although it's love for my car, not me.

"You took good care of it?" I ask as I reach into my pocket for my wallet.

He nods enthusiastically. "Didn't let it out of my sight, sir."

I slip him a hundred-dollar-bill. "Good job," I

say, patting his shoulder before sliding into the driver's seat.

The kid closes the door and I drive onto the rainy street. I'm weaving through traffic to return to the house, to what should be my home. The place I love. The place I've stayed away from for too long.

All because of them.

Isabelle Bishop's electric blue eyes dance before me. I wonder if it was fear that lit them up or if that's their color. Like broken glass. Shards and shards of it.

My dick twitches in anticipation of those eyes staring up at me when I push her to her knees. When I take her. Own her. I smile at the images. Look forward to them. And I have to force myself to come back to the why of this. To the fact that she's a Bishop. I remind myself why I was in that chapel in the first place. To remember. To pay my respects. To tell the dead that they are not forgotten. That the time for vengeance has come. Finally.

This is what I need to keep at the forefront of my mind. Not the Bishop girl's pretty eyes.

I turn onto the drive of the house and the gates slide open. It's the only house on several acres of land a few miles outside of the city. The only drawback is the property it backs into. Bishop land.

The car whines as I slow. It's built for speed. Wants it. I drive along the circular drive where the front door opens and Dex, my right-hand-man, steps out to greet me.

I climb out of the car and toss him the keys. He's been with me for five years. He's closer to me than my brother.

"All good?" he asks.

I nod. "What happened here?"

"She wants you. Your mother's been up there with her for a while but she's struggling."

I nod, go inside. Although we've lived well these last five years, she's not used to this scale of things. Or the age of the ancient mansion. The St. James estate is several centuries old and although modernized, there are plenty of dark corners and ghosts. I will teach her they don't mean her harm. But five is a tender age.

The house is lit in soft golden light. My shoes sound as I make my way across the marble floor to the grand staircase standing as the centerpiece of the round foyer. I hurry up to her room, remembering the feel of the banister beneath my hand, the dips in the marble where it's worn over centuries. Carpet softens my footfalls as I make my way down the curving hallway to Angelique's room. I set my hand on the doorknob and take a breath in, banishing thoughts of The Society, of the Bishops. Of the girl with eyes like blue glass. I put on a smile and open the bedroom door.

"Daddy!" Angelique calls from the bed.

I force my smile to widen even as I take in her pale face, the shadows in her eyes. They don't belong in a child her age and I mean to banish them. The only thing she has done wrong is being born to me for a father.

My heart constricts as I make my way across the large, primarily yellow room. My brother outdid himself.

"What are you still doing awake, sweetheart?" I ask as softly as I can while my mother quietly stands from the bed, comforting my daughter. "It's very late."

Angelique glances at her grandmother, then back at me. I study her eyes. Familiar. A carbon copy of my own. But that's all she inherited from me. Her beauty comes from her mother. As does her gentle nature.

"I was scared," she confesses. "It's too dark here."

I brush her wild curls over her shoulders and hug her. She feels so small. So vulnerable. "You're safe here, Angelique. I'm here. Uncle Zeke is here. Your grandmother is here."

I wonder sometimes if she inherited her instinctual fear the moment she was born. The day she was ripped from the safety of her mother's womb into a violent, cruel world.

I draw in a deep, tight breath. My arms stiffen and it takes all I have to relax. To hide this part of myself from her. Because I don't want to be on the list of things she fears.

"I'll leave this light on for you," my mother says,

switching on a lamp across the room. "Will that make you feel better?"

"And open the curtain?" Angelique asks.

"No moon or stars tonight," I tell her. "Only rain."

She shrugs a shoulder. "I like rain."

"Then we'll leave the curtains open."

She smiles and lays down. I bend to kiss her forehead and tuck her in.

"How long will we stay this time?" she asks. She has moved from house to house, hotel to hotel, for all her life. A girl in hiding. A girl who didn't exist until just a few days ago.

"This is home," I say, standing. It's time for her to come out of hiding. Time for her to live. "We're here to stay, Angelique."

"You too?"

Fuck. She hasn't forgotten how often I disappeared. Left her with her grandmother and a slew of soldiers to guard her while I tracked down her mother's killers.

"Me too," I tell her. And I mean it. I'm home too. It's time for me to live, too.

She nods and I watch her eyelids flutter closed.

"Goodnight, sweet girl," her grandmother says and, after giving her a kiss on the cheek, we walk out into the hallway, and I pull the bedroom door closed.

"You're tired," I say to my mother. It's obvious. "You should be in bed." Her hair's growing in. Soft white wisps of it. And she's got some color back since the treatments stopped. Finally.

She smiles. "I'm glad to be home and I'll be fine."

"Zeke?" I ask.

"Downstairs."

I nod. "Goodnight," I tell her, and hug her. She still feels frail even for the weight she's put back on.

"It's good you brought her home." She draws back. "I hope you meant what you said to her."

"I did. We're here for good." My voice comes out hard and she hears it. I see it in the crease between her eyebrows.

"Past is past, Jericho."

"The dead will be avenged." I turn and walk toward the stairs. This isn't the first time we're having this conversation and I'm tired of it.

"She wouldn't have wanted that," she calls out when I get to the stairs.

I stop, grit my teeth, jaw clenching. "Go to bed," I say, although I want to say a hundred other things.

"Son," she starts.

I shift my gaze to her. "It's the only way to keep her safe," I tell her, although it's not my only reason. But it ends the conversation.

I walk down the stairs and toward my brother's study to wait for Councilor Hildebrand and the rest of our guests.

3

ISABELLE

"Where have you been?" Carlton asks. He's standing just outside the entrance of the ballroom. He's a half-brother, actually. That's where the *half* comment came from earlier. I'm only half-Bishop. People can't seem to let that go but for the wrong reasons if you ask me. I'm not sad to not be a full-blooded Bishop. The opposite. I'm sad I have any Bishop blood in me at all.

He forces a smile at a passerby, nods as if we're having a normal conversation. I wonder if that smile hurts him. But appearances matter to Carlton.

"Freshening up after all the dancing," I lie.

He looks me over, nods. "Good. You look a little wilted."

"I'm tired. Can we go home?"

He glances over my shoulder, scans the crowd.

"You'll go home after dinner."

"I can't dance anymore. My feet hurt."

"It's important we find you a suitable match."

"Does it matter that I don't want a suitable match? Or any match?"

"You know we need to do this. It's for everyone's benefit."

"You mean for your benefit. How will it benefit me?"

He tugs me away from a couple who passes too close on their way to their seats. "You're a Bishop, Isabelle."

"Half."

"That doesn't matter. You have a duty, just like I do. Just like every Bishop."

"To enrich the family coffers."

His light-blue gaze goes flat, eyes dull. He's no longer wearing his mask so I can see his face fully and he's not pleased.

"I didn't hear you complain when I took you in and paid your school fees, not to mention your clothes, the car you drive, your beautiful room, the food you eat. Should I go on?"

"No," I say tightly. I never asked for those things. Extenuating circumstances put us both in a position neither of us wanted to be in. And now it's too late to pull out. The money is spent. And I have no means of paying it back.

"Good." His phone dings and he reaches into his

pocket. I can see what he reads pisses him off, although he's been on edge lately. More so than usual. "Fucking Hildebrand," he mutters, looking over my shoulder into the crowd. His posture tenses and I watch the effort it takes for him to smile.

I follow his gaze and turn to find an older, unpleasant looking man heading toward us with two guards in tow. You can always tell The Society guards from the way they move. And I know instantly whatever is coming is no good.

"Councilor Hildebrand," Carlton says, extending his hand.

Councilor? As in The Tribunal?

I don't miss the hush that falls over those standing within earshot and people passing by who slow down and strain to hear.

"Carlton," the older man says. He glances at me but doesn't actually acknowledge me. "There's been a change of location. I hoped you'd be ready."

"I only just received your message, or I would be."

"Well, shall we, then?" he gestures to the exit.

"If you'll let me know the location, I'll have my driver—"

"I have a car for you," Hildebrand says and although I don't know him, I know his word is final.

The Tribunal is the judicial arm of The Society. IVI seems to stand apart from the law, having their own rules, their own courts. Their own system of punishments.

I shudder at the thought. At the things I've heard from my cousin, Julia, who studies The Society's history like it's her bible.

Carlton watches the older man closely and it takes him a moment to acquiesce. He's not used to taking orders. "Of course. I'll just arrange for the driver to take my dear sister home."

"She'll accompany us."

Carlton's eyes narrow. "What the hell is this? All this cloak and dagger—"

"You'll do well to watch your mouth, Bishop," Hildebrand says and turns to walk away, gesturing to the two men who I know would, without question, drag my brother and me if we don't move.

Carlton takes a step, but I grab his arm and tug. He turns to me.

"What's going on?"

"Come," Hildebrand calls over his shoulder.

My brother follows the older man without a word to me and I'm left with the guards, one of whom clears his throat and gestures for me to walk ahead of him. I do, trying not to look at the curious gazes, grateful for the mask that covers my face because my cheeks are burning underneath, my heart hammering.

But I follow obediently because that's what I do. It's what most women in The Society do. We're not quite second-class citizens but this is a patriarchy. And I'm not only a woman but I only half-belong.

Carlton's father had an affair with his maid who happened to be my mother. At least it was described as an affair. I'm not so sure when I recall their relationship in the years I was old enough to pay attention.

Anyway, she got pregnant. And for the first sixteen years of my life, I didn't know I was a Bishop. I was simply a York. But then my parents died, and, within a year of their deaths, Christian, my brother who had guardianship of me, was killed, and Carlton took me in. I was an orphan and then not, all within 48 hours of my brother's death.

When we reach the gates of the courtyard something distracts me from my thoughts. I'm grateful for it because those thoughts never lead to a good place. And as Councilor Hildebrand climbs into the first of two Rolls Royce's awaiting us, I see the mask with its devil's horns on the ground. I take a step toward it and gasp. Because it's *the* mask. The horned devil from the chapel. He must have left the compound. Taken it off here. Would I recognize him if I saw him again? Heard his voice? I'm sure I would. Hell, I'll know if I'm ever in the same room as him because even looking at the discarded mask I feel it, that shivering sensation along my spine raising the hairs on the back of my neck.

"Sister," Carlton snaps, startling me.

He's waiting at the open door of the second Rolls Royce, the two guards behind me.

Glancing once more at the mask, I turn and walk into the waiting vehicle somehow knowing wherever we're going, whatever it is, tonight, everything will change for me.

4

JERICHO

"I told you that you shouldn't have gone," Ezekiel, my brother, says. "You're not yourself." He hands me a tumbler of whiskey.

I take it from him and drink a sip. "I'm fine. Everything looks good?" I ask, moving around the desk to look at the papers spread across it. They must have arrived while I was at the compound.

"Exactly as discussed. Just needs a couple of signatures," he says. "Hildebrand was good with the change in location? Just readily agreed?"

I hear his tone and glance up, meet his grin with my own. "I have no idea. I switched off my phone."

"I'm sure he'll be in fine form." He swallows the last of his whiskey and pours another.

I study my brother in profile. I haven't seen him in five years, but he hasn't changed much. Most would say not at all, but I'm not most. He's built like me. I'm roughly two years older than him and we've always been close. Well, except for those months we weren't but that's water under the bridge.

"Zeke," I say. He turns to face me. "Her room looks nice. If a bit yellow."

He smiles. "Just a bit? I was going for over-the-top."

"Thank you," I say. "Thank you for doing it."

All joking is gone. "She's my niece. I'm happy to have her home where she belongs. Along with my brother."

I do smile this time, a real smile.

He nods and reaches into his pocket to retrieve his cell phone. He reads a text. "Two Rolls Royce's pulling up to the house."

"Get Hildebrand in first. Bishops can wait outside," I say, taking off my suit jacket and hanging it over the back of the desk chair, then rolling up my sleeves.

He types out a reply and pockets his phone. "Jericho," he says, drawing my attention from the sheets on the desk. He takes in the ink on both forearms. It's actually one tattoo. Two dragons coiled on my back, tails extended over my arms. Chaos and kinship. Destruction. Power. He has the same so I'm not sure why he's staring. "You sure you're ready for this?"

I square my gaze on him. "I've been ready for five years. I just needed the evidence."

He nods. He's heard the recording. Knows Carlton Bishop's role in Kimberly's death. Her accidental murder. I was the target. She just got in the way. She was twenty-four years old. Twenty-fucking-four. Pregnant with our first baby. We were engaged to be married. Fantasizing about living on a fucking beach in Mexico and leaving everything behind.

Fuck.

Fuck me.

And fuck Carlton Bishop. I'm going to bury him.

"Brother." I startle at Zeke's touch on my shoulder. I don't know when he moved. I'm too caught up in the past.

"I'm fine," I say, not looking at him.

"Are you?"

I meet his eyes. His are steel gray like our mother's. Hers are softer though. Kinder than his.

"I said I'm fine," I say, voice thick, my throat coated with the memory of that day.

"Don't let them see it."

"See what?"

"Your pain. It shows weakness."

I clench my jaw, take a deep breath in. He's right. I need to master this. Can't let my mind take me there. Not in front of them.

I close my eyes, take a deep breath in and nod just as a knock comes at the door.

"Showtime," Zeke says, a wide smile on his face.

He's better at this part than I am. He swaps out his masks more easily. "Come in," he calls out as he walks back around the desk and picks up his whiskey.

We both watch as Dex opens the door and Councilor Hildebrand enters. He looks at me, at my brother, around the study. He's irritated but I think that may just be his resting face. He's a self-important man and as far as I've known from when our father was alive, he's never had much affection for our family. Probably thinks we're imposters. Not a founding family but one with money and ultimately, all bow to money. Everyone and everything can be bought no matter how much The Society may want to deny it. Even status within IVI.

Now the Bishops, they're the real deal. One of the thirteen original Founding Families. They're not only members of The Society but are part of the groundwork. Carlton Bishop, a bona fide Sovereign Son. Me and Zeke and our father when he was alive, we bought our place. And Hildebrand has never forgotten it.

Which makes this all the sweeter.

I paste a smile on my face. "Councilor," I say. "I appreciate you coming on such short notice."

Dex closes the door and Hildebrand meets my gaze. "In future, you should know matters of this importance will be handled at the Tribunal building."

"Considering the delicacy of the situation, I didn't think you'd mind."

His jaw tightens. I have him by the balls. A Sovereign Son, a founding family member, making deals with mobsters. Well, it's not so much that as getting caught at it. That would not go over well if word got out. Which is why he's here. Which is why he'll do exactly as I say.

"Of course," he says.

"Sit, please," I say, stacking the pages on the desk and walking around it to gesture to the leather couch in the sitting area.

He sits. "Drink?" Zeke asks.

He nods and my brother pours him a whiskey.

"How is your daughter?" Hildebrand asks tightly.

"Doing well." Considering. The councilor's support is necessary for this part of my plan, but I won't tell him any more than he needs to know about my family.

"You'll bring her to the compound for a formal introduction, I presume."

"When the time is right, and I have secured her safety." The first part is a lie. The second a little pressure on him. Let him know just how delicate this matter is for IVI.

"She's been baptized?"

"Are you concerned for her soul?"

"Of course," he replies with a smile about as warm as mine.

This will go nowhere good, so I change the topic. "You've vetted the evidence against Carlton Bishop, I presume?" I ask. He has or he wouldn't be here. The evidence is a recording of Carlton with some very bad men initiating the attempt on my life that killed Kimberly. It also suggests he may have had a hand in my father's fatal car crash.

"Yes. You'll hand it over once the papers are signed tonight, as agreed?"

"As agreed." I feel my brother's presence beside me, but I need to ask. "The girl?"

"Waiting on your command along with her brother."

I don't glance at Zeke. He's clearly surprised by this. Tonight was about confronting Carlton. Signing the papers. Showing him the game has changed. Taking Isabelle wasn't supposed to happen yet. But my plans have evolved.

"Good." I collect the paperwork Councilor Hildebrand had drawn up and spread them over the coffee table in the sitting area. The oversized sheets of parchment take up the entire surface. I uncap the fountain pen and set it in front of Hildebrand.

He puts his drink aside and scoots forward, picking up the pen, looking over the pages. I haven't made any changes so this part should be quick, and it is. Not a moment later I hear the scratch of the pen tip scrawling his signature. He wants his part done and over with.

He sets the pen down and reclines in his seat. "Discretion is of the utmost importance here, St. James."

"Oh," I say, taking a seat and picking up the pen, my gaze falling to the name Isabelle Bishop mentioned in several places throughout the document. "I couldn't agree more." I sign.

Zeke opens the door and, with one glance at Dex, instructs him to bring the Bishops in.

"Tell me something," Hildebrand starts as we wait. He leans closer. "Why do you want the girl? She's not even full-blooded. Her mother was a simple maid who reached above her station."

I flex my hands, counting to ten, breathing. "Well, then you won't mind so much considering my place within The Society's upper echelon was bought." I don't bother to look friendly as I say this. It's a truth he wishes he could deny.

His face goes an angry shade of red. I've hit my mark.

"Discretion," he mutters.

The door opens. I stand and turn to watch Carlton Bishop enter the study. When his gaze lands on me, there's only a split second where I glimpse a reaction. If he hadn't heard the rumors of my return until tonight, he knew the instant the car bringing him, and his pretty half-sister turned onto the long, lonely road that leads to the St. James property that the time for his reckoning has come.

I see the effort it takes for him to shift his gaze to Hildebrand. "Councilor. It appears we've both been inconvenienced," he says tightly. He doesn't know what I have yet. Most likely doesn't know the recording exists. Felix Pérez was good at that. Secret recordings.

"Sit," Hildebrand orders, not even bothering to stand himself.

Carlton Bishop's gaze lands on the official sheets of parchment scattered across the coffee table. The uncapped fountain pen. The still drying ink of our signatures. Does he see Isabelle's name all over the document? Will he wonder what I want? What I'm planning?

Either way, I've got Carlton Bishop by the balls.

I smile a wide smile and turn back to the door. I don't care about Carlton Bishop. I don't give a fuck if he sits or stands or does fucking cartwheels around the room. It's her I'm curious about.

And here she is in that ridiculously inappropriate dress, considering the reason she's here, her chainmail mask gone, those too-pretty eyes set in a too-pretty face and locked on me. And fuck me if the moment our eyes meet something doesn't tighten in my gut. A sensation similar to what I'd felt when she'd laid her hand in mine earlier tonight.

Does she recognize me, I wonder? Does she know I was the masked devil she has to thank for saving her ass earlier?

Dex closes the door behind her, and she jumps. Literally jumps.

I keep watching. I can't seem to look away.

Zeke clears his throat and I turn to the seated men, find Carlton Bishop's icy-blue gaze studying me closely. I narrow my eyes. Lock him out. But I'm already too late, I know that. He saw how I looked at her.

But fuck it. As far as he's concerned, I'm looking at my next fuck toy. Because that's what she'll be, at least in part. She'll suck my dick when I tell her to suck my dick. She'll spread her legs when I tell her to spread her legs. And she'll scrub my floors when I tell her to scrub my fucking floors. Because in this house, a Bishop is nothing. Less than nothing. Less than the dirt on the bottom of my shoe.

Although this Bishop will serve a purpose.

Because she is the key to wiping out the Bishop name. To taking every fucking thing they have ever owned.

"Isabelle. Why are you standing by the door like that? Greet the Councilor," Carlton barks.

I watch her reaction. She looks at her brother with contempt. I'm not even sure she's trying to hide her disdain of him. She drags her gaze to Hildebrand.

"Councilor," she says but I notice how it takes her a minute to lower her gaze.

Her brother turns to Hildebrand, but my eyes are

locked on her. I see how she shifts her gaze and her eyes lift to mine momentarily, thick lashes working fast when she blinks away. Caught.

"What is the meaning of this?" Carlton asks as he skims the documents on the table.

Hildebrand glances at me. He opens his mouth to speak but I don't let him. Because this is too important. This first step to bringing Carlton Bishop to his knees.

And I want to be the one to say the words.

"I initiate the Rite."

I *initiate the Rite.*

The words echo, like earlier tonight.

She's not yours to break.

I reach for the edge of the chair closest to me because my knees threaten to buckle. My mind works frantically.

My brother's ruddy complexion has gone crimson. And I understand why I'm here. Why it was necessary for me to be brought here. Because Councilor Hildebrand or any of the Councilors wouldn't ever deign to talk to me. A mere woman. A half-woman in their eyes since only one parent was a member of their precious Society.

This man, the stranger from the chapel, has just initiated The Rite. An ancient, archaic, non-sensical law within The Society. A power bestowed on a trusted friend. A godparent relationship almost. One party taking custody of another, a minor in a normal-world sense. But within IVI's convoluted laws, it means taking custody of a child or a woman —no matter her age. Because each household needs a male head. That's why it was so easy for Carlton to take guardianship of me, although I was a minor then. But my family was all gone. There was no one. And once it was determined that I was a Bishop, it gave IVI rights over me.

Or maybe I allowed it. But those were dark days. I was sixteen. My brother had just been murdered before my eyes. I'd been left for dead.

Now though? I'm nineteen years old. An adult.

But we don't live in the normal world. And these men do not play by normal rules.

"You cannot initiate the Rite," Carlton spits, taking up the sheets of ancient looking parchment that seem as though they may disintegrate in his hands. He scans the text.

"I can. I just did," my horned devil of earlier says.

I force my knees to lock, wipe my sweaty palms on the feathers of my dress. They're still damp from the rain.

It's quiet while Carlton reads whatever is on those sheets of paper. "Councilor, this is unacceptable. I don't know what lies St. James has told you, but I can assure you they are only that!" He's on his feet, pages clutched in his fists.

"You tear that, and you'll be answering to the

entire Tribunal. It is an official document. It will be treated as such." Hildebrand takes a breath. "And you'll be grateful it's all he has asked for. It is his right. And you are the only one to blame for giving it to him."

Carlton purses his lips.

My devil looks at me, eyes unreadable, mouth unsmiling. He hates my brother. I know that without a doubt. He abhors him. I shudder as his gaze seems to settle deep under my skin. It takes all I have to remain upright as I wonder if he hates me too, if only for my name, the blood I share with Carlton.

"Dex," he says, eyes still on me.

The door behind me opens. I step deeper into the room to put space between myself and Dex.

"Sir," Dex says, unbothered by the palpable tension in the room.

"Take the girl downstairs."

Downstairs? We're already on the ground floor.

Dex nods and when I glance at him, he gestures for me to move.

I don't. I can't. My mouth opens and closes but nothing comes out. My brother is reading through those sheets of paper for the second or third time but the rest of them are watching me. Will Carlton save me? I'm not sure he could if he wanted to. For the Tribunal to be here means this man, my devil, has their blessing to do what he's about to do. And Carlton will bend to IVI law.

My gaze shifts to the stranger who gives an almost imperceptible nod. Dex wraps a hand around my arm.

"Wait!" I cry out as he tugs me toward the door.

They all look at me. The one who hasn't spoken, who looks so much like my devil I'd guess they were brothers, casually sips his drink, and watches the scene. I can't read his expression. Can't tell what he's thinking.

My mouth and throat are dry. I lick my lips as I force myself to look at my devil. He's the one making the decisions here. He's the one dictating what happens. But what do I say?

When I am silent, he raises his eyebrows.

"I... I don't understand," I manage.

"Then your brother hasn't done a very good job educating you in the ways of The Society. I'll be sure to remedy that." He shifts his gaze over me. "Dex."

"Let's go," Dex says.

"But... Carlton?" I ask as I stumble toward the door.

Carlton glances at me then back down at the sheet as if I haven't spoken at all. As if these men kidnapping me, and let's be clear that is exactly what they're doing, is totally normal. Acceptable.

"Dex," my devil calls out and we stop. "If she gives you any trouble, keep her in the dark."

Dark? Where the hell does he plan on taking me?

Dex nods and we're out the door, his grip painful

around my arm. When he closes the door behind us, I hear Carlton's angry tone, his out-of-control tone. The one that tells me he won't be getting his way, not tonight. Not against these men.

I look around as Dex leads me to the foyer. My heels clicking loudly on the onyx-veined white and gray marble. I think he's going to take me up the marble staircase, but we pass it and the farther we move from the double front doors, the more urgent my fight becomes.

"You're hurting me!"

He doesn't bother to reply, just drags me toward a dimly lit corridor.

"Where are we going?" I ask, trying to pry his fingers from my arm as panic sends adrenaline through my veins.

He turns to me and I find myself leaning back. "Keep your voice down," he says calmly. He unlocks and opens a steel door at the very end of the corridor.

I peer around him as he switches on the lights, but I don't have to see anything to know we're going into a basement. I smell the cool, earthy scent of an underground space. He keeps hold of me as we descend and I clutch my free hand around the uneven railing nailed into the stone wall.

"Where are you taking me?" I try again, counting my steps, looking in either direction once we're at the bottom. A light blinks at the far end of the corridor to my left like the bulb is about to burn out. The other to my right is better lit and I see it's lined by a row of old doors.

"Catacombs."

I freeze. "What?"

He grins when he gets a look at my face. I'm sure I've gone white as a ghost.

"Catacombs?"

"Just kidding. We won't go that deep."

Kidding? I struggle against him, but he carries on, dragging me to the right. I'm grateful for that at least as I crane my neck to look behind me. I watch that bulb flicker once more then go out, plunging that other corridor into darkness.

When we reach the last door, he opens it, reaching in to switch on the light. A single light bulb brightens the room. It hangs naked from a wire at the center of the ceiling in this windowless room. A small bed is pushed against one wall, beside it, a nightstand with worn legs and a drawer that hangs askew. On it sits a shadeless lamp without a bulb inside. On the floor is a threadbare rug.

I turn to Dex who is watching me.

"What is this?"

"Old servant's quarters. Not in use anymore, obviously. This is the half you want to be in, trust me."

Trust him?

I look at the opposite corridor, the darker of the two, then back at him.

He gestures for me to enter.

I shake my head. "I need to talk to my brother. I need—"

"I can take the bulb away. I promise you, you do not want that. Pitch black is pitch black down here."

I swallow. "Why? Why does he want me?"

"Bulb or no bulb?"

I won't get anything out of him. I know that. So when he takes a step into the room, I cry out for him to stop because I know he's not messing around. And I don't want to be in the dark, not down here.

"How long?" I ask when he releases me once I'm fully inside the room.

He shrugs his shoulders, reaching for the doorknob. I see the key in the lock on his side. "Until Jericho decides it's time to come for you." And before I can get another word in, he pulls the door closed and locks it.

I wrap my arms around myself. I look around this small, haunted place, chilled to the bone in this stupid dress. And terrified of what's to come.

6

JERICHO

L ike a chastised child, Bishop is silent as he and Hildebrand leave the house. He heard the evidence. Bits and pieces I selected just for him. The most damning fragments. He didn't look at me once after that. Barely met the Councilor's gaze. I wonder if Hildebrand is relieved not to have to stand him before The Tribunal. A Bishop. Founding family member and sovereign son plotting the execution of another member of The Society. The IVI justice system is an extreme one. Operating outside the norms of society, somehow above the law. Their punishments often exceed those of the outside world and this particular offense is a death sentence penalty.

In this modern day just a few years ago, an execution was carried out on IVI grounds for a similar offense. Granted, one with consequences that reached farther than Carlton Bishop's limited imagination could conjure up. A man was executed and although proceedings of The Tribunal are secret, the details circulated among the members of The Society and serve as a warning to all, even Carlton Bishop.

The door closes and I turn to find Zeke watching me.

"Get the outcome you wanted?" he asks.

"What I wanted was for Angelique to have a mother."

Zeke drinks a sip of whiskey, taking his time. "You're not the only one who lost her, you know. She was my best friend. More."

More.

Yeah, I know. Kimberly was more to him once upon a time. Her falling in love with me was not something either of us had planned. Neither had consciously wanted or sought it. But it happened and my brother and I moved past it. I think we did, at least. Although there were some tough months, especially when she started to show.

Zeke and I watch each other as images of the past pass like a slideshow through my mind. Is he thinking the same things? Watching that same slideshow play out? Does he blame me? I blame myself. And hell, maybe I deserve his blame too. She died because of me. He had warned me, too. Being with me wouldn't be safe for her. Just like I warned

Dante Grigori not too long ago that the woman he was in love with was in danger simply for his affection.

"I'm sorry," I tell Zeke. "Every fucking day."

"I know." He drinks another sip and it's a long time before he speaks. "She's young."

Change of topic. He's talking about Isabelle Bishop.

"An adult," I clarify.

"Technically. She's also twelve years your junior."

"And most importantly, she's a Bishop." I swallow the last of my drink and set the tumbler down. "You're not growing a heart for the Bishops, are you? Overwriting Kimberly's memory?"

His jaw tightens. "I'm just telling you she's young and if you didn't see it, I can also tell you from the few moments I spent in the same room with the girl, that she's no match for you."

Something about the comment gets my hackles up. I straighten, step toward him. He narrows his gaze infinitesimally, cocking his head to the side, waiting for my reaction.

"Is she a better match for you, then?" I ask.

"Are you fucking serious?"

"Is that what this is?" I continue. I don't know why.

"Get your head out of your ass, brother. She's barely a woman. And I know you. I have some idea what you're planning."

"Do you? What am I planning then?"

"There's only one thing that makes sense."

I raise my eyebrows. Give nothing away.

"I'm just saying she's young. You want to bury her brother. I get that. Are you willing to destroy an innocent girl to do it?"

"She's a fucking Bishop. There is no such thing as an innocent Bishop."

"And how do you plan to explain it all to your daughter? Have you considered Angelique?"

"I'll handle it. You don't have to worry about Angelique. She's my first priority."

"Is she?"

Fury burns inside me. "You do not get to question that," I bark through gritted teeth.

"She's my niece," he says, setting his drink down and stepping toward me. "She's my first priority too. And I think you're making a mistake. I think something about this girl has caught your eye. Just don't let your need to wet your dick cloud your priorities."

I grab him by the collar. "Don't you fucking dare—"

He knocks my hands off. "I will not stand by and watch you fuck this up."

"I don't plan on fucking it up."

"You're not focused, Jericho."

"I'm one-hundred percent focused, Zeke. You just stay the hell out of my way if the thought of punishing Isabelle Bishop makes you queasy. All you have to do is make sure to keep your hands to yourself."

"Like you did with Kimberly?"

The door opens then, and we both turn to find our mother standing there looking more fierce than she's looked in a long time. She's downright furious. I recognize the blazing eyes. I see them every time I look at my reflection. At least in one of my eyes.

She takes in the scene, her mouth falling open, and I realize how close we are to coming to blows.

She enters and closes the door behind her.

"Why are you out of bed?" I ask, as Zeke and I put space between us.

"Have you two lost your minds?" she asks instead of answering my question.

Fuck.

I look down at the Persian rug covering a large section of the floor. Zeke always liked those. My office, which is across the foyer, has a slightly more modern design.

With a sigh I shift my gaze to my brother. "I'm sorry. I didn't mean any of that."

"Me either," he says, looking as sheepish as I feel.

He steps toward me, extending his hand. I shake it.

"We're in this together. I am your ally. Don't forget it," he says.

"I won't," I tell him.

"Better," my mother says.

"You need to get some rest," Zeke tells her. "Your doctor said—"

"I know what she said, Ezekiel," she says, then turns to me. "Tell me something, did I hear correctly?" She raises an eyebrow and doesn't take her eyes off me. "The Bishop girl is here?"

Zeke snorts.

I clench my jaw. I don't owe anyone an explanation. Not even my family. "She is."

"Where is she?" my mother asks, eyes bright.

I grit my jaw and she knows exactly where.

Her face pales. "Jericho."

I stand there and manage my breathing.

"You cannot leave her down there," my mother starts, her tone already setting me off. She's softened over the last few years. But this is not a time for softness. Her words blur into background noise for a minute until she makes a mistake. "Kimberly would not—"

"Enough!" I slam my hand on the edge of the desk and my mother jumps. I see her face and know I need to rein it in. The girl already has us at each other's throats. It's what Bishops do.

I look at my brother, then my mother and I hold her gaze as I speak. "You did not watch Kimberly die." My voice is more controlled but I'm not calm. Nowhere close to it. "You did not hold her as her life drained from her body. As her eyes lost their light. I did. Neither of you. You do not get to say what happens to the Bishop girl."

With that, I gather up the signed parchment and stalk past my mother leaving both her and Zeke in his study.

I walk toward the cellar. I brace myself when I reach the steel door. Force in a breath. Force memories back down. I remind myself why I'm here. Why I need to go down there. I need to be as cold and as unforgiving as this door. I unlock it and push it open. I banish all those thoughts as I descend the stairs to deal with Isabelle Bishop.

7

ISABELLE

The door slams against the wall, startling me. I blink once, twice, my back sore and cold against the stone wall. My eyes land on the devil of a man looming in the hall. I instantly remember where I am. What brought me here.

Survival instinct has me jumping to my feet and shuffling to the opposite end of the tiny room. The carpet scratches my bare feet as I gather my senses to put space between us. I'm registering the pounding of my heart, the adrenaline rushing through my veins.

He looks furious. His jaw is clenched, the line of it somehow sharper for that tightness and barely hidden beneath the five-o'clock shadow. His eyes are on fire, one almost black with rage, the other a feral, animal silver. I drag my eyes from his and my gaze catches on his bare forearms, the sleeves rolled up to his elbows. They're corded with muscle, and hugging the skin tight are the coiling tails of serpents. His giant hands fists at his sides.

I fell asleep. How in the hell did I manage to fall asleep knowing where I was? What awaited me?

He takes a step toward me but when I take one back, he stops. He pushes his hand through his dark hair and I get the feeling he's rattled by something. This man is fierce. Savage. The raw rage coming off him is palpable. I wonder if this is how he experiences every emotion. Intensely. Passionately. I know being on the wrong end of that passion is lethal. And I'm there, in his sights, the object of his hate.

I want to run but there's nowhere for me to go. The small bathroom is the size of a shower stall with barely enough room for the toilet and sink. And there's no lock on the door. Although I know no door or lock would stop this man from advancing. I have never been around someone like him before. Never felt so much crackling, animal energy from any human being.

"It's done," he says, tossing the papers he's holding onto the bed. His voice is different than it was in the chapel. Even the threat he made sounds like child's play compared to his tone now. There's an edge to it. Something wild. Something he is trying to rein in.

"What's done?" I ask, glancing at the pages,

noticing one has slipped off the bed and landed on the floor.

I initiate the Rite.

He can't do that. The Rite is not something one can take. It's given and only to a trusted friend.

He takes a breath in, shifts his gaze around the room, not bothered by the sparseness, the cold, the old. He then settles his gaze on me. The tension in his shoulders subsides a little. Hands flex then relax. My gaze falls to those hands and inevitably to the inked forearms. To the powerful muscle beneath the skin.

"You belong to me, Isabelle Bishop."

I can't help my quick glance to those sheets of paper on the bed, but I can't read more than a few words from this angle. It's written in an old, ornate script and upside down. What I do see are the words Rite and my own name.

And a signature I recognize. My brother's.

Christian wouldn't have allowed this to happen. He wouldn't sign anything that would give me away.

But Christian is dead, and Carlton is a very different man than Christian was.

I don't need to read the details to know he's not lying. That I do belong to him. It's how The Society works. If it had been another man, another sort of contract, it would probably be much the same albeit with less animosity. Because this man hates me. Loathes me.

"Why did you help me?" I ask before I can think about what I'm doing.

He looks confused. "What?"

"At the chapel. Why did you help me if you hate me? Why not let those men do what they wanted to do to me?"

"Ah."

I take a step away from him and feel the wall at my back. There's nowhere for me to go.

He sees my disadvantage. Sees he has me cornered. And like any good predator, he advances, only stopping when he's closer than he was at the chapel. When I can almost feel the heat coming off him. The sheer power of him like waves of electric energy ready to zap me.

"Isabelle Bishop," he says, noting the dozen hair pins I dropped on the nightstand before taking a thick lock of my hair into his hand. I'd taken it out of its chignon. It was so tight it gave me a headache. But now as I watch him, I wonder if I should have left it in that bun because he begins to twist a handful of it around his fist. I count one, two, three, four turns. My hair reaches my waist and he'll use even that to his advantage.

I expect him to pull, to hurt me, and I brace myself.

His gaze meets mine and I study him. This close, I can see the specks of gold in his eyes, the ring of black around the gray one. He tugs my hair, holding it taut forcing my head to tilt backward.

"You weren't his to break. You're mine."

I swallow as my shoulders shiver. I wrap my arms around myself, too much of me exposed in this wilting, ruined dress, too much of me left unprotected.

He unwinds my hair, knuckles purposefully grazing my bare shoulder and then sliding across to my collarbone, to the long, ugly scar there. His eyebrows furrow as he studies it, touches the scar tissue, the dark tracks of the stitches.

When his eyes meet mine again, that shiver turns into a full shudder and my chest heaves with each breath.

His gaze drops to watch the swell of my breasts.

I try not to hyperventilate while his knuckles leave a trail of goosebumps down my arm, over the crease of my elbow. He takes my hand and turns it over, brushing the backs of his fingers back and forth from wrist to elbow and back again and again and again. The sensation is sensual and utterly terrifying.

"It fits you, that scar," he says. "Something ugly on something so very beautiful. A warning."

I struggle to follow, but I can't think right now. Not with the way he's touching me.

"I plan to break you slowly, Isabelle Bishop."

My knees wobble.

"I will enjoy every moment," he says.

I lean against the wall for support.

"It wouldn't do to let that boy touch you. So, I wasn't so much helping *you* as I was helping myself. Making sure the goods weren't damaged before I took possession."

He lets my arm drop, and his gaze shifts once again to my collarbone.

"Tell me about this scar."

"I fell." It's true but only half and I'm not wasting my words on him. I was pushed, took a tumble down the stairs and broke my clavicle, for starters, the night Christian was killed. I was lucky, though, because I'm sure that man would have broken much more if he wasn't interrupted by the wail of sirens. One of our neighbors had heard my screams and called the police.

"Any other flaws you're hiding?" he asks.

I'm not sure he's waiting for my reply, but I shake my head anyway.

"Hm. I'll see for myself, I think." He takes a step back but there's no relief when he sets one hand on the wall over my head and leans his weight into it. I note, however, that the door is still open behind him and Dex is gone. "Take off your dress, Isabelle."

My throat goes dry, my entire body tense, nipples hard, belly doing strange flips.

"I... What?"

He grins, never once blinking and I wonder about the mask he'd worn earlier. How I'd thought him some sort of beast. A devil. I wonder if he's those things now. Not human at all.

"Undress and show me your scars," he says.

I hug myself tight, glance over his shoulder. See the obstacle of my discarded heels at the foot of the rickety old bed.

He's watching me when I return my eyes to his and when I lick my lips to speak, his gaze falls to them. I see desire in his eyes, and I think about all the women at the masquerade ball. So many who are so much more beautiful than me. More elegant than me. More *Society* than me. And I wonder why he chose me. What he'd want with someone like me.

"Isabelle."

I blink, glance again at the open door before returning my eyes to his.

"Do you want to run for it?" he asks as if he's just noted my interest in that exit.

I don't answer. He's playing with me.

"Freedom is just a few feet away." He smiles wide and steps aside. "You're considering it. I would too." He extends his arm, gesturing to the door. "You can try, I suppose. You won't get far, but you can try."

I don't move and all I hear is the pumping of blood through my veins, my ears ringing with adrenaline.

It's a game. He's playing a game. The voice inside my head screams. Every logical molecule of my being knows it.

"Go on. You want to."

He's goading me. He leans closer, cheek alongside mine, scruff brushing my skin, breath a whisper along my ear. "But if you do, know when I catch you, I will punish you. And I will catch you."

I shudder at his words.

Fight or flight.

I know I will lose both fight and flight, but I'm not thinking anymore. Instinct has taken over. Survival is the goal, so I choose flight and my legs move. I spring forward knowing he'll catch me, knowing I won't make it or if I do, there will be a trap waiting for me. But I run anyway, and I hear his laughter, or is it a growl? The low rumble of a beast springing to action as his prey does exactly what he expects, what he wants, and the chase is on.

I sprint across the bedroom, muscles moving in a familiar motion. I'm a runner, but this is unfamiliar terrain, and when I step out into the hall, I pause because it's even darker than it was earlier.

He doesn't come after me, not right away. I know because I hear his chuckle. When I glance back, I see he hasn't moved but the moment his eyes meet mine, he takes a step.

I bolt. He's behind me but he's in no rush. He's taking his time. I run toward the stairs. I know the corridor runs farther past the stairs, but it's too dark and I'm too scared to go there.

When I get to the stairs, he's still down the hall. I

can make it. Thirteen steps. I can make it. I take hold of the rail and run up, tripping in my haste when he calls my name, voice calm and taunting. I'm almost to the top though and I don't need to look back to know he isn't sprinting to catch up with me.

It's a trap. A game. An excuse to punish me. I know it. I know it before my hand closes around the doorknob, know it before I try the door. I know it's locked. And no matter how much I pull and pound, it won't give.

A moment later powerful arms wrap around my middle. He lifts me effortlessly, carrying me back down the stairs, arms trapped, my back pressed to his hard chest. I scream. I scream and fight, half-crazed with fright as he carries me calmly, almost patiently, back down the corridor. That light at the opposite end somehow, impossibly, flicking on again, it, too, taunting me, blinking, as if watching the devil drag me back into that room.

He drops me onto the bed, and I bounce, the springs whining. He closes the door and not a hair is out of place, not a drop of sweat beads his forehead as he pushes his hands into his pockets, watching me. His expression dark and curious and unhurried as I get back to my feet and wipe my eyes.

"Why are you doing this to me?" I scream the words, but my voice has dried up, my throat like sandpaper.

He shrugs a shoulder. "Because I can. Now strip."

8

JERICHO

She can't be more than five-and-a-half feet barefoot. I like this difference in size between us. Liked the feel of her slight weight against me when I carried her down the stairs and back into this room. Her cell for the night. I appreciate how her narrow shoulders tremble as her gaze shifts from my eyes to the ink on my forearms. Inevitably they move to a point anywhere in the room. Anywhere but on me. Though each time she is drawn back. Each time she begins the cycle anew, vivid blue eyes growing more and more panicked each time they meet mine, her entire body shuddering as she hugs herself tight.

"Isabelle," I start, leaning on one leg, cocking my head to the side as I study her. As I watch the heave of her breasts above the dress. "What did I just say?"

She seems to shrink back into herself even more.

She's already cornered herself twice now and I admit, letting her run was cruel. Toying with her wasn't nice. But I'm not nice and I wanted to watch.

No, not just to watch. It's not that simple. Those last few minutes in the study rattled me. The exchange with Zeke. Old feelings I thought were buried deep rising back to the surface. How does he truly feel now, years later? Has he forgiven me? Because he hasn't forgotten. That's obvious. But I can't exactly blame him for that, can I?

My mother is another story. She won't like what I have to do to Isabelle. She already doesn't. But she won't interfere, either.

I shake my head to clear it. I need to focus. Need to deal with Isabelle Bishop now because she'll meet my daughter tomorrow. And I need to get her in line before that. I will do what I need to do to protect Angelique. And I can't care about the cost to the Bishop trembling before me.

"Isabelle?" I raise my eyebrows.

She squeezes her eyes shut, presses the heels of her hands to her eyes and I watch her drag in a deep breath. She's steeling herself. Good girl. When she opens those eyes again, she has mascara smeared across her skin. And the blue of those eyes is like blazing shards of glass. Christ. She's fucking beautiful.

"Why?" she asks, voice coming across stronger than earlier.

"Why what?" I ask, aware she can hear the taunt in my tone. It only makes her angrier and I'm entertained.

"Why me? Why this? What did I do to you?"

"Fair questions," I say, turning a circle around the tiny room, noting the cobwebs in the corner. The bare, stained mattress on the rickety bed frame. I pick up the sheet of parchment that had fallen and set it with the others on top of the bed. When I look back she's folded her arms across her chest. "Why not you?"

Her eyebrows furrow. It's not what she expected. "Carlton did something to you."

It's a statement, not a question. And it isn't what I expect. My jaw tenses and I know she sees it. I see the way her eyes shift, how her back straightens just a little.

I take my hands out of my pockets and step toward her. Her shoulders curl in protectively. I smile, take her wrists, and draw her folded arms to her sides. I look at her mouth and I wonder if she realizes she licks her lips when I do. I let my gaze drop farther to the swell of her breasts and she tries to pull her wrists free. I don't let her. Instead, I watch her as I slowly turn her to face away from me.

"I want your hands on the wall," I tell her, raising her arms above her head, pressing her palms to the cool stone. I don't let go of her wrists as I take her in, her shoulders tensed, skin stretched tight, shoulder blades protruding. I hold both wrists in one hand and with the other, brush her waist-length black hair over one shoulder to bare her back.

She sucks in a breath at my touch. That sound, the tremble of her body when I bring my nose to her pulse and take a deep breath in, makes my dick hard. My own breath is short and she's not even naked yet. I swallow, catalog her scent. Springtime and innocence camouflaging acrid fear. Barely.

I run my chin over the curve of her neck, and she whimpers. I draw back to look at how her pale olive skin reddens where the stubble irritated it then lean my mouth to her ear.

"Don't move," I instruct as I slide my hands down over her arms, watching goosebumps rise in their wake, fingertips feeling the contour of long limbs, slender muscle.

When I lift my fingers from her, she fists her hands, and I can almost hear the battle she must be having. Stay or move? Do as she's told or fight?

"I said stay," I whisper against the jumping pulse at her neck, letting my breath tickle her, feeling the warm shudder of her skin against my lips.

A moment later, her palms are flat against the wall, and I look at the back of the dress. It's a corset top held together by some sort of ribbon. Silk. I pull that ribbon to undo the bow and begin to unbind her. The corset was too tight. I can see how her skin has creased against the bonds of the dress.

"Please don't," she says, still not moving her hands.

"Shh."

I swallow as I pull the top of the dress apart, see the bare skin of her back. The curve to her hips. My own breath is ragged. I hope she can't hear that. I'm also glad she can't see me as I tug the two sides wider, wide enough that I can push the dress down over her hips and let it drop to the floor.

Isabelle whimpers, shuddering, and drags her arms down a little.

"No," I tell her, and she stops their progress. She's obedient. Probably because she's terrified. I know what she's thinking I'll do. And there's a part of me that hates myself for it. Hates that I'm letting her think it. Only a monster could.

I fist my hands, close my eyes, and clear my head.

She is a Bishop.

She does not deserve your pity.

"Nor shall she have it," I say under my breath and look her over. See the jagged scar running down her spine. Another flaw. One I have to force myself to look away from. I study the contours of her body instead, the taut muscle, the narrowing to her waist, the swell of her hips, her long, slender legs, ankles tickled by the feathers of her dress pooling around her feet.

"Another mark," I say, my voice hoarse as I bring the tips of two fingers to the top of that scar. I can feel the thickened tissue beneath my fingers, hear her hiss of breath as I trace the rough line of it. The skin over her clavicle was stitched. The doctor did a shit job of it. This has no stitch marks. "This one?" I ask.

"Fell," she says.

"You fall a lot."

She remains silent.

There's more to this story. But tonight isn't the time to hear it. And besides, I don't care.

"You should be more careful," I say and slip my fingers into the band of her panties to push them down, letting them drop once they're over the swell of her hips.

She gasps, is about to move to cover herself but I close my hands over hers and press against her. Can she feel the length of my cock against her back? Fuck.

"Don't. Move."

She turns her head a little and I see the wet skin around her eyes.

"Please don't... Please..." her voice breaks.

"Be still. I'm only looking," I say quickly, wondering why I do it. Why I give her any comfort. "But you must be still, or I'll do more than look."

There's no point in fighting me. I have proven that already. She nods. I draw back and my breath catches at the sight of her standing against the wall, arms raised, her naked body exposed.

Fuck.

"Turn around." I don't sound like myself.

She glances over her shoulder before slowly turning. She doesn't know what to do with her arms and instinctively moves to cover herself.

"No, Isabelle."

She drops her arms to her sides and I let my eyes feast. Her hair is still over her shoulder obscuring one breast. It reaches to her waist.

"Push your hair back. I want to see."

Her throat works to swallow as she raises her arms to obey me. I see the trembling of her hands. The sight makes me harder.

Her nipples are taut, breasts small but high and full. Less than a handful but I'll manage. Her stomach is tight and her pussy shaved bare so I can see the slit of her sex between her legs. Fuck me, I can't remember the last time I was so fucking hard for a woman.

I force myself to look at her eyes and find hers on my length. I wait, give her a chance to take it in, let her know I caught her looking when she drags her gaze back up to mine. I drag in a breath and wonder if I were to slip my fingers between her legs if she'd be wet.

I can smell her. A hint of arousal beneath that fear.

A low groan rumbles against my chest and she presses her back into the wall.

"Pick up your dress and panties."

Confused, she steps out of them and lowers herself down, keeping one eye on me as she gathers them up.

"Shoes too." They're closer to me but rather than coming nearer, she sets her bare knees on the threadbare, disgusting rug and extends her arm to snatch them up. I watch her ass spread, wishing I was behind her to see more.

I adjust my dick. Tell it to be patient. It will come. She is mine. No need to rush.

She stands up, hugging her things to her body and I see the goosebumps across her skin. It's cold down here. Even on the hottest summer day, it's always cold and dank in this cellar. I remember it from when Zeke, Zoë and I would play down here before our father put the steel door in place. Before he locked it. Not that Zeke or I would ever come down here again after what happened, at least not when we were young. I wonder if he has since.

I blink, see her watching me, her head tilted a little. I have to be careful around this one. She's observant. Too much so. I let my gaze drop to her breasts as I unbutton the top few buttons of my shirt.

"You said—"

Her eyes grow wide and she hugs the dress to herself as if it could protect her from me. I don't answer her but pull the shirt over my head and toss it onto the mattress. It's a kindness. She'd better be fucking grateful.

Her eyes dart across my chest, my stomach, mouth growing wider at the ink curling around my shoulders. More of the dragons. But she hasn't seen anything yet.

I take the sheets of parchment from the bed and roll them up in one hand. "Hand me your clothes." I hold out a hand.

"You said you were just looking," her voice is barely a whisper.

"Hand them to me."

She extends the clothes toward me as a tear slides from each eye.

I take the clothes and shoes and watch the path of those tears. "You'll spend the night here. Your punishment for running. I'll be back for you tomorrow morning. If you try to run again, you'll spend two more nights. Are you following my math?" I ask more firmly than I need to. "Or do I need to dumb it down."

She nods.

"Dumb it down or you understand?"

She grits her teeth. "I understand." Her eyes dart around the creepy room and although there is fear, I also see relief in them. Relief I won't touch her.

Should I tell her the reprieve is temporary?

I don't. Another kindness. Instead, I turn and walk to the door, barely pausing when I hear her audible gasp at the sight of my back. I step out into the chilly corridor, closing and locking the door behind me. I ignore the ghost that trails me back up the stairs. She'll stop at the steel door. I don't know why she doesn't leave the cellar. Doesn't return to the happier places.

Happier. I think sometimes happiness is erased from memory. In a way, it's more painful to remember those moments. To know what you lost.

I shake my head and drag that heavy door closed. It takes all I have to lock it again.

For Angelique, I tell myself. To keep her safe. I don't ever want her going down there. Ever.

9

ISABELLE

The lightbulb swings with the jarring of the door against the doorframe. I hear the lock turn and listen for his retreating steps. I don't cry out for him to come back. I've been robbed of my voice. But a few moments later, when the light settles, I walk to the door and try it. Locked tight. Am I safer for it? Will whatever it is I felt out there stay out there? On the other side of my locked door? Because I swear there's something.

Christian used to laugh at how jumpy I've always been. He loved horror movies and I always watched them with him, even knowing I'd have nightmares later. He'd make a giant tub of popcorn and we'd sit under blankets and watch. He'd laugh while I covered my eyes at the worst moments. And for days after I'd swear I'd see ghosts or hear them. But it was always worth it. My brother and I were close, especially after we lost our parents. I miss him so much. It's been three years and I still miss him every day.

I shudder with the damp cold typical of cellars and grab the shirt Jericho St. James dropped on the bed. Why did he leave it? It's not as if it's much protection against the cold. I hesitate for a moment but only a moment because being down here is fucking with me. I slide it over my head, tucking my arms into it. The sleeves come to my wrists only because he'd had them folded up to his elbows and the shirt itself reaches to mid-thigh. It's still warm from him. It still smells like him.

The springs of the bed creak as I sit on the edge and draw my legs up. I hug my knees and am weirdly grateful he left his shirt. I don't feel so alone. And I know how ridiculous that sounds. He hates me. I would be safer alone than I am with him. Didn't he just prove that?

Heat flushes my face at what happened. How he held me against the wall. How he stripped me. How it felt when he touched me. I'm still damp between my legs, and I can't even begin to process that. I tell myself it's not arousal. It's humiliation.

I push my fingers into my hair and pull at my scalp as I remember the rest of it. Like how I didn't move when he told me not to move. Like how he didn't exactly have to hold me down to rip off my clothes. How I didn't fight. I should have. But when it comes to strength, he'll win hands down. It made no sense for me to fight.

I picture that tattoo on his back. I only saw it for a moment, but I don't think I'll ever forget it. Two giant dragons coiled around one another. Fighting? I'm not sure. Embracing? Entwined in love maybe? I need to study it to know. I doubt I'll get the chance and I can't even believe I'm thinking about it. It spanned the whole of his back in vivid color, the muscle moving beneath the ink somehow making those dragons come to life.

I lean back against the wall, not sure I want to lie down on this mattress. He said he'd come back in the morning. It's already late, isn't it? When we left IVI it was after nine. Dinner is always served late there so maybe it'll just be a few hours before he returns. Do I want him to return?

These thoughts circle for what seems like eternity, and I don't think I'll be able to sleep until the turning of the key in the lock wakes me some time later. I straighten up, wipe at the corners of my mouth and rub my eyes as the door opens carrying that chill draft with it, the lightbulb swaying on its wire. It's the same feeling as last night. I didn't imagine it. But whatever that chill is, it stayed out of my room until he returned. Is it attracted to him?

Jericho St. James looks freshly showered, hair still damp, face shaved clean. He's dressed casually in dark blue jeans and a charcoal cashmere sweater.

From the V-neck I see the creeping edges of the tattoo on his back.

He tucks his hands into his pockets. His sleeves are rolled up, so I see those tails again. This time, I note the watch, expensive, and the bracelet he wears on the same wrist. It's too delicate for him. Doesn't quite fit. But my gaze again moves to that ink and he stands there to let me take him in.

I feel my face flush and look away, embarrassed. I can't seem to take my eyes off this man. I was used to how Carlton was. Domineering. Bullying maybe. But Jericho St. James is different than that. He is the definition of power. A force like a deadly storm.

"Good morning," he says.

I don't reply.

"Sleep well?" One corner of his mouth curves upward

"What do you think?" I ask. I'm exhausted, thirsty, my throat so dry I can barely swallow not to mention how cold I am.

"Would you like to spend two more nights down here?"

I fold my arms across my chest as a voice in my head tells me to tread carefully.

"Is your silence a yes? If so, I'll..." he trails off and takes a step backward.

"No!" I jump off the bed. "I don't want to be down here." I grit my jaw but he's waiting so I swallow the shredded remains of my pride. "Please."

He smiles. "Better." He steps aside and gestures to the hall.

I hesitate, knowing he could still be playing with me, but I have no choice. I walk past him, taking care not to touch him, which is hard considering his size. Once I'm in the hallway he captures my arm and turns me to face him.

"Not a sound, understand?"

"Why? So whoever else is upstairs doesn't know you kidnapped me?"

He smiles. "Oh, they already know. But it's early. My daughter is still sleeping."

That takes me back. "Your...daughter?"

He gestures to the stairs. "Move."

He has a child? Does that mean he has a wife? Is she lying in his bed now? Then why did he do what he did last night? Why strip me? Touch me? He was hard. I saw and felt it. Weirdly, this feels like a betrayal although I don't know how it could. If anyone should feel betrayed it would be his wife.

I walk, glancing over my shoulder at him.

Maybe they have an open relationship? Maybe she doesn't mind if he's with other women?

But then I remind myself he wasn't *with* me. He humiliated me. It was what he wanted to do, and he succeeded. That's all.

I pause at the bottom of the stairs because the door above is open, and I see light.

He nods and I hurry up. Once we're out in the

hallway, I look around, see light coming from around a corner where I hear the sounds of pots and pans. Of water running. Someone lighting a gas stove. The normal noises of a normal household.

I wait as he closes and locks the steel door. I follow him back down the hallway Dex dragged me through last night. All the doors I pass are closed and I'm glad they're all old, wooden doors, not steel. We reach the circular foyer and ahead of me I see the double front doors.

"Remember, if you run, you spend two more nights down there," he says, not bothering to look at me as he begins to ascend the stairs.

I look at his back as he climbs, glance at the doors and I know there's no point in running. The house is set on a huge parcel of land. It took several minutes for the Rolls Royce to make it from the gate to the circular drive. So I follow him up the stairs, the marble like ice under my feet. On the landing is a rich, deep royal blue runner to cushion the sound of his shoes and to provide me some protection against the cold. He turns left and I follow him, counting doors, six of them on this side of the staircase, before he reaches the double doors at the very end.

He opens one and gestures for me to enter.

I glance inside, my eyes landing on the huge four-poster bed in the center before I step inside. I stop and take in the room as he follows and closes the door, locking it. He doesn't pocket the key but leaves it in the lock and I wonder if it's to make sure his daughter doesn't enter. Which brings me back to thoughts of his wife, but only one side of the huge bed has been slept in. All I see are masculine things, furniture, a jacket over the back of a chair, the scent of cologne—his cologne—hanging in the air.

I'll always associate that scent with him. It's not one I've smelled before—black leather and earth and wood and darkness—but I know if I ever smell it again, I'll remember Jericho St. James.

I take in the papered walls, a rich black on midnight damask with velvet curtains in obsidian that must be twelve feet long. It's how high the ceilings are, and the drapes hang from ceiling to floor. They're still closed tight blocking out any natural light. The only light in here is from the bedside lamp that's still on. The furnishings are minimal, rich cognac leather chairs and ottomans, dark wooden dresser and nightstands, all clean lines, although not quite modern, but stylish. And all entirely masculine.

He's watching me when I turn to him.

"You need a shower," he says, and I narrow my eyes.

"Do I smell like damp cellar? Or molding mattress?"

"All of the above and fear," he says, leading the

way to the bathroom door which stands open. He switches on the light and waits for me.

I walk toward it. I would love a shower, but I don't tell him that. I pass him into the large bathroom with its black and gray tiled floors and walls. A rectangular mirror spans the length of the counter with its double sinks and a black claw-footed tub stands against the far wall. The shower stall is glassed and built for two.

The Bishop mansion is large and there's obviously been money for centuries, but the style is completely different, with more of the rooms needing TLC than not. My own bedroom is on the small side, maybe a little larger than this oversized bathroom. I always wondered why Carlton gave me that one while so many larger, better furnished ones sat empty. Not that I cared, I was just curious. I knew to be grateful because the alternative to him taking me in was probably the street.

"Not to mention the residual musk of arousal," Jericho says, drawing me back to the here and now. I realize what he means. He's talking about how I smell.

My heart races. He knew. "What a keen sense of smell, but you're off on that last one. I'll give you fear though. Your cellar is haunted."

That makes his face go funny for a split second, but it passes so quickly I'm doubting I saw it at all. But I take my advantage and continue.

"This is your bedroom. Your bathroom."

He nods and I note how his face is not set in that arrogant way he has. What I said has thrown him.

"Won't your wife mind that I'm going to shower in your shower?" My heart pounds as I watch the play of emotions across his face. Again, they last a moment but it's enough to give me a glimpse into this man who wants to appear as if he's made of steel. He's not.

But then his mouth settles into a hard line and his eyes narrow, their laser-like glare on me.

I've hit on something.

And I'm about to pay for it.

"Strip," he says, voice tight, almost hoarse. His hands are fists at his sides, and I see his chest move as he drags in a long breath, exhales as slowly.

I try to swallow but my throat is too dry. I see a glass on the counter by the sink. "Can I have some water first?"

He studies me. Nods once.

I go to the sink, exhaling with relief. I turn the tap, cup my hands beneath the flow of water and drink. The running water reminds me I have to use the toilet, but I won't ask for permission. That's going too far, even given what he's already done.

When I look back at him, he's standing exactly where he was, those hard eyes trained on me as if he's reciting inside his head all the reasons he hates me. The sight of him like this, looking at me like this, sends a shiver down my spine.

"What did Carlton do to you?" I ask, my voice quiet. Because whatever it was, it was bad. And God, I hope it didn't have to do with this man's wife. Because there is no wife, I am ninety-nine-point-nine-percent sure of that. Please don't let Carlton be the reason for that.

Jericho St. James doesn't answer my question. "Strip."

I nod, start to unbutton his shirt, my fingers fumbling when I alternate between looking at him and concentrating on the task of unbuttoning. I give up and pull it over my head. I hold it out to him, and he takes it.

His gaze doesn't leave my eyes this time as he gestures to the shower and leans against the door frame, folds his arms across his chest.

I step into the all-glass shower enclosure, and switch on the water, jumping out of the way when the first icy blast hits me before it warms up. I look over my shoulder as I step under the flow and confirm he's still there, still as stone, watching me.

So, I shower. I scrub my face then shampoo my hair with his shampoo, note the absence of conditioner, and pick up the still-sudsy bar of soap and wash myself. It's strange this part. Too intimate. Using his bar of soap, rubbing it over my skin. Is he thinking about that?

When I'm finished, I switch off the water and glance to the rack of folded towels. He doesn't move so I step out of the stall and reach for a towel, aware of the water sliding off my body, aware of his eyes on me.

That's when he moves.

Our eyes meet as he lifts a towel, lets it unfold. I look up at him. He wraps it around my shoulders tight, too tight, and tugs me toward him. I instinctively put my wet hands on his chest to stop from falling into him. I can feel the contour of muscle beneath the soft sweater, feel the heat of his skin. I swallow and meet his midnight and steel eyes.

"You don't get to mention her. Ever."

Shit. I was right.

"Do you understand?"

I nod.

He tugs, pulling the towel tighter, uncomfortably squeezing my arms and shoulders. "You don't ask questions about her. And you don't say a word to my daughter about her mother. Do you understand me, Isabelle Bishop?"

The way he says my name it's like he's spitting it. He hates me. God. He *hates* me.

He shakes me once.

"Yes!" I answer.

"Good. Because if you do, if you ever fucking do, you'll be begging me to let you live out your days in that room in the cellar to escape my punishment. Am I very fucking clear?"

I swallow hard, my entire body shuddering, the bathroom suddenly freezing. I nod. I don't stop nodding until he releases me letting the towel drop and turning to walk out of the bathroom, slamming the door shut behind him.

10

ISABELLE

My hands tremble as I bend to pick up the towel. I lock the bathroom door although he's gone. I know that. But I need to do it.

Hugging the towel around my shoulders I sit down on the closed toilet seat. I'm shivering, so I draw my legs up to hug my knees.

He hates me.

Before my family was killed, I had only ever been loved. My parents and Christian, we all loved each other. Then Carlton took me in. I still wonder why he did it. At first, I'd thought it was because I am his half-sister. That he felt something for me given we share blood. But later, as I got to know him, as I saw how he was with Julia, our cousin, versus how he was with me, it became obvious he took me in because he had to. He's cooler with me, cold even. Like he is with his wife, Monique. Although she was mostly gone the three years I lived at the Bishop house during their trial separation. I don't know how long that trial will last. According to Julia, her miscarriages had driven them apart.

But that's not what's on my mind now. It's Jericho St. James.

His hate for me is different than Carlton's. No, it's not that Carlton hates me. He's indifferent to me or at worst, dislikes me. Jericho St. James hates me. And to be hated is a terrible feeling.

I shudder and force myself to stand, to dry off completely. Securing the towel around me, I look at my reflection in the mirror which is still slightly foggy around the edges. I look tired, the skin under my eyes tinged blue, my face pale. My hair needs to be combed out but a quick glance through the two drawers only reveals a comb with teeth too close together so I gather it up and twist it, wringing out as much moisture as I can before setting it over my shoulder.

I don't know what he expects of me. Am I supposed to go back out there? Go downstairs? Wait here for him? And what does he want from me? Why am I here at all?

Before I can decide what to do I hear the door in the bedroom open and close. My heartbeat picks up although I'm not sure it's him. The two times he's made an entrance or exit with me he's slammed the doors.

But when there's a soft knock on the bathroom door, I jump back.

"Isabelle?" comes a woman's voice. "I have some clothes for you. Come on out. I'm sure you're hungry, too, and breakfast is ready."

She sounds older. And her tone is not unkind.

"He's not here," she adds as if she might know why I'm holed up in here.

I force myself to walk to the door, unlock and open it. On the other side the woman steps back giving me space. When our eyes meet, she smiles and although it's a neutral smile, I see the worry in her eyes.

"I'm Leontine St. James," she says. "Jericho is my son."

"Oh." He has a mother. Even monsters have mothers.

She takes a breath in, walks to the bed, and starts to straighten the covers. I guess Jericho St. James is above making his own bed.

I see familiar clothes lying on top of it. A pair of jeans and a cornflower blue top, mine, along with a pair of sandals. Also mine.

"Where did you get those?" I ask her when she's finished with the bed.

"Jericho had your things brought over early this morning. And your room is almost ready. I'm sure he'll show it to you after breakfast. Why don't you get dressed and I'll take you downstairs." She steps closer and glances at the mess that is my hair. "I'll give you a few minutes to dress and I'll see if I can find you a brush, all right?"

I nod.

She smiles and leaves the room. I consider locking it but instead I hurry to get dressed, seeing a pair of light pink panties and a matching bra underneath the clothes. They're not mine but the tags are still on, so I quickly tug them off and dress. Better than going without. I've just zipped up my jeans when the soft knock on the door comes again before she opens it to peek her head in, only entering once she's seen I'm dressed.

"That's a lovely color on you," she says of the blue Henley. I glance down, consider buttoning the top button which I usually leave undone but leave it.

She hands over a wooden hairbrush and a spray bottle of detangler.

"My hair used to need it but not at the moment," she says, touching the soft wisps of white hair on her head. It's short, like it's just growing in, and I get the feeling she's been sick. That may be the reason she has a silk scarf wrapped around her neck in this heat. "It's coming in white," she says, "but it used to be as dark as yours."

"Thank you," I say. "I'll just go to the bathroom to brush it out."

"Sure." She sits on the edge of the bed. "I'll wait for you."

I walk toward the bathroom and pause at the door, turning back to her. She smiles when she meets my eyes, but it's not a carefree smile.

"I don't understand why..." I trail off. What do I say? I don't understand why your son kidnapped me? Isn't she complicit if she's here?

But she saves me from continuing. "Jericho will explain everything." She looks at her watch. "We'd better hurry. Angelique will be down by now."

"Angelique is his daughter?"

She nods.

"How old is she?"

"Five."

"Oh." So young. I walk into the bathroom, grateful for both detangler and brush as I brush out my hair. I pleat it into a long braid over my right shoulder, securing it with a rubber band I'd seen in one of the drawers. It'll take forever to dry this way but it's the best I can do with the small rubber band. I return to the bedroom and hand both brush and detangler back to Leontine St. James.

"I'll put them in your room once it's ready. I have no use for either."

My room. So I don't have to sleep in here? I don't ask her, though. "Thank you," I say instead.

"You're welcome." She walks to the door, opens it and gestures for me to follow her out. We head downstairs where I can already smell French toast, bacon, eggs and, most importantly, coffee.

I'm anxious as I follow Mrs. St. James around the grand staircase, past the study I was brought to first thing last night and toward the kitchen. Turning, we enter the dining room through an arched opening. I barely notice the vaulted ceilings, the marble pillars, the faces around the table bright in the morning sun, because all I see is the face of my devil sitting at the head of the table. Any warmth there vanishes the instant his eyes fall on me.

11

JERICHO

Angelique stops speaking when Isabelle walks in. She stares at her, her eyes wide her mouth open into a tiny O.

I look back at Isabelle Bishop and take her in. She's inherited her looks from her mother. That's a blessing. The Bishops are ruddy-skinned, with pale hair and eyes. Her skin has an undertone of olive, and her hair is as black as night, blacker now that it's wet, the thick strands braided into a long plait over her shoulder. She's not wearing any makeup this morning and she's still as beautiful as she was last night. Maybe more for the vulnerability in her eyes.

Zeke clears his throat and stands. I don't.

"Isabelle," he says, coming around the table. He extends his hand to her. Actually fucking extends a hand. I'm going to need to discuss loyalties with my brother. "I'm Ezekiel, Jericho's brother."

She looks from his face to his hand and back. She must be as surprised as me at this gesture, so it takes her a moment to slip her hand into his. The instant she does, some primordial savage inside me growls. I set my hands on the table and get to my feet, my eyes on Zeke who turns to me before releasing her hand.

"Mom," Zeke says and moves toward our mother, obscuring Isabelle from my line of vision for a moment as he seats her.

"I'm not an invalid. I'm not sure how many times I have to tell you boys that."

"Sit," I tell Isabelle, gesturing to the chair at the foot of the table. I'm not so chivalrous as my brother.

She glances at it, moving on stiff legs as I look her over, taking in the cornflower blue top with the buttons going all the way down the front, the top one undone. It matches some of the blue shades in her eyes. She's also wearing jeans and flat shoes. I had her things brought over. I'll go through them myself and decide what she'll keep.

Isabelle's eyes settle on my daughter, and I see her make an effort to smile.

I sit down, reach out to touch Angelique's hand. "This is Isabelle," I tell her, tucking a curl behind her ear. "She's going to stay with us for a while."

"Belle?" she asks. "Like in my book?"

I smile tightly and nod. I want to tell her Isabelle Bishop is no princess but don't.

"Isabelle, this is my daughter, Angelique."

"Nice to meet you," Isabelle says. "My little cousin calls me Belle."

"It's my favorite name," Angelique says, surprising me. She's very shy, probably my own doing. I've kept her apart from society for all her life. She's known my mother, Zeke, Dex, a handful of guards and staff, but no one else. Ever. And on the rare occasion she meets someone, she mostly hides behind her stuffed bear, which is always with her, or me.

"Angelique might be my favorite name, too," Isabelle says.

Angelique beams. "Really?"

"M-hm," Isabelle says with a smile, and I wonder how kind she'll be to my daughter once she comes to truly hate me. Because she doesn't yet. She may fear me. And that won't change. But she doesn't know me. Doesn't know what I plan to do with her. No one does. Because The Rite offers her some protections. I plan to strip her of those. Her brother will agree. He'll have no choice when he sees the rest of the ammunition I'm collecting against him. I just need Santiago to come through for me and when he does, I'll act.

Catherine, the cook who's been with the family since I was a little boy, walks in with a huge platter of French toast. Angelique's request. I see how she winks at my daughter and hear Angelique's delighted gasp as she sets the dish at the center of the table.

"Oh wow!" Angelique exclaims at the mound covered in powdered sugar.

"There," Catherine says.

I look up at her. "Is there anything healthy?"

She raises her eyebrows. "I remember your sweet tooth, Jericho," she mutters. "But yes, of course." And several maids enter carrying trays of eggs, bacon, sliced fruit and various freshly squeezed juices.

She makes a plate for Angelique and pours coffee for the adults before leaving. I watch my daughter's delighted face as she eats the sweet breakfast, sugar coating her lips and cheeks, falling onto the head of her teddy bear sitting in her lap. My mother walks over to clip her hair back from her face before sitting down to butter a slice of bread. I sip my coffee and watch her. She takes a bite then sets the bread down.

I get to my feet, pick up her plate and scoop scrambled eggs onto it along with several strips of bacon.

"Protein. You need to eat to keep up your strength," I tell her. She's recovering from chemotherapy and while I'm glad it's over, it's a long, slow recovery. A few months ago, we weren't sure she'd come this far, so every day I'm grateful for it.

She smiles up at me. "I do eat." She gestures

toward Isabelle who is also sitting with an empty plate. "Perhaps you need to make your guest feel welcome enough to eat."

My guest. She's not my fucking guest. And she's not welcome.

Grudgingly, I make my way to the foot of the table. Isabelle stiffens when I reach her and lean down, picking up her dish. "You'll need your strength, too," I whisper so only she can hear. I load her plate with eggs, bacon, French toast, and fruit and set it in front of her. It's a mountain but she'll eat it. She missed dinner last night and she can stand to put on a few pounds. I straighten, look down at the top of her head as she takes in the heaping dish. "Eat," I tell her.

Zeke watches without a word then turns to help Angelique with her knife and fork. She's young but she watches the adults and mimics. She's never been around other children, only adults. I wonder how she'd appear to them. If they'd find her odd. If they'd make fun of her for the mismatched eyes, the blue and gray that I passed on to her. She won't ever be subjected to that though. Nothing will change for her now that we're home. The tutor I've hired will begin her work this week and she'll be safe where I can watch her, protect her.

I kiss the top of her head before resuming my seat and eating my own breakfast of eggs and bacon.

Zeke gets a call a few minutes later and leaves

the room to take it. Once Angelique has finished eating, my mother takes her from the table, leaving only Isabelle and me.

"You'll finish your plate before you leave the table," I tell her when she puts the fork and knife down. She's eaten everything but the bacon.

"I'm finished."

"I don't know how you were brought up, but we don't waste food in this house."

"I was brought up fine and don't waste food either, but since you scooped a mountain of it on my plate without bothering to ask if I eat meat maybe you can finish it for me."

That's unexpected. I'm glad to see she's got a spine.

I smile, get up and move toward the foot of the table. She isn't expecting that and squirms in her seat as I take the chair closest to hers.

"Vegetarian?"

She nods.

I am surprised she ate the rest of it. It was, I admit, a lot. I pick up the strips of bacon one at a time and eat them while she watches. I am wiping my hands on a napkin when Dex comes to the entrance of the dining room.

Isabelle stiffens, her hands gripping the wooden arms of the chair hard.

"Room's ready," Dex says, not sparing her a glance.

I nod, rise to my feet then turn to Isabelle. "Up." I pull her chair out and she rises. With the tips of my fingers just brushing her lower back I guide her toward the stairs. When we pass the hallway which ends at the steel door leading down to the cellar, I feel her stiffen. Good. I walk more slowly, only feeling her relax once we've passed that corridor and are climbing the stairs.

"Left," I say at the top of the stairs.

She casts a suspicious glance over her shoulder but moves. When we get to the door beside mine, I stop her with a hand on her shoulder and take the key out of my pocket to unlock the door. I push it open. She steps inside and I follow her in, closing and locking the door behind us, making a point to tuck the key back into my pocket.

She's watching me when I turn back to her, but I leave her standing there while I go into the bathroom to wash my hands. When I return, she hasn't moved. She's looking around, forehead furrowed as she takes in the room dotted with her belongings.

"My things," she says to me.

"Some of them."

"Your mother said someone brought them." She walks to the far wall where her violin case is resting, touches it.

"You play violin?" I ask. I don't know the first thing about the instrument or her level of proficiency. I guess low considering she hasn't enrolled in any school since graduating high school.

She glances at me, nods, but doesn't elaborate. She moves to the desk, peers inside the backpack at the notebooks there. A glance at the notebooks earlier showed they're full of sheets of music.

"My cell phone?" she asks.

"You won't need that. You're a vegetarian. Anything else I should know?"

"Like what?"

"Like medications, allergies, etc."

"Nothing. How long am I staying? If you brought my things—"

"You're mine. You'll stay until I put you out."

She winces at the ice in my voice and it takes her a moment to recover. "When do you think you'll be *putting me out*?"

"Why? You have plans?"

"Your family seems nice enough," she says, walking into the closet which is sparse even with all her clothes in it. "Are you adopted?"

"Funny. A word of warning. Watch out for my brother," I say, remembering last night, the conversation still bugging me.

She doesn't remark.

"You'll remain inside the house while you're here. You may venture outside with permission and then only within the walls of the property."

"Permission?"

"Permission."

"From you?"

I grin.

"How long do I have to be here really?"

"Indefinitely. You're in my care now, Isabelle."

"Care is a stretch."

"It's a matter of perspective."

"Why?"

"Why what?"

"Why did you do it? Take me? Why do you want *me*?"

"You mean is there something special about you?" I watch her as I say it, knowing my purpose is to wound. And it does. I see it in the flush of her cheeks, in the embarrassed way she looks away.

It takes her a minute to steel herself and square her shoulders to face me. "I don't think I'm special. I just want to know what's going on. What you intend to do to me. When I can plan on resuming my life."

"You're a means to an end," I say, walking closer to her. I can see she wants to move away but she doesn't. Instead, she folds her arms across her chest. I pick up the end of the braid and pull out the rubber band. It's still damp as I unwind it, watch the waves it makes as I set it loose over her shoulder. "I intend to do a great many things to you. And there won't be a need for you to make plans on resuming your life." I watch her process. Her eyes search mine and I feel that strange sensation I've felt off and on with her. "This is your life now, Isabelle. You will be kind to my daughter, polite and respectful to my family. Subservient to me."

"What does that last part mean?"

"It means you'll do what I tell you to do. If that means getting on your hands and knees to scrub a floor, then you'll get on your hands and knees and scrub the floor."

"So, I'm a glorified maid."

"Not glorified, no. And I haven't told you your most important duty."

Her arms fall to her sides when I put a finger on her stomach and nudge her back two steps to the wall. I lean my shoulder against it, trapping her. "Most importantly, you will please me. In fact, if you forget everything else, remember only those two words and let all your actions come back to that thought. Pleasing me."

Her jaw is locked so tight I wonder if she's going to crack a tooth.

I dip my head close. "I like your hair loose. That'll be one way you can please me," I say. "To show me the river of black spilling down your naked back."

"I'm not sleeping with you," she blurts.

"Sleep wasn't what I had in mind." I let my gaze drop to the open neck of her Henley. It's wide but not so wide her scar is visible. I reach to undo a button.

One arm shoots up to stop me.

I glance down at it, her hand appearing smaller now that it's wrapped around my forearm. I take her wrist, pull her hand off, then take her other wrist with my free hand and draw both arms over her head. Without taking my eyes off her, I shift both wrists to one hand and stretch them higher, high enough she has to stand on tiptoe.

She squeezes her eyes shut like she's steeling herself so when she opens them again, she stares straight ahead at the middle of my chest. Her breathing is labored, the pulse at her neck throbbing. I undo another button, watch her thick, black lashes flutter as she follows the workings of my fingers. I undo a third button, a fourth, fifth and sixth. It's enough to pull the top over her collarbone, enough to draw the two sides apart to expose her breasts, the pretty pink bra.

"I chose it," I say and when her eyes flick up to mine, the sight of them is breathtaking. A fine, fiery line of blue around dilated pupils glaring up at me, hating me, hating herself. "The bra and panties. I'm glad to see you wore them. *If* you're wearing the panties that is. I shouldn't make assumptions."

"I didn't exactly have a choice," she hisses, struggling against my grip.

"Well, you did. You could have chosen not to wear anything. You always have a choice. All of life is a choice," I say, unwilling to drag my gaze from her eyes as I let my fingertips explore the soft flesh in the valley between her breasts, the taut skin of her abdomen, her belly button a small oval, the jeans low.

"Stop," she croaks out as I let my fingers hover over the button there.

"But I want to know two more things." I pop the button.

"Stop!"

"I want to know," I say, slowly drawing the zipper down. "One, if you wore the matching panties," I start, letting my gaze drop down to her stomach as I nudge the denim over just a little, just enough to expose a little bit of the soft pink lace. "And two..." I let my words trail off as I tickle the place just at the band of her panties.

She swallows, looks up at me and I hold her gaze. Her neck and face are flushed pink, eyes almost wholly black now.

"I think I can guess but just to be sure... I mean I could ask you, of course," I continue, letting my fingers dip just a little lower as she squirms. "Should I ask you?"

"What?" She wants to sound angry, but it's choked.

I lean my face toward hers, nudge her cheek with my chin then bring my mouth to her ear. I feel her shudder as I tickle the shell of her ear with my tongue before I ask. "Are you wet, Isabelle?"

"No!" she blurts, and I simultaneously draw back and lock eyes with her as I slide my hand into her panties and hear her sharp intake of breath when I cup the sweet, tell-tale damp of her sex.

"You little liar," I taunt, drawing my fingers through her folds and dragging them up to the hard nub hidden between her lips. I circle it, hear the catching of her breath, watch her face as her knees buckle. "Dirty, dirty little liar. You're soaked."

I drag my hand out of her panties smearing her arousal over her belly before bringing those fingers between us as if to show us both how wet they are.

She glances at them then turns away but there's no denying it.

"If you weren't such a liar, I'd make you come," I say, placing those fingers on her cheek to turn her face back to me before I smear her arousal over her lips. "But I can't stand lies or liars."

"Fuck you, you're an asshole!"

She tries to wrench her head out of my grasp, but I bury my fingers in her jaw and press the back of her head against the wall.

"Watch your mouth, little liar. I don't like girls who swear."

"You don't have to like me. In fact, I'm sure there's no risk of that happening."

"You're right about that but I don't want to put my dick in so foul a place so let's start a list of rules. You can think of them as your commandments.

Think you can remember them, or do we need to write them down? I noticed your brother didn't bother enrolling you in any university program. I hope there's not a cognitive problem."

"Fuck. You."

I dig my fingers in. "Thou. Shalt. Not. Swear."

"Fuck. You. Asshole." She matches my tone although her words come out slightly strange with me squeezing her cheeks like I am.

"I'll tell you what, I'll fuck *your* asshole if you say it one more time. What do you think? You want to try me? Because I can guarantee two things." I hold on up one finger. "One. You will not enjoy it." I hold up the second. "Two. I will."

She exhales through her nose keeping her lips sealed tight.

"Come on. Try me, Isabelle. Let's make this a fun morning. Tell me to fuck off again. Go on."

Nothing. Nothing but daggers shooting from her eyes.

"Just once? You're not scared of me, are you?"

"I think you'll look for any excuse to punish me and I'm not going to make it easy for you, Jericho St. James."

I study her, ignoring the buzzing of my phone in my pocket. I smile, then lean my face close and kiss her full on the mouth, tasting her lips, the sweet musk of her pussy. Then the copper of blood as she opens her mouth and snaps her teeth shut over my lower lip, drawing blood and daring to meet my eyes as she does it.

I grin, kiss her deeper and when her teeth drop away, I take her lip between mine and tease it, play with it, but I don't bite, not yet. Instead, I drag my bloody lip over her cheek, smear my blood like war paint on her beautiful face before dropping her arms and stepping away, watching as her legs give out at the unexpected release and she falls to hands and knees.

She looks up at me, face flushed, a smear of red across one cheek, breath short. She sits back on her heels. I like her like this. I'll have her there tonight, I decide. On her knees. My cock down her throat. Choking on my come.

My phone buzzes again and I draw it out of my pocket, read the text. My brother. They're waiting on me.

"I'm tempted to bend you over the bed and fuck you now, but it'll have to wait. Do try to keep your hands out of your pants until I'm back."

Her mouth falls open as if she's offended.

I walk to the door, unlock it, but turn back to her before I open it. "Don't do anything stupid."

I know from the look on her face she's screaming every foul word she knows at me, but she's smart. She knows I'm not screwing around. I will fuck her in the ass to punish her and she's clever enough to know that is not a punishment she wants to earn.

"See how well this is working already?" I ask her.

She gets to her feet, picks up the first thing she can reach, which happens to be the lamp on the nightstand, tugs it so hard that the plug comes out of the wall socket, and she hurls it at me. Her aim is shit and she misses. It crashes against the wall, and I can't help but laugh.

But my phone buzzes again. I need to get downstairs. So, I put a stern look on my face and turn back to her. When I take one step toward her, she backs up three.

"That was an antique," I pause. "Get it cleaned up. We can decide how you're going to pay me for the damage tonight." I open the door, purposely crunching glass under my shoe before I step out into the hallway. I turn back to her. "And it bears repeating. Don't do anything stupid."

"Drop dead, Jericho St. James. Just drop dead."

I close the door and walk away with a smile on my face because this has just shaped up to be a hundred times more fun than I imagined.

12

ISABELLE

I glare after him while buttoning my clothes. I swear it feels like his hand is still on my skin. Inside my panties. Rough fingers rubbing my clit.

Me liking the sensation.

Me fucking liking it!

"Fuck you, Jericho St. James," I say, my face hot with humiliation as I tuck my shirt back into my jeans and go into the bathroom to wash my face. I can't help but catch a glimpse of my reflection, though. The streak of blood smeared across my cheek. His blood.

I stop. Look straight at myself.

His blood.

He bleeds. He's human.

Which means I can hurt him.

I press a finger through the red streak. I did this. I

bled him. And I don't know what he expected in taking me, but this will not be a one-way street. I will hurt him back every time he hurts me. I will not just take it. He's a bully. A kidnapper. Probably more and worse things.

But then I see Angelique's little face at the breakfast table. Her well-loved bear in her lap, two fingers rubbing the ear as she stared at me like she'd never seen anyone outside of her family before. And I see his face as he watched her. As he tucked her hair behind her ear with the gentlest touch of those giant, menacing hands. As he kissed the top of her head.

This is like two different men.

Her father.

My devil.

I shake my head, adjusting the water as hot as I can stand it in the sink and scrub my face. I tell myself how much I hate that he touched me. That he laid his hands on me. I don't remind myself the point he was trying to make. The point he proved. And I quash the thought that I enjoyed it because I did not.

I switch off the water and grab a towel to roughly dry my face. I glance to the clock on the bedside table. It's a little after nine in the morning.

My toiletry bag is here on the counter. I rifle through it, grabbing my toothbrush and toothpaste to brush my teeth as I search through the drawers beneath the sink. I find my razors, tampons, shampoo, and conditioner. Everything from my bathroom at home. Well, most things. My scissors are missing. Probably doesn't want to take a chance I'll stab him.

I switch off the electric toothbrush and rinse, then dry my hands again and hunt through my makeup bag. There I find the little plastic package of birth control pills. Carlton made sure I was on them as soon as I moved into his house even though I told him there was no need. Now I wonder if there's going to be a need. I pop the next pill in the cycle, swallow it with a handful of water. I've always been lax about taking them, but now I'll make a point to do it right. Because I know what just happened is only a prelude. I have no doubt Jericho St. James plans on having me in his bed.

I return to the bedroom and take a quick look inside the small interior pocket of my backpack to confirm two more sets of pills are still there. I always get them from the pharmacy in three-month increments.

After zipping the pocket, I look out the window. I must be at the back of the house and from what I can see, the large garden is bordered by dense woods surrounded by a wall that seems to go on for miles. There are a few areas where the trees thin out and far to the east of the house, I see what appears to be a crumbling stone structure. Or maybe it was once a structure. It's too distant to tell from here. I don't see the house on the other side of that wall. Only more trees. The Bishop and St. James properties stand back-to-back, a wall the dividing line between them. This place is like a fortress. Why does he need a fortress?

The Bishop house is probably as large, but the garden doesn't look nearly as well kept as this one below with its large, turquoise swimming pool, the beautiful furniture along the wide, curved patio overlooking it and the neat garden with what seems to be miles and miles of roses along the walls. It's beautiful. Like a fairy tale.

A knock comes on the door, and I'm startled. I turn but I know it's not him. He wouldn't knock so I tell my heart to slow down.

"Yes?"

"Isabelle, it's us. Leontine and Angelique. May we come in?"

I walk to the door, picking my way around the shattered lamp to open it. I see Leontine standing there with her hand on Angelique's head. Angelique is holding her bear and a very large book with a beautiful binding that looks like it may weigh more than she does.

"What happened?" Leontine asks as she looks down.

"Oh, I um dropped a lamp."

Her eyebrows, which are almost non-existent, rise high on her forehead. She smiles. "Well, I'll send someone up to clean it. Why don't we go downstairs and Angelique can show you her book."

"My room, Nana," Angelique says to her grandmother.

"Of course, dear," Leontine says with a warm smile.

"I can clean it up if I can borrow a vacuum cleaner. I'm the one who broke it."

"Well, I get the feeling you had good reason," she says, her gray eyes brighter than I expect. They almost match Jericho's gray one. I wonder if the midnight is from his father. But then I remind myself I don't care.

"I'll ask someone to help us. Angelique has been wanting to show you—"

"The princess with almost your name," says the little girl, drawing my attention. She's very pretty with her little heart-shaped face. Very sweet. "Her name is Belle. I'll show you."

I crouch down as she tries to open the book to a certain page. It's too bulky for her. "Let's go look at it in your room," I tell her before she drops it in the broken glass.

Leontine guides Angelique into the hallway and I move around the glass before closing the door behind me. I spare one glance at the double doors next to my room, remembering they lead to his bedroom, then follow Angelique down the hall. Leontine disappears downstairs to get someone to clean up my mess. I do feel bad about it but there's nothing to be done.

"This is my room," Angelique says, reaching up to open the door. She's small for being five. "It's new."

"New?" I ask as we step into the yellow bedroom.

"We just moved here," she says, and I make a mental note the next time I see Julia to ask her about it. I'm sure she is researching the St. James family since what happened last night. I wonder what Carlton told her. My cousin has a strange obsession with IVI. She knows all the founding families, the Sovereign Sons. I don't think she'd mind Carlton matching her up with one.

Angelique's room is large. Larger than mine, and the centerpiece is a double bed draped with yellow gauze. Fairy lights line the edges of the ceiling, and I am sure any toy a girl could ever want is in this room, most of the boxes not yet unpacked. But for all of that, the room is neat and on the nightstand are several storybooks stacked one on top of another. On the floor against the wall are two more stacks of books that appear to be well loved.

Angelique walks to the bed, climbs up and sits down against the pillows. She sets her bear beside her and opens the book on her lap. She pushes a dark curl behind her ear, and I see how her tiny feet turn in and swing a little as she focuses on a page of a very elaborate pop-up book.

I sit down beside her, and she points to the castle with its layers of detail. A peek inside one of the windows shows the princess Belle in her signature yellow ball gown.

"That's her," she says. "Belle. The Beast kidnaps her and then he falls in love with her," she explains simply. "Do you know the story?"

"I do. It's a beautiful story. And a beautiful book. Would you like me to read it to you?"

She smiles wide and nods, handing it over to me.

I turn to the first page taking a moment to appreciate the village scene that pops up before I begin to read.

Angelique sighs and lays her head on my arm. I'm so surprised I pause to look down at her and wonder if she realizes she's doing it. I don't think she does. Her attention is fully on the book. She's careful as she reaches out to touch one of the town folks as I read her the story. I wonder how many times this story has been read to her when she follows along whispering the words with me.

I also wonder how she can be that terrible man's daughter. How this gentle, sweet girl can be his offspring.

The door opens quietly, and Leontine enters, smiling when she sees us. After adjusting the curtains on one of the windows she comes to sit beside Angelique. When I finish reading and close the book, Angelique sighs heavily and takes it from me.

"It's my favorite story," she says to me.

"Is it?"

She watches me the way children do. No sense of awkwardness.

"You're pretty and even though your name is like Belle, you look more like Snow White." She runs her hand over my long hair which I'd left as Jericho had wanted. But only because it hadn't occurred to me to braid it again.

"Thank you. You're very pretty, too, Angelique."

"Isabelle, would you like to take Angelique for a walk in the garden?" Leontine asks. "My appointment has been moved up a few hours, so I'll need to be away for a while longer than I planned. Would you mind?"

"Mind? Not at all. I'd love it," I say as we stand, and Angelique slides her hand into mine. As I follow the older woman out, I recall Jericho's words about needing his permission to go outside and I mentally flip him off.

Before we're out in the hallway, Leontine turns to the little girl and crouches down. "Shall we leave Baby Bear in your bedroom? Let her get a little rest?"

Angelique hugs her bear and shakes her head. "She doesn't like to be alone."

"All right then," she says and straightens. I catch her eye, see a hint of worry.

We make our way downstairs, Angelique taking each step slowly with her little legs as she holds my hand and the banister. Her bear's paw is crushed between our palms.

I wonder if Leontine's appointment has to do with her hair growing back and the comments she'd made earlier but don't mention anything. We make our way toward the living room which is an expansive, bright room that overlooks the garden and pool through three sets of double French doors.

"This house is beautiful," I can't help but say.

"Thank you," Leontine says. "It's been in the family for generations. It was built by Draca St. James over four hundred years ago," she says, turning to glance at me as she opens the French doors leading to the patio. "Our combined history goes back that far, but you probably already know that."

I wonder if I hear something in her tone or if I imagine it. Her smile is as gentle as it's been.

"I don't, actually. I only just learned that I'm half-Bishop a few years ago."

She mutters a *hm* but doesn't comment and now I'm more anxious than ever to talk to Julia.

"Oh, goodness, the heat today," she says, turning away and walking ahead of us before I can get a read on her.

It's the last day of August and it's a hot one. September will bring with it slightly cooler temperatures. I feel a cloud descend at the thought of September. School starts in just a few weeks. But Carlton told me he had unenrolled me. He'd done it sometime during the summer break but hadn't bothered to mention it, so I only learned about it when I called to check about books and classes. He'd explained that it was no longer necessary. That he was going to find me a match and I'd be married soon. So because this is apparently the middle ages, I wouldn't need a career. I shake my head at the memory of our conversation but when Carlton has an idea, there's no talking him out of it.

It was the point of the masquerade ball. Me in that ridiculous feather dress. It was him showing off the goods to potential buyers. I wonder how close he'd come before Jericho St. James upended his plans.

Either way, it does me no good. I have a feeling that for as much as my devil hates Carlton, they'd be aligned in this. It only makes my life a little more miserable and isn't that what he wants? Isn't that part of this strange punishment I'm on the receiving end of, even though I don't know what I've done?

A man comes to the door then and clears his throat. "The car is ready, Ma'am."

"Just a minute," Leontine tells him and turns to us. "You're sure you don't mind watching her, Isabelle?"

"I'd really love it, actually."

"Good. Catherine is inside if you need anything. There are guards all around." I'm not sure if that part is said as a warning or to make me feel safe. Although why do they need all this protection?

"Okay," I say.

"I will be back in a few hours." She turns to Angelique and crouches down. "You help Isabelle find her way out there and remember, you're not allowed in the woods, all right?"

"Okay, Nana." She hugs her grandmother.

I see how tightly Leontine hugs her, almost like she's not sure she'll see her again. It's strange. But then she straightens, says goodbye to me and is gone.

Angelique and I spend the next few hours exploring the garden, picking roses, and reading. We have lunch together inside and I assume she'll nap afterwards. I'm not sure at what age children stop napping but she doesn't. Instead, we're back outside in the heat.

"Shall we explore?" I ask her. "It'll be cooler under the trees."

She eyes the cropping of trees warily and turns back to me. "I'm not allowed in the woods. My daddy doesn't want me to go there without him."

"Oh." I remember Leontine's reminder about the woods then. "Even with me? I'm a grown up."

She shakes her head.

"That's okay. Um…" I look back at the sparkling

turquoise pool. "How about a swim. Do you like to swim?"

She eyes the pool too and her smile grows huge but quickly dims. "I can't swim," she says.

"I can't remember if I knew how to swim when I was five. But I'm an excellent swimmer and I can teach you if you like?"

"Really?"

I nod. "Really."

"I'd like that very much."

"Great! Let's go get our swimsuits on," I say, hoping whoever packed my things packed my bathing suit.

I help Angelique with hers first. She has a—surprise—yellow swimsuit with ruffles which she clearly loves. In her bathroom I brush out her hair and tie it into a curly ponytail to keep it out of her face. Then we walk toward my bedroom where I find the glass has been cleaned up. Angelique follows me inside and looks around as I go through the dresser drawers to find a swimsuit.

Some of my things have been unpacked and some of the drawers contain new clothes. I don't find any of my own suits, but I do see three brand new bikinis. They're all a little smaller than I'd choose for myself but they're my size, so I pick a yellow one to match Angelique and slip into the bathroom to change.

When I return, I find her sitting at my desk flipping through one of my notebooks.

"What are these?" she asks, her little finger tracing the notes on a page. "They're not words."

"No, they're music."

"Music?"

I smile and nod. "I play the violin," I tell her, pointing to my violin still in its case. I pick it up, set it on the desk and unzip it to show her. "See."

"Oh."

She climbs up to stand on the chair and leans toward the instrument. A few moments later, she reaches out a tentative hand to touch the old wood. It's a used violin and was well-loved when my parents bought it for me years ago. I don't mind. I love it. In fact, I prefer a used, old violin to a brand new one. I can just imagine how much it was loved before I loved it.

"It's so pretty. Can I hear you play it Belle? I mean Isabelle."

"You can call me Belle. I'm used to it."

"Really?"

"Yep."

"Thank you, Belle. I've never heard the violin," she says.

"You probably have but don't know it. I'll play for you later, okay?"

"I'd like that." She glances at my bikini and

smiles. "I love your bathing suit," she says. "It's like mine."

"We match," I tell her and pull on my robe. She wears one too. "Sunscreen?" I ask.

She shrugs her shoulders, and we make our way downstairs, still carrying Baby Bear. In the kitchen I find Catherine, the woman who served breakfast. She seems surprised to see us dressed to swim.

"I'm not sure about that," the older woman says.

"Belle can swim," Angelique says. "And we'll be careful."

"I'll take good care of her," I tell the woman. "Please don't worry. I'm an excellent swimmer. Was even on the swim team throughout high school and a lifeguard at the local pool over summer breaks."

She seems hesitant but hands us the sunscreen. "All right."

"Are there any pool toys?" I ask.

She appears confused. "Toys?"

"Um, yes, like floats?"

She shakes her head like it's the first time she's ever heard anything like it.

"Well, shall we?" I ask Angelique who smiles wide as we head back out to the pool. She sets Baby Bear on a lounge chair and covers him with her robe.

"You love her, huh?"

She nods. "I'm her mommy. She gets scared when she can't see me. She thinks I'm leaving and won't come back." She turns her face up to mine and I glimpse a sadness that I'm weirdly not surprised to see even though it doesn't belong to a child her age. But before I can ponder her words, she speaks again. "Do you think we can bring the chair closer to the pool, Isabelle?"

"I think we can definitely do that. We'll put it under that umbrella, so she has some shade. What do you think?"

"That's a really good idea."

Once we get Baby Bear situated and I've lathered us both in sunscreen, I take her hand and we take the first step into the swimming pool. When we get to the second, she hesitates, and I look back at her.

"All right?" I ask.

She squints her eyes against the sun. "Maybe I should sit with Baby Bear so she's not scared."

"She's fine," I say, waving to the bear. "She's not scared, sweetheart. And I won't let go of you, so you don't need to be either, okay? I promise."

She looks over the sparkling water. "Okay," she finally says, and she sucks in a breath at the next steps which brings the water up to her stomach.

I take both her hands and face her as I walk backwards down the last two steps. She stays where she is as I dunk my head under. The water feels great on this hot, sticky day. I shake out my hair and splash her, making her giggle.

"Come on, you just hold on to me," I tell her. I take her in a hug and carry her into the pool.

She wraps her arms around my neck seeming amazed as I bob us around, staying in the area where I can stand, not yet going into the deep end. Whenever I test if she's ready for me to loosen my hold on her, she only tightens hers and glances at her bear.

"Have you ever played starfish, Angelique?"

"What's that?" she asks.

"It's when you lay on your back in the water and pretend you're a starfish. It's easy. Want me to show you?"

She nods.

"Okay. I'm going to put you down on the edge of the pool, okay? You don't come in without me, understand?"

She nods as I set her down, her tiny feet in the water. I stay within arm's reach and float on my back, extending my arms and legs to make a star shape.

"See, like this?"

She watches me and I make sure to keep one hand on her as I float.

"Do you see that?" I ask, pointing up at a cloud. "I think it looks like an ice cream cone. Do you think so too?"

She turns her face to it, and I watch her squint, wondering if she's even been in a pool before. Wondering how any five-year-old is more afraid of the water than she is excited to get in it. I blame Jericho St. James for her fear.

"I see it!" she exclaims. "And look at that one. It looks like Baby Bear!"

"Oh my goodness, it really does! Want to play starfish and find shapes in the clouds?"

She looks me over and nods.

I straighten, collect her in my arms again and pull her into the water.

"Belle?"

I smile down at her. "Yes, sweetheart?"

"I'm a little scared."

I hug her. "I'll be right here. I won't let you go for a second. I promise, okay? You're safe with me. Do you feel safe with me?"

She nods.

"Okay then, here we go. You're just going to lie down, okay? Just lie down and my hand will be like a pillow for your head. All you have to do is breathe like normal. If you fill up your belly with air, you'll float just like I did, okay?"

"You won't let me go?"

"Nope."

It takes a moment and I feel the tension in her body, but then I see her decide to do it. Feel her relax just enough to lay back. A few minutes later as she lies with arms and legs extended, I see her smile. I draw my hand out from under her head and intertwine our fingers as I join her and we float, two starfish in the water.

"That one's a unicorn," she says, and I glance over at her with a smile. I wonder about her life, about her mom, about the darkness I glimpse in eyes too young to know anything but light.

"Definitely," I say and am about to point out a hippopotamus when a dark shadow falls over us.

I gasp, straightening, my feet not touching down because we've floated into the deep end. As soon as I go under, Angelique panics and flails her arms to get hold of me. I catch her before her head even goes under, but a huge splash sends us bobbing. A moment later, two powerful arms wrap around us and we're dragged to the shallow end where Angelique is snatched away from me.

We're both sputtering water and coughing. I wipe my eyes with wet hands before opening them to find Jericho St. James in the water still fully dressed in his suit holding his daughter tight to his chest, glaring daggers at me.

"What the fuck were you thinking?"

Isabelle startles, stopping short when she comes out of her bathroom clutching a towel with one hand.

I showered and changed into jeans and a T-shirt after making sure Angelique was all right. I've been pacing in here ever since. I take Isabelle in, looking her over as she tightens her hold on that towel, long wet hair sticking to her shoulders and arms. I see the effort it takes her not to go scurrying back into the bathroom to escape my wrath.

Seeing them out there when I came home, seeing Angelique lying in the pool like that, fuck, my heart almost gave out.

"She can't swim," I tell Isabelle. "She's five years old!"

"We were just having fun. I was there. I didn't let her out of my sight. I didn't let go of her once!"

I stalk right up to her, catching up with her in what seems to be our natural stance: her back pressed against a wall, me towering over her. It conjures an image similar to some of the pictures in Angelique's fairy tales. Beauty and the Beast. I realize how unflattering it is to me, but I don't care.

I squeeze my hands then flex them and finally shove them into my pockets to keep from wrapping them around her neck. I'm so angry. So fucking angry I don't know what I'll do otherwise.

"Who gave you permission to go outside? I told you—"

"What, is that a commandment too? Should we add it to your list after thou shalt not swear?"

My hands turn into fists in my pockets and a growl comes from inside my chest.

She hears it and shuts her mouth, leaning a little farther from me although there's nowhere to go.

I count to ten. "Who gave you permission to take my daughter into the pool?"

"No one," she says. "I just... Your mother asked me to look after her," she starts, voice growing more anxious as she continues. "It was so hot, and she's not allowed in the woods even with your thousand guards and impenetrable wall!" This part sounds like some sort of accusation. "And I get that if she's alone, but she wouldn't even go with me because you won't let her!"

"She's scared of the water."

"Because she doesn't know how to swim. I don't know many five-year-old's who do but I know even less who are more afraid than excited to jump into a swimming pool! You've got her scared of her own shadow—"

My right hand closes around her throat. It's not even conscious. "And you know this after spending a few hours with her. She's *my* daughter. Mine!"

She's gone too far. She knows it. "We were just floating. Playing a game," she says, both hands around my forearm, her towel dropping to the floor.

I look down at her, naked, vulnerable. At my mercy. I loosen my grip on her neck.

"She was safe the whole time. She was having fun." The whites of her eyes are pink, the skin around them wet. When I let go of her neck, she realizes she lost her towel and covers herself with her arms. "Until you decided to jump in fully clothed and send us under with that tsunami! Why would you do that?"

She wipes tears with the back of one hand and I think they're tears of frustration and anger even if they started as fear.

She's at least a little right, but fuck, she has no right to be. No right to say these things.

"You don't know us, Isabelle. You don't know anything about us."

"And here I am thrust into your family. I didn't ask for this."

I push my hand into my hair and walk away.

"What did you think I was doing?" she asks, sounding indignant now.

When I turn back to her, I find her clutching that towel again.

"What could you possibly think I would do to your little girl? To any child?"

"You're a Bishop," I spit and walk to the door. I need to be away from her.

"And you're unbelievable!" she cries out. "Did you think I'd let anything happen to her? Think I'd hurt a little girl because I'm a Bishop? I've never heard anything more fucked up than that, Jericho St. James!"

I spin to face her, and she stumbles backward. "I know what Bishops are capable of. I've seen it with my own two eyes." My voice is raspy, the words sounding strange, but she shudders, and she doesn't even know their meaning.

"I wouldn't hurt her. What is wrong with you that you think I could?" she asks more quietly.

I close my hand over the too-small bracelet on my arm. Kimberly's. And I remember that day. Remember the sound of the gun. The look on her face when she was jolted into my arms. Remember the weight of her body going limp there.

I make myself remember it. And I stare at the Bishop before me. And I remind myself why she's here. What she's capable of. What they're all capable of.

She must feel the aggression growing inside me because she takes two steps away, wide eyes locked on me. She's ready to make her move when I make mine. But I don't make any move. Not toward her. I need to get away from here. Away from her. Before I do more damage than I intend.

I turn to the door again, digging out my key as I do. When I open it and step into the hallway, she runs toward it.

"Wait!"

I stop, key in hand, the door open just a few inches.

"Is she okay?" she asks, surprising me. I thought she'd beg me not to lock her in. Thought she'd plead her innocence. "At least tell me she's okay."

"She's not your concern," I tell her and before she can say anything else, I close the door and lock it, pocketing the key.

14

ISABELLE

It's hours later and full dark when I finally hear the lock in the door turn. I quickly close the notebook on my lap, shoving the pencil in the page and rubbing black smears off my hands. My eraser drops to the floor and my stomach growls loudly. I'm starving. I think part of his plan is to starve me. And for what? For taking his daughter swimming? How unbelievably ridiculous is that?

The smell of the food makes the already loud growling louder. The door is pushed open and a woman I saw helping in the kitchen earlier pushes a cart in. It's laid with a beige linen tablecloth, topped with a dish covered by a stainless-steel dome as well as an uncorked bottle of wine, another of water and two sets of glasses, a basket of bread.

My mood would lift to see this except that

Jericho St. James follows her. His gaze barely brushes over me but even in that moment he does deign to look in my direction, he manages to show his disapproval of me. He can go fuck himself. I disapprove of him, too.

He stands there with his hands in his pockets just watching the woman set up the tray. The smell is even more enticing once she removes the dome lid. I press my arms into my stomach to stop its loud rumbling at the sight and smell of vegetables roasted with herbs layered with melted cheese and potatoes.

"Thank you, May," Jericho says when she's finished and walks her out, locking the door behind her and pocketing his little key. Dickhead.

"You don't have to worry I'll try to run past you, you know," I tell him, bending to pick up the fallen eraser and setting it on the nightstand. I don't wait for an invitation to eat. I'm too hungry.

"It's to make sure no one comes in," he says calmly. "No little girls wandering into rooms they shouldn't wander into. Not tonight anyway."

My heart drops to my stomach at his words. At their meaning. I stop short of the table.

"Sit down and eat," he says, lifting my desk chair and setting it in front of the tray table. He picks up the wine and pours two glasses.

"I'm underage," I remind him, picking up my fork. I'm guessing he's about ten years older than me. I drink wine and beer, but I don't overdo it primarily because I don't love it. However, with him, I feel like I need to keep my wits about me.

"As your guardian, I give you permission," he says with a smirk as he raises the other glass in a mock toast and sips.

Fuck you Jericho St. James.

I think it but don't say it. I should though. He wouldn't do what he threatened earlier. I just don't believe he would. He has a daughter. He can't be that much of a monster.

But maybe that's stupidity talking. And better safe than sorry.

"You're very easy to read, Isabelle," he says with a that same grin. "I can just about hear the *fuck you* you're hurling at me."

"Me? No. I wouldn't dream of breaking one of your sacred commandments, oh great sir." I pick up my glass and drink a bit. It tastes good, a deep, rich red.

"I like the sir. Very much."

Fuck you. Fuck you. Drop dead. Fuck you.

"Eat."

I am about to take a bite, but feel his eyes on me so I put my fork down. "Is it poisoned? Is that why you're not eating? Is it going to make me sick?"

He walks over, picks up the fork on which I'd speared a piece of potato and sticks it into his mouth. He makes a point of chewing and swallowing before replacing the fork.

"Nope, no poison. I already ate with my family."

"Ah. So this is part of my punishment, my humiliation. I'm to be sent to my room like a misbehaving child." I don't know why the thought upsets me. I'd rather be here alone than down there with him anyway. But it's hard to swallow around the lump in my throat. Maybe it's the part about his family. The fact that mine is gone. Because Carlton and Julia aren't family. Not in the way that matters.

I keep my eyes on my plate as I manage the tide of emotion. I pick up my glass, drink another sip to calm my nerves then set it down.

He moves toward the bed, opens a page of the notebook. "What were you doing?"

"Dancing," I say.

"Funny. What is this?" He flips through a couple pages.

"Music." I get up, take the notebook from him. Feeling weirdly embarrassed to have him flip through my notebook, I set it aside then sit back down.

"Your hands are dirty."

I look down at the heel of my hand which is still smeared with pencil marks. I shrug a shoulder, knife in hand. Leaning back against my seat, I watch him as I turn the knife over, considering the sharpness of the blade. I then shift my gaze to his and tilt my head to the side.

"Are you trying to appear remotely threatening?" he asks. At least he's forgotten about the music. "Because if so, you're failing. Miserably."

I stand up, walk toward him. I take his glass and set it down. "I'm tired. It's been a really long day."

He chuckles. "Longer for me," he says, holding my gaze as he closes his hand over mine and relieves me of the knife. "Let me take that before you hurt yourself."

"Does go to hell count as foul language?" I ask as he sets the knife down.

He considers. "Try me."

I don't.

He takes hold of my hands, shifts them behind my back and holds both in one of his. His grip isn't tight, but I know it can be. His gaze moves over my face, hovering at my lips, then lower to the exposed skin of my chest before returning to my eyes.

"I like your eyes, Isabelle."

I blink, unsure how to respond and look away.

"They're beautiful. I like beautiful things."

I force myself to look at him. To glare.

He grins. "And they're very expressive. They make reading you very easy. Too easy."

He's right. I've never been very good at hiding my emotions. My thoughts. He touches his free hand to the collar of my shirt and pushes it over sightly.

"What I mean is," he says, his touch feather light as he brushes my hair back from my shoulder to expose the scar. He leans closer, hovering so near I can feel his body heat as he lowers his mouth to that scar. I gasp when he traces the length of it with his tongue. That's when his grip on my wrists tightens and I watch as he licks that line before closing his mouth over the thundering pulse at my neck, leaving my skin wet. He draws away to stand at his full height just inches from me. "I can tell from the look in your eyes that your pussy is wet."

I swallow hard, fisting my hands although he can't see them since they're behind my back.

"Should I..." he trails off, his free hand moving to undo my jeans like earlier that day.

"Stop."

He doesn't but he brings his face closer, inhales deeply like he's some animal and can scent me. And then he does it. Like earlier. He slides his hand into my panties. Unlike earlier, I feel myself moving toward him, my legs not closing, my body respond-ing, again, to him. To his presence. His closeness. His touch.

He makes a sound as his thumb flicks my clit. I whimper and his eyes never leave mine. I want to tell him to stop. I want to scream it. I should. God. I need to! But all I do is stand there while his fingers play with me, while they dip inside me and turn circles around the hard nub of my clit, my legs trembling, his touch feeling good.

He leans close, his mouth brushing mine. "Say my name," he says, his breath warm against my lips.

"I…"

"Say it and I'll make you come."

I shake my head, but my mouth opens and when it does, he kisses me. It's light, just a brushing of lips on lips, the flick of a tongue, not deep. He stops, draws back to watch me.

"Please… I… Stop."

I gasp when he pushes his fingers inside me and I rise on tiptoe. He pauses just for a second and his expression changes. He exhales, eyebrows coming together.

"Isabelle," he starts, a knowing smile forming on his lips, thumb circling my clit. He lets go of my wrists and I set my hands on his shoulders and lean my forehead against his chest because it's too much. Too hard. I want to come. I want him to make me come. When what I should want is for him to go. What I should feel is repulsion at his touch. But this is insanity. He is my enemy. He is a devil, a monster. A cruel jailor. I know this.

I squeeze my eyes shut and will myself to stop feeling. To think.

"Isabelle," he repeats my name then brings his mouth to my ear. "Are you a virgin?" he whispers, and I hear the taunt in his tone, his words.

My head snaps up and I see how his eyes have gone dark, one ringed with silver, the other wholly black.

I don't answer.

He clucks his tongue. "Are you?"

"Will you take it from me? Hold me down, force my legs open and take it?"

His fingers stop moving. "I'm not forcing you now, am I?" he asks, but his tone isn't light anymore. And he's right. He's not holding me down. I'm holding on to him.

"Will you do that and say it's because I'm a Bishop?" I press on because I have to.

He slips his hand out from inside my jeans and his eyes grow dark. It's not arousal I see in them, though. It's something else. Anger. Rage. He grips my upper arms painfully.

"You should learn the true history of your family rather than believe your own lies, Isabelle Bishop," he says, my name like something terrible on his lips. Like something rotten.

"Will the fact that I'm a Bishop make it somehow better for you? Easier? Is that the point of this?"

He snorts. "You have no idea, do you?" he spits and leans his face so close, his eyes so full of malice that my entire body begins to shudder. He opens his mouth to speak, to curse me or declare his hate of me. I don't know what, but then he draws back, shakes his head and tosses me onto the bed. For a brief moment, I think this is it. I think he's really going to do it. Take what I don't give.

I'm about to scream when he leans over me and clasps his hand over my mouth, muffling the sound when it finally comes.

"You have no idea." He finally says and spins on his heel to leave.

15

JERICHO

I sit in a corner table at the Cat House in IVI's compound. The clock chimes and I look up to see it's two in the morning. This place is alive though. Always.

The Cat House is one of the perks of being a member of The Society. Our own personal whore house, albeit as high end as they come, with the most beautiful of courtesans at our disposal.

I watch from my shadowed corner. See the men, some masked, some not. Most drunk by this point, having their little lap dances or their dicks sucked right out in the open. I never understand why they don't go to the private rooms. But the women are paid to indulge any fantasy. Paid well. So, our wish is their command and if exhibitionism is the wish, well, it could be worse.

I should use one of them. Let off a little steam. I

have in the past. But not a single one of the beauties catches my eye tonight.

A waitress returns to refill my empty glass.

"No," I tell her and stand. I set a hundred-dollar-bill on the table, walk out through the courtyard and exit the compound. Dex is waiting beyond the gates with the car.

I'm not drunk but I'm in no shape to drive and although I slip into the front seat beside him, he knows I'm in no mood to talk.

Seeing Angelique like that in the pool today fucked with me. Instinct kicked in sending me diving into the water to rescue her. But she wasn't drowning. She didn't need rescuing. And neither did Isabelle when she went under. In fact, my dive was what sent her there. What sent my little girl into a panic.

I've protected Angelique all her life. No one knew of her existence apart from a handful of trusted staff and security. My mother thinks it's damaged her. She should be with other children, not shut up in house after house with us. Only us. At least when I was around it was us. Mostly, it was her, though. That's another thing. Angelique is terrified I'll leave and not come back. And what Isabelle said hit a nerve.

I don't believe we remember our birth on any level conscious or subconscious. I never have. But Angelique's birth, her violent introduction to this world, maybe it left its traces in her psyche. Maybe it damaged her more than I know.

Her mother, Kimberly and I had been engaged to be married. I asked her a few months after she became pregnant. We'd been in Mexico. I'd taken her with me on a business trip that we turned into a vacation. If I hadn't taken her, she'd be here now. Angelique would have her mother. She may not have me, but she'd have her. I have no doubt Kimberly would be an infinitely better mother to her than I am a father.

The morning we were to leave we'd been having breakfast at a café on the beach. Kimberly wanted to feel the sand between her toes one last time. She'd looked so happy. She'd glowed, with her belly beautifully rounded, her skin tanned and her smile brighter than ever. I've never known anyone to be as happy as she was in those last months.

I left her sitting there while I went inside to pay except that I'd forgotten my wallet on the table. When I went back to get it, she'd already realized my mistake and was bringing it to me.

I saw them just before it happened. I think I did. Or maybe I'm making that part up, a thought made into memory. I felt it though, the change in the air, the darkness coming toward us. To invade our lives. To steal hers.

She was smiling, holding up my wallet. She may have been commenting on how absent minded we both had become, so drunk were we with joy. The happiness we were sure to have.

Maybe that's what caused it. Our sureness. As if the gods above looked down on us and shook their heads. Maybe we were too happy.

They wore black suits. That's all I remember. Two men who stood out on that beach of blue ocean and bluer sky and golden sunshine. I saw the gun. Saw the one draw it from under his jacket. And before I could think, before I could throw my body over hers, it was done. He pulled the trigger and her body jerked. I heard her breath catch as her face lost that smile, lost all expression but shock.

There was a second shot. That bullet hit my shoulder because I was dropping to me knees with her in my arms. Wanting to catch her. To not let her fall. And then they were gone and the panicked screams of strangers rushed back into my last moments with her.

She had died by the time we got her into the ambulance, and I thought for sure I'd lost our baby too. I remember screaming at the paramedic when I saw the knife, when I saw him cut her. I remember being held back by another paramedic.

And then I heard that tiny, strangled cry.

The car slows, drawing me back to reality. I blink my eyes as we approach the front entrance of the house.

"Are you going to be okay?" Dex asks me.

I brush my hand through my hair. "Fine. Thanks." I get out, walk into the house. It's dead quiet. I stand in the foyer for a minute and listen to that silence, thinking about Angelique's cry the morning she was born. How it sounded against the roar of sirens.

I think about why it happened.

Why a man who didn't know me pulled a gun from inside his jacket but missed his target and instead killed Kimberly.

I think about Carlton Bishop. I wonder what he was doing when the assassination took place. Was he getting a play-by-play? And what did he do when he realized they had missed me but killed her? What did he do when he knew he'd killed a mother and her unborn child? Because as far as anyone knew, the child had died before ever once seeing the light of day.

And I think about the Bishop in my house now and why she's here.

Carlton Bishop thinks this is it. Taking her as my own to punish him. Humiliate him perhaps. But my plans go far beyond simply taking her. His punishment has only just begun because when I'm finished, there will be one more Bishop in the ground. At least.

As I stalk up the stairs, my mind focuses on that thought. I reach into my pocket to take out the key to her bedroom, unlock the door and open it.

Moonlight spills in from the split between the curtains. It casts its silvery light over Isabelle's face. I step closer. She's asleep on her back, the blanket covering her stomach, one arm over her head the other resting on her belly. Her dark hair is spread like a raven's wing across the white pillow. Alongside her on the bed is that same notebook I'd seen earlier. A small ruler, a worn eraser and a pencil sit on top of it. I glance at it, see the notes and the faded marks of pencil the eraser left behind. Is she writing her own music? I don't know the first thing.

She mutters something then, calling my attention back to her face. It's a moment before she quiets. I watch her sleep. Listen to her calm, even breathing. So peaceful. I'm envious of it. Of her peace. A peace no Bishop deserves.

As if sensing this shift in the air, Isabelle stirs, opens her eyes. It takes her a split second to register that she's not alone and she gasps, bolting upright and clutching the blanket to her.

"Up," I say, standing to the side.

She looks around the room, glances at the clock.

"I said up."

She pushes the blanket away and sits up, rubs her face, then stands. The T-shirt she's wearing comes to mid-thigh. It's threadbare and has the faded remnants of some band on the front. She's barefoot. If I were a better man, I'd let her get dressed.

"Shoes," I tell her, pointing to the pair I see by the desk. Does this win me any points in the better man area? I doubt it. Not for what I have in mind.

She looks confused but slips her feet into the flats. Running shoes would be better. More appropriate. But I don't bother telling her that.

"Not a sound," I say and gesture for her to go out into the hallway and down the stairs.

"Can I get dressed at—"

I grip a handful of hair and tug her head backward. "I said not a fucking sound."

She swallows hard and when I release her, she grips the banister with both hands, keeps one eye on me as she hurries down the stairs. I wonder if she thinks I'll push her.

I can take several routes to the exit, so I choose the one that will walk us by the steel door to the cellar. She instantly hesitates but I nudge her forward.

"I don't want to go down there," she starts as we get nearer. "I didn't mean to do anything."

I don't say a word but feel her exhale of breath when we pass that door and keep going. I wonder if she'd prefer the cellar to where I'm taking her, though. Around the next corner we arrive at the kitchen. I unlock the door and let her step outside onto the patio.

"What are we doing?" she asks, confused, as I take her arm and walk her across the patio, past the pool and onto the grass. I keep walking her toward the woods and she hesitates. But she doesn't have a choice. Not in any of this. She should know that by now.

I follow the path. It's lit by the moon in the moments the clouds part and casts its light on us. The cropping of trees is dense, but I know this way well enough without it. It's well-worn and maintained. Although for the last five years only my brother has tread on it, and I doubt he's done it often.

The only sounds are those of the insects and the branches crushed beneath my shoes. Her footfalls barely register. But her breathing grows louder as she tries to keep up. She's not quite struggling. I don't think she can at the pace we're moving. But she is holding back so I have to keep a firm grip on her. It would be easier if I just hauled her over my shoulder and carried her. Kinder, too. But I don't.

A soft rain begins to fall but we're protected beneath the canopy of trees. The sound is gentle. Isabelle, in just her threadbare T-shirt, shivers and wraps her free arm around herself.

We slow as the path widens.

"Where are we?" she asks, peering out into the darkness, holding back.

I wonder if she can smell the incense out here. I can. Or maybe it's memory, a trick of the mind telling me I smell something that isn't there.

A wind blows, uncovering the moon. The rain is little more than mist clinging to her face and hair, but she is wet, her shirt sticking to her. I look down at her feet clad in those ballet flats. See the grass and dirt stuck to the shoes and her legs. She shudders and I wonder if it's with cold or the sight before her as I follow her gaze to the chapel. The cemetery before it. Tall stones mark the graves and just beyond are the marble vaults holding the bodies of St. James's of generations past.

I look back at her, see the lines on her forehead, feel her try to pull free, to back away.

"Why are we here?" she asks, having to drag her gaze from the graveyard to me.

"Are you afraid of a few ghosts?"

She shudders and I remember what she'd said about the cellar, how it's haunted. And I think about Zoë. Even the cemetery would be a cheerier place to haunt than that cellar.

"Why are we here?" she asks again, trepidation in her voice.

"We're here so you can understand why *you're* here. So you can see what the Bishops have done. What they, and *you*, are capable of."

"I'm not—"

"It's what you wanted to know, isn't it? Why I took you? Why I hate you?"

She shudders at that word and I'm not sure it fits,

but all it takes is a glance at one of the grave markers to shove those thoughts away.

I pull Isabelle with me as I cross the clearing toward the iron gate. She resists but I never expected her to come willingly. It's her guilt, her subconscious guilt inherited from her ancestors.

I open the gate. It creaks just like in horror films and I'm surprised when Isabelle moves a little closer to me. I wonder if she realizes she does it.

We walk past the gravestones. I don't look at those yet. Instead, I take her directly to the chapel. It was built on a hill. She'll see why in a few minutes. She's quiet as we walk, but her breathing is short, and every sound makes her jump. Her hair clings to her face now. She's soaked through. The shivering, though, is probably a combination of fear and cold.

Two stone steps lead to the chapel door. They're worn and uneven. We climb up and push the heavy, wooden door open. The scent of incense clings to the place, to every stone here. It's been burnt here for centuries, the chapel used for Sunday mass weekly. Until six years ago, that is. I wonder if my mother will take up the tradition again.

Once we're inside, I close the door and look around. I haven't come here myself since my return to New Orleans. I'll see it for the first time along with her.

I take it in, the ancient stone walls, the crooked windows with their stained-glass depicting scenes from the bible. Those are a more recent addition. Zeke must have updated them because I remember they'd been damaged by a storm before I'd left home. Six pews, three on each side of the aisle take up most of the space with a small baptismal font in one corner. The tabernacle lamp burns red on the altar but apart from that the candles are out, and no cloth is laid out on the ornate wooden altar. Zeke hasn't been using it. I wonder when he was last here. When was the last time he came to tend to the graves, at least to Zoë and Kimberly. Probably hasn't if I know my brother. And I don't blame him.

I turn to Isabelle who is as still as the Christ over the altar. She stopped her struggling and is looking around curiously. She looks up at me and I find I can't read her expression. I blame the lack of light.

I loosen my grip on her and we walk up the center aisle, coming to a stop before the carving in the large stone beneath our feet just before the altar. It's why the chapel is built on a hill.

She turns her gaze to it.

"This is the grave of Draca St. James, the oldest recorded member of the St. James family, the one who bought this land from the Bishops and built his house upon it. He would be buried inside the chapel beside his wife. His first wife, that is. Not the second or the third."

She glances up at me as I read the dates.

Draca St. James was born in 1682 and died in

1740. His wife, Mary, was born in 1690 and died in 1709.

I watch Isabelle as she reads their names, the dates of birth and death. She shudders. "She was nineteen when she died."

"Your age," I tell her. It's a cruelty I allow myself.

I release her. Her eyes search mine in the dim tabernacle light.

"We bought the land from the Bishops. Did you know that?"

She swallows. Shakes her head.

"Your brother didn't teach you?" I ask, walking a few paces to the altar where I see the familiar heavy tome that is the bible of the St. James family. Draca St. James's diary. A ledger of his struggles, his victories. I set my fingers on the ornate wood etched with silver, caress it, open it to peer inside, to smell the scent of something old and decaying.

"I only learned I was half-Bishop three years ago," she says, and I return to her.

"That's three years. A family like the Bishops. You weren't curious? Not even to know your neighbors?"

"There are miles between our houses. And I was dealing with the loss of my family."

"Carlton Bishop *is* your family."

"He's not," is all she says after a long moment.

I lean toward her. "Your blood would say differently."

We turn and walk back out into the night where mist has once again turned to rain. It's still light though and won't interfere with my work.

She's quiet as I lead her back outside although the resistance has begun again. That and her shivering.

"I'm cold," she says.

"They're colder," I tell her as we walk to the farthest point in the cemetery on the west side of the chapel. The mausoleum is on the east side. Here lies a single grave marker and this grave is not tended. It's overgrown with weeds and surrounded by its own rotting iron fence. The only thing kept intact are the name and dates of birth and death of the grave's inhabitant.

"This one," I start, pointing to it, feeling the cold creep over me, just the same as when I was taught our history as a child. "This is Nellie Bishop." 1690 – 1711. "She lived two years more than Mary. They were supposed to be friends if you can believe it. A Bishop and a St. James. Friends."

"I'm really cold. Can we please go back?"

"No." I release her, and she rubs her bare arms. "You see, you Bishops have always been a greedy lot. The men coveted their neighbor's possessions. Their wives. And as founding members of IVI, they had power. Power they abused. Although they underestimated Draca St. James."

"I don't know what you're talking about."

"Do you know the name Reginald Bishop?"

She nods. "I've seen his portrait in the house."

"He, like your father, had a hard time keeping his dick in his pants. Except that Mary wasn't his. She'd worked for him, though, before she married into the St. James family. Imagine that. A servant in one household who becomes queen in another. Draca St. James fell in love with her on sight. I'll show you a portrait later. You'll see why. He married her within weeks of having laid eyes on her. But Reginald, like most Bishops, was an entitled man. I'm sure selling off half his land to what he considered the help in order to keep afloat didn't help. Maybe that's why he did it. Who knows? What is certain, is him believing himself entitled to Mary. Even when she no longer worked in his household, he felt he had some claim to her. Even after she was a St. James, a member of IVI. The same Society his family had founded, he felt himself above any law. He took her. And when she wouldn't have him, he raped her."

Isabelle looks horrified.

"And when he was finished with her, he sent her back barefoot and pregnant. He waited until her stomach swelled with his bastard to do it. I imagine he took some sick pride in it. In impregnating the wife of another. A man he deemed lesser."

I don't realize I've grown quiet until she speaks. "What happened then?"

"Draca took her back. He loved her. And he was

the one to discover her hanging in that cellar not one week later."

She gasps, covers her mouth with her hand.

"Is she what I felt? The ghost?"

I study her but don't tell her there is more than one. We have a history with rope, my family. An obsession with it.

"She couldn't stand the thought of bringing another Bishop into the world," I say instead, ignoring her question altogether. "She felt shame. Shame at what he'd done to her. Shame at being raped."

"What did Draca do?"

"He initiated The Rite." I watch her as I say it. Her face blanches and she hugs her arms tightly around herself. "He took Nellie Bishop, Reginald's daughter. And he married her. They never had children, thank goodness. He wouldn't pollute our bloodline."

"But The Rite safeguards against an abuse of power. And marriage is an abuse of power in a case like that," she says, and I get the feeling she's arguing her own case.

"IVI supported it. Just like they supported my initiation of The Rite."

"But—"

"See, Bishop did make a mistake. It's always an error to think yourself above the law. He was an arrogant man. And not well-liked within The Society.

He'd made enemies. Like your brother has," I add. "And when it came to The Rite, The Tribunal sided with St. James. It was to punish Reginald Bishop as much as anything else. And at that point, our family's fortunes far exceeded those of the Bishops. Similar to today, actually."

She shakes her head. "Did he hurt Nellie?"

I remain wordless, studying her.

She shudders. "I want to go back."

"When your history lesson is over." I turn back to the grave. "Nellie died two years after the marriage. Threw herself into the well and drowned. Or so it's said. Draca married again but only to continue the family line. His one true love was Mary." I pause, look at Isabelle who is studying the inscription on Nellie's grave. "There's space for one more beside hers," I tell her. She looks at me, confused. "Another Bishop to keep Nellie company."

Any remaining color drains from her face.

I take her arm and walk her to the Mausoleum to point out the names of my ancestors, uncles, aunts, and cousins. I see Zoë's marker. I take a moment to read the dates. Sixteen. Even younger than Mary St. James. I see Isabelle's eyes on that marker. It's the only one with a bunch of rotting roses that were probably laid here a week or so ago. I turn her away before she can comment.

"And we come to why you're here. Why I initiated The Rite."

I hear her swallow and, as if on cue, the rain picks up suddenly and gloriously. It soaks us both through, but I walk at the same pace to Kimberly's grave marker. I'm not in a rush. She's not in the mausoleum. We weren't married. Only those who carry the St. James name can be laid to rest in the mausoleum.

I stand before the stone, see the roses about the same age as those on Zoë's laid in front of it. But thinking of Zeke out there picking roses and walking them to the cemetery is too lonely an image so I shove it aside.

"This is Angelique's mother," I say flatly. "Kimberly Anders."

I watch her take in the dates and when she looks up at me it's with something strange in her eyes. Something like pity. I want to wipe that pity off her face.

"How did she die?"

"She was murdered."

She winces and I'm not sure she's aware that her hand has just moved up to that scar on her collarbone. Her parents and brother were killed. Parents in a car accident. Brother in a break-in. Does that count as murder? I guess so. Even if it's not the intent of the robbery. I realize that's when she must have gotten her scars. They're not from a fall. But they could be from a push.

A gust of wind blows so cold that it breaks into

my thoughts. I blink, look at Kimberly's name on the stone. Too young to be dead. Too young to be bones in the earth. And I harden myself. Because my mother is wrong. Kimberly would want this. She'd want revenge.

"Carlton?" she asks, then shakes her head. "He's not capable of something that like. It's not in his DNA."

My eyebrows rise to the top of my forehead. "No? I think you may be surprised what your brother is capable of. What's in your DNA."

She stares up at me and when she doesn't argue, I wonder what she truly believes.

"But that doesn't matter for you. It makes no difference. We have other business tonight."

"What business?"

"Come, Isabelle. It's time to spill the first drops of Bishop blood."

16

ISABELLE

nother cold gust accompanies his words. I'm not sure if it's that or his words that turn my blood to ice. When he faces me, the look in his eyes sends a shiver down my spine.

It's time to spill the first drops of Bishop blood.

I take a step backward. My feet hurt. These shoes weren't made for a stroll in the woods much less what we're doing tonight.

"We're going to play a game, Isabelle Bishop."

"I don't want to play any game, Jericho St. James."

He grins at that. "You're going to run. And I'm going to chase you."

"I said I don't want to."

"You need to find the well where Nellie's body was found."

"What?" God. I feel sick.

"If you get to it before I catch up with you, you'll be safe from me tonight. But if I catch you or get to the well before you," he continues, stepping toward me. "I will bleed you."

He shifts his gaze to his watch, turns the knob on it casually like we aren't standing in the middle of a cemetery while rain pours down on us in the middle of the night talking about an idiotic game. About bleeding me.

"I don't want to play this game! I want to go home."

"Home?"

I shake my head. "My house. Away from you!"

He shrugs a shoulder. "I'm even going to give you a five-minute head start," he says, turning his wrist so I see the face of his watch. See the timer counting down.

"That's not... I won't play."

He shrugs his shoulders and moves to pick up the dead roses on Kimberly's grave making a show of consulting his watch. "Four minutes and thirty seconds."

I look at his broad back, his muscular shoulders. The rain makes his sweater stick to him soaking his dark hair, turning it black. I take a step back, look around this haunted place with its grave markers, its eerie chapel. To Nellie Bishop's grave separated from the others by a rusted, rotting fence and grass so high you almost don't see the stone. She's all but forgotten. Although I don't think forgetting is the point. I think remembering is.

Nellie threw herself into a well and drowned? Or was she thrown in? Maybe killed before that. I take a step away from him as he straightens, wipes off his hands. He glances at me, then at his watch. And I don't need another reminder of the time I have left. Because this game is going on whether I want to play or not.

I turn and run out of the cemetery gates. I'm tempted to backtrack to the path we came from and go to the house to burrow in my bed. But I know he'd easily follow me. And going to the house? *His* house. To my bedroom to which he has the key? No, I can't go back there. I have to find the well.

So, I run away from the cemetery into the dense woods, the sound of rain all around me, the light that of the moon through the cloud cover. I can only see a few feet ahead of me. I stumble over fallen branches and thorn bushes scratching my bare legs. I run deeper into the woods, my only thought to put some distance between us.

I think back to when I'd surveyed the property from my window. I hadn't seen the cemetery or the roof of the church from there. The path we took curved, so I guess they were around the corner and not behind it. But I did see a stone structure. A circle within a circle. It looked crumbled from my vantage point, but the trees weren't as dense, and it was to the east of the house. I don't know if it's the well he's talking about but it's all I have to go on, so I slow my step and try to get my bearings. I don't have a horrible sense of direction but it's not great either. And I need to find the house in order to know which way to go.

I stop and listen for a few moments. I listen for him. But the rain muffles all other sounds. A part of me wonders if this is some sort of trick on his part. He could easily have gone back into the house, to his warm bed and left me out here to search for a non-existent well all night. But I don't think he'd do that. I think he truly wants to play his little game of chase.

I think, looking back at the path I came from. Walk back and head in the direction I think is the house. If I can just get a glimpse of it, that's all I'll need. But it's the middle of the night and it was so dark when he came for me. The gray stone will only stand out if the clouds clear the moon.

A branch breaks nearby. I gasp and sprint away making too much noise. I glance behind me relieved when all I see is darkness. By the time I turn to watch where I'm going, I'm too late. Although I'm not sure I'd have seen it anyway on this forest floor. I catch my foot on a root and pitch forward, the shoe slipping off my foot as I land heavily, the ground knocking the wind from me. I cry out, I can't help it and it takes me a moment to sit up, to register the throbbing pain on my right shin.

I touch the spot, feel the wet warmth of blood.

I push myself up to stand and am grateful that I can put weight on it. It's a cut, just a cut. I haven't sprained my ankle. But I have lost one shoe and when I can't locate it after a quick search, I keep moving, my eyes on the ground scanning as best as I can in the darkness.

I don't know how long this goes on. How long I run. At one point I find I've circled back to the cemetery and am briefly horrified, but I force myself to breathe. To calm down and just breathe.

From here I can find the path to the house. From here I can get my bearings. Keeping to the cover of trees, I locate that path and walk alongside it. Then, it's not long until I see it. A light. A light going on in one of the upstairs bedrooms of the house.

Relief floods me, filling me with a new energy. I know where the house is. And from the location of the cemetery, I think I can find that clearing. The collapsed wall.

I pick up my pace and run. Aware now that the rain has slowed to a mist. I don't know when that happened but suddenly, I feel like things are working in my favor. My leg hurts, as do my feet, but I see that light and I can find that well. I know it.

I'm feeling a little more confident. A little stronger. But then, in the sudden and utter stillness of the night, I step on another branch that breaks underfoot. I swear the sound echoes for miles and miles throughout the forest, giving away my location. I think I hear him stalking at a steady pace. Unrushed. Confident. Because he knows he'll win.

I turn to where the sound is coming from and that light that had gone on is suddenly out. And at the same moment, a thick layer of clouds closes over the moon pitching me into complete darkness.

Another branch breaks and I spin to look for it, for him, sure he's going to be right there. Right behind me. But he's not. Just more darkness. Never-ending darkness. More trees. More night. And I'm disoriented again. I've lost the path. The house. All I know is I need to move, and I walk and walk and run and run. I swear I hear him behind me. I'm not even sure if I'm moving in circles anymore. I am exhausted and freezing cold and scared. So scared.

And then somehow, some way, the trees become less dense and the moon shines again. I stop. Because I see it. The crumbling stones I glimpsed from my room in the house. But they're not crumbling. They're laid in a pattern. A circle surrounding another, smaller circle.

The ground feels colder here, I look down to find I have lost my second shoe somewhere during our chase. But it doesn't matter because I'm here. I made it. It's the well. And I'm safe.

Except that the instant I think I'm safe, there's

movement from the shadow of the ancient structure. I gasp because there, emerging, is Jericho St. James, hands in his pockets, a grim look on his face. But not satisfaction. I don't know what it is.

"Boo!"

I scream, back away. I hear the words he spoke at the cemetery.

It's time to spill the first drops of Bishop blood.

"I made it. I found it," I say as he stalks toward me. I should run again. I should. But I can't I'm so cold and my feet hurt and my shin throbs. "I'm safe. You said—"

"You're not safe, Isabelle. You'll never be safe again," he says. I don't know if it's his words or their warning or the fact that I know they're true, but I shake my head. A sound begins in my ears, like a drumming. The drumming of my heart, the pumping of blood. The *thud thud thud* of chaos inside me.

"Careful," he calls out.

I'm backing away from him because I don't want him to bleed me. I don't want to be the next Bishop they bury in their cemetery.

"Isabelle, stop!"

He picks up his pace and then he's running. There's something else in his eyes, an urgency in his stride. I keep going, because he's too close. I'm ready to sprint away, only I've run out of ground. There's no earth to meet my step and I scream as I fall backward. The last thing I see is Jericho St. James's face as he reaches out to catch me, fingertips brushing fingertips as my arms flail, long black hair in wisps floating through air, and the sensation of falling. Falling. Falling. And then...nothing.

17

JERICHO

"Fuck."

I drop down into the small embankment where Isabelle lies still, eyes closed. "Isabelle?"

No answer. I crouch down bedside her and watch her chest move up and down. I look her over before touching her. It's only a three-foot drop but still. Arms and legs are at normal angles. I feel them, nothing seems to be broken. Hardly any blood but for a couple of scratches and the gash on her shin which looks like it's already closing up. She must have gotten that one earlier.

"Isabelle? Can you hear me?" I gently lift her head to feel the back of it. Mutter a curse as I look at the smear of blood on my palm. Although it's not bleeding heavily. I lift her and am relieved she landed like she did. The rock just inches away would have caused more damage.

I run my hand over her spine as she flops forward into me. When she groans, I exhale with relief.

"I'm going to lift you up," I tell her. She doesn't respond and doesn't move as I set one arm at her back and the other under her knees. Her head drops against my chest and her arms hang limp as I carry her back to the house.

This wasn't the kind of bloodletting I was talking about.

I walk in through the same door we exited and carry her upstairs. It's still dark, everyone will still be sleeping. I'm grateful for that. The last thing Angelique needs to see is me carrying a bloody, dirt-covered Isabelle upstairs. She's already become attached to her. Something I hadn't counted on. And definitely not for it to happen as quickly as it has.

I bypass Isabelle's door and carry her into my room, drawing the blankets back and laying her in my bed. I look down at her. She looks so small. So fragile. More breakable than I thought.

With a sigh I walk into the bathroom stripping off my soaked sweater as I go and tossing it on top of the hamper. I grab a few towels, the first-aid kit and walk back into the bedroom. She hasn't stirred. I set the towels down and sit her up to pull the T-shirt she's wearing over her head. I drop it to the floor and peel off her panties.

I take a moment to look at her, then get to work. She's cold. Her skin icy. I dry her off, wiping away dirt as best as I can before dropping the soiled towels on the floor and choosing a warm sweater from my dresser for her. I slip it over her head and cover her with the blanket. Then cradling the back of her head, I feel the bump there. My fingers come away dry. Again, I'm relieved.

She stirs then, a sound of protest. The bump is tender, I'm sure.

"Shh, relax," I tell her as she blinks her eyes open. They're heavy and I imagine she'll fall asleep again but then she looks at me. For a moment, it's as though she doesn't recognize me. Just for a moment. Then her eyes go wide and she tries to sit up, but can't. I watch her, see the effort it takes her to keep her eyes open.

"Just close your eyes, Isabelle," I tell her.

"You..." She's drifting but fighting it. She manages to put a hand to my chest. I think she means to push me away but her arm flops back onto the bed.

"I'm going to take care of you. You're safe," I say without thinking.

"I'm not," she mutters but her eyes don't open again. I look at her face, her pretty face. There's a cut across her cheek. It's superficial. I'll tend to that too but first the one on the back of her head.

I turn her head slightly and clean the dried blood as best I can without irritating the cut. It's matted into her hair, but it could have been worse. Once it's as clean as I can get it, I leave her in the bedroom and go downstairs for ice. When I return, she still hasn't moved, and her breathing is even. I set the ice at the back of her head, she winces, tries to pull away.

"Shh," I tell her, cupping her cheek. "Sleep."

She does and I get to work on the other injuries, cleaning cuts and bandaging what needs to be bandaged. By the time it's done I'm tired. Fucking exhausted. I walk around to the other side of the bed —I'd put her on my side without thinking—and climb in. She still doesn't stir so I turn out the light and listen to her steady, even breathing, feel the warmth of her body beside mine. I let myself drift off knowing it will be a fitful sleep.

18

ISABELLE

I wake up to the chirping of birds outside. It's a sound that's familiar. There's a nest of finches on one of the trees by my window and I love hearing them first thing in the morning.

Although I'm neither in my room nor am I in my bed. I know from the light even through closed eyes. I know from the smell. And when I remember where I am, I bolt upright with a gasp and instantly regret it.

"Ah. Fuck!" I touch the back of my head gingerly, hissing when my fingers brush against the tender bump.

"Headache?"

My gaze snaps to him. Jericho St. James. He's standing against the wall, leaning his full weight on it, one hand in his pocket, mug of coffee I can smell from here in the other. He's wearing a suit, black like his soul, dark hair still wet from a shower, watching me. Just watching me.

And I remember last night.

I remember him walking into my bedroom at God knows what hour of night. Taking me to that chapel, the cemetery to show me my ancestor's forgotten grave. Tell me the ugly history of the Bishops and the St. James's. And to play that stupid game to find the well where Nellie's body had most likely been thrown after she'd been murdered. I remember the dark of the woods, the cold of the rain. And then falling.

"You fucking bastard."

He nods as if in agreement and sips his coffee. "Aspirin is there. With water. Also not poisoned."

I feel the bump at the back of my head. "I need a doctor. I could have a concussion."

"You don't have a concussion. It's barely a bump."

"You jerk, I could have died!"

"Died is a bit much, Isabelle." He finishes his coffee and pushes off the wall to come toward me. "Let me see." He sits on the edge of the bed. I have a vague and strange memory like this has happened before except that last time he was naked from the waist up and my hands were on him. Feeling the swell of muscle beneath his warm skin.

I close my eyes and force the image of him half-naked with that dragon tattoo curling around his arms and shoulders away.

"Don't touch me," I snap, slapping at his arm and jerking away but that jerking costs me. "It hurts. Shit."

"Here." He holds up the aspirin and the glass of water.

I look at them, then at him.

"The bottle is right there. They're just aspirin."

I glance to the nightstand where I see the bottle. I reach out and take them from him, pop them in my mouth and swallow them with one gulp of water.

"Drink it all. It's good for you."

"You almost killed me last night. You now want me to believe you care what's good for me?"

"I didn't almost kill you. You're fine."

I drink the water but not because he tells me to. I'm just very thirsty. When I'm finished, he takes the glass and sets it aside, then cups my jaw. His touch isn't hard like the last time he did it. He's being careful. Is that guilt?

He turns my head and I feel his fingers near the spot that's currently throbbing but he's gentle when he touches it.

"Swelling hasn't gotten worse, but I'd leave it alone if I were you."

"I didn't know you were a doctor." I say when he straightens.

"Just a concerned citizen."

"Fuck you."

"Careful. Remember the commandments. I'll let

you go on it considering you just hit your head but watch your mouth."

"Really? Considering I just hit my head? You're so fucking kind. Fuck. You."

He grits his teeth and I know I should stop while I'm ahead.

"Why did you do that? What was that last night?" I ask.

The bottoms of my feet hurt. My shin. I remember losing my shoes and falling. My whole body aches. And I realize I don't recognize the sweater I'm wearing. And I know instantly whose it is when I sniff the sleeve.

When I look up at him, he's watching me, amused.

"Did you undress me?"

"I did. Nothing I hadn't seen before." He winks.

Fucking bastard.

I look past him for my clothes. Well, clothes. T-shirt and panties because I am pretty sure he took those off too.

"Where's my T-shirt?"

"That ratty thing? What's the matter? Don't tell me things are so dire at the Bishop house you can't afford to buy a proper—"

"Where is it?" I push the blankets off to swing my legs over the edge of the bed and stand but it's too soon. Pain and dizziness throw me off balance and I stumble forward right into Jericho St. James's very wide, very muscular chest. He catches me and I want to pull my hands off him, to tear myself out of his grasp but I do neither.

"Relax, Isabelle. Get back in bed." He puts me back into his bed and I see the scrapes on my legs, see where some are bandaged.

"Where's my shirt?" I ask again.

"I'm having it laundered."

"You're washing it? Why?"

"It was filthy from our game."

"It wasn't a game. Not to me." My voice breaks, the fear of last night and the energy of it all, this whole thing, catching up with me. I wipe the backs of my hands over my eyes. I will not cry. I will not fucking cry. Not in front of him. "I want my shirt back."

"You'll get it back once it's cleaned. It's a fucking T-shirt."

"It's not just any T-shirt." I start to tell him it's Christian's. That I have been wearing it since he died. That it took me months to even wash it. But I don't. He doesn't deserve to know that. To know anything about me. I touch the bruise on my shin around the bandage. "Did you do this? Bandage me up?"

He nods solemnly, expression all seriousness.

"Why? Isn't it what you wanted? To spill Bishop blood?"

"That wasn't the blood I would have spilled. My plans were of a more intimate nature."

At first, I don't follow but after a moment, I understand. My virginity. He would have taken it last night if I hadn't knocked myself out. I feel my face grow warm and I'm sure my skin has flushed red.

"Well, I'm not sorry I spoiled your little game of bloodletting, you sick prick. I could have been seriously hurt."

"You weren't."

"I was."

"And now I know to take better care with you considering your...fragility."

"I'm not fragile. I'm just not used to being told horrible stories about my family and yours and then being made to run for my life."

"You were never in danger of losing your life."

"Only my virginity?" I don't know why I ask it and the instant I do that warmth of embarrassment I'd felt moments ago turns into bright red heat.

Jericho St. James watches me. He doesn't speak. Doesn't deny it. Doesn't defend himself.

I look away from him because I can't hold his gaze. It's too much. He's too much. Last night in the graveyard, I felt like he blamed me. Hated me. But now, it's not that. It's not hate.

I take a deep breath in, steel myself and stand slowly.

He watches, ready to catch me, I guess.

I sway for a moment but steady myself. He's close, inches away. And he doesn't move back. I square my shoulders and meet his gaze.

"Why didn't you take it then? While I was knocked out? While I couldn't fight."

His gaze intensifies, searches.

"It was my blood you wanted. Why didn't you take it? You could have. I was in your bed. Naked. Incapacitated." I shrug a shoulder gaining some backbone from his silence. "Yours."

He snorts, gaze moving over me as he shakes his head before meeting my eyes again.

"Why didn't I rape you?" he asks and when he says it like that, uses that word, it makes me blanch and I can't hold his gaze.

But he doesn't let me off the hook. That'd be too easy. He brings one finger to my chin and turns my face up to his. He gives me that cold grin I'm getting used to. The one I hate. The one that shows how much he hates me.

"I didn't rape you because I'm not a Bishop."

H er mouth hangs open. She clearly wasn't
expecting that response.

"Go to your room and get showered,"
I tell her. "After breakfast you'll be watching
Angelique along with my mother."

"Wait. What?"

"She was upset yesterday after the swimming
pool incident."

"Shocker."

"Careful."

"You're giving me whiplash here. One minute
you accuse me of almost drowning your daughter—"

"I never accused you of trying to drown her."

"Now you want me to babysit?"

I feel my eyebrows rise. "Babysit? No, my mother
will take care of her. I wouldn't leave her in your hands."

"Because I'm a Bishop."

"And somehow regardless of that, she seems to have taken a liking to you and with my mother present, perhaps you can play your little game in the pool. What was it called?"

"You mean before you dove in fully clothed and created a tidal wave?"

I raise my eyebrows.

"Starfish," she says, studying me suspiciously.

"It's probably not a bad idea since we're home that she learns to be comfortable in the water. But I do not want her left alone—"

"I wouldn't leave any five-year-old alone in or near a pool."

"I'm glad to hear that."

"Shouldn't she be going to school anyway? Kindergarten? She's five. I think that's when they start."

"Thanks for your expert opinion which means nothing to me. She will be educated at home. If you're above spending time—"

"That's not why I said it. She's a sweet girl. And a very nervous little girl. It might help her—"

"Don't dictate to me how I raise my daughter," I tell her in no uncertain terms.

"I just think it would be good for her to be around other kids her age," she says, tone and expression serious and possibly a little concerned.

"Don't think." My gaze doesn't waver from hers and a few moments later, she blinks away.

"Your mom's sick," she says. It's not phrased as a question.

"She was. She's better now, although not as strong as she likes to let on."

"Chemo?"

"That's really none of your business. You just take care with my daughter."

"You don't have to tell me to take care with her. I would anyway. With any child." She walks to the door.

"Use this one," I tell her, opening the other door. It's the one that connects our rooms.

She peers into her room then turns back to me, eyebrows raised.

"Easy access when I require use of you."

"Jerk," she mutters under her breath as she walks toward her room.

"What was that?"

She looks back at me. "Nothing."

"Good girl. You're learning."

She sucks in a deep breath, nostrils flaring, hands fisting at her sides.

I smile. "We have a party tonight at the compound. You'll be ready to go by seven o'clock. I'll have a dress sent up."

"A party? What kind of party?"

"Dinner. Drinks."

"You don't strike me as the mingling type, and I definitely am not. Is this to rub my brother's nose in your acquisition of me?"

"Would that bother you then? If that were my intention, which it's not."

"Carlton isn't losing sleep over me not being in his house. He took me in because he had to. That's all. What you're doing to me, you hurting me, he won't care about that."

"You think I don't know that? He doesn't care about you, Isabelle." Her expression changes infinitesimally although I know I'm not telling her anything she doesn't already know. Still, it's kind of a jerk move. I check my watch. "Maybe my brother's right."

"Right about what?"

I glance back at her. "You really aren't a match for me, are you?"

She sighs. "In your games, no, probably not," she says and walks stiffly toward her room.

"Seven o'clock, Isabelle. You'll be ready to go."

She doesn't bother to reply, just slams the door shut loudly behind her.

At seven o'clock on the dot I enter Isabelle's room via the connecting door between ours. She's sitting at the vanity, back to me, with the hairdresser applying the final touches to her hair. I'm glad to see her wearing the floor length deep lilac sheath dress. When the hairdresser pushes the final pin into place, she moves and I meet Isabelle's eyes in the reflection in the mirror.

For a moment, we stay just like that. Her seated, back to me, eyes locked on me, the expression in them at first cautious then fixed in irritation.

I adjust a cuff and dismiss the woman who just did her hair and makeup. I don't take my eyes off Isabelle as she stands, turns to face me. I let my gaze sweep over her, and she folds her arms across her chest.

She looks good, makeup heavier than I like during the day but for this event, it fits. The dark liner around her eyes seems to make her eyes appear even bluer, like the brightest of sapphires. Her hair is swept across her forehead and to the side in soft waves. It hides the scar on her collarbone perfectly.

"What you wanted?" she asks. "To put me on display?"

"You're very attractive. I'm sure you're used to men looking at you," I say. "Put your arms at your sides."

She sets her jaw, drops her arms. Her hands in fists.

I look her over, see the rounds of her nipples outlined against the fine material of the dress, see the tips poke against it. I have an urge to flick one, but I don't. I let my gaze move lower then walk closer, inhaling the soft scent of perfume same as the first night in that church. Brushing my knuckles over the scar beneath her hair, I study her.

"You hide it."

Her mouth moves into what I think she hopes is a casual, careless smile but it doesn't work. "Just turned out that way."

"No, I don't think that's it," I say, dropping it.

I turn a slow circle around her but when I get behind her, she pivots, keeping her eyes locked on mine. She doesn't want me at her back. I get it.

"You do look very nice," I tell her, leaning my face close to hers and bringing my mouth to her ear. "There's only one problem."

She stiffens. I'm not touching her, but we're close enough that when I speak the hair on the back of her neck stands on end.

I set the tips of my fingers on her thigh and begin to gather the dress up.

Her breath catches as I brush the skin of her bare leg before cupping an ass cheek. I'm not gentle.

"I sent up what you were to wear. You added to it."

"Panties. I added panties."

"But that wasn't up to you. Slide them off and hand them to me," I say, brushing my fingers along the crease under her cheek, moving toward her center.

She sucks in a breath and closes her hand over my forearm then turns her head to glance at me from the corner of her eye. "The dress may as well be see-through."

"Take them off, Isabelle."

"Or what, Jericho?"

"Do it."

"No."

"Are you testing me?"

"I wouldn't dream of it."

"Because I have to warn you that if you force my hand, I'll have no choice but to leave you with something to remind you how important obedience is."

She turns to face me holding my forearm between us. I let go of the dress and it drops down to her shins. I expect her to back away so when she doesn't, I lean deeper into her space and glance down at her hand around my arm.

She follows my gaze and as if just realizing she's still holding on to me, she drops my arm.

I grin. "Don't test me, Isabelle."

Her eyes search mine and there's a moment I see her falter, but she steels herself. Stands up taller.

"Are you threatening me?"

I tilt my head to the side. "A challenge. I like it. Is this because of my comment earlier? That you're no match for me?"

"No. I don't care what you think." It's a lie. I see it in the way her jaw tenses and her posture shifts.

"Have you been stewing all day over something I said?"

She searches my eyes. "Like I said, I don't care what you think of me."

"No, of course not."

I look down at those nipples again, straining against the fabric of the dress. I bring the back of my hand to one, brush it lightly and instantly, she steps back. A flush of red creeps up her neck, the blue of her eyes darken as the pulse at her neck throbs.

I smell adrenaline, fear and rebellion. And underneath it all, arousal. I breathe it in. "Now slip off your panties and hand them to me."

"What will you do if I don't? Put me back in that cellar room? And then I miss the party? I may prefer the ghost downstairs to—"

"No." I walk toward her, and she backs right into one of the posts of her bed, trapping herself. Her hands move to my chest, and she tests, pushing a little. I don't budge. But she doesn't pull her hands away. "I'm talking about a different sort of reminder. You're going to the party. Make your choice."

She clears her throat, tilts her head back to look up at me. "I won't be complicit in your weird game."

"Funny, because you know what I think?"

"I don't care what you think."

"I think my *weird game* is turning you on. A taste," I say and reach my hand behind her to smack her ass.

She gasps, her body jerks into mine. She's clearly not expecting that. Her hands move to cover her butt.

"What are you doing?"

Using my chest to pin her to the post, I tilt my head to look at her. Her gaze falters when it meets mine. She's embarrassed.

"Like I said, that was a taste. Would you like the real reminder before you do as I say because either way, you will obey. Ball is in your court."

Her neck and cheeks are bright red and she presses her lips together.

I raise my eyebrows in anticipation of her answer.

"I'd rather you put me down in that cellar than obey you."

"I'm glad you said that," I say and reach around to take her wrists in one hand. I sit down on the bed, hauling her over my lap. She struggles but it takes hardly any effort at all to hold her down.

I look at her like this, over my lap, both wrists in one of my hands as she twists and turns. She cranes her neck to look up at me and I drag my gaze from her ass to her face. "Ready?" I smile, raise my free arm to spank her ass.

"Wait!" She calls out as my hand comes down. It's not a hard smack. I think she's more embarrassed than anything else, but she still yelps. I give her a minute then do it again.

"Stop!"

"I can go all night," I tell her casually.

"I hate you."

"Again or..." I let my words drift.

"Let me go."

"Are you going to do it?"

"Let me go and I will," she says, wriggling to get free.

"Just to be sure," I say, smacking her ass one more time before releasing her.

She stumbles to her feet.

I remain where I am and watch as she takes two steps away and reaches under her dress. Her eyes are locked on me, hair a little out of place, hate in her eyes. She tugs at the panties. They get caught on a heel and she hops, catching herself on the edge of the vanity. I try not to laugh as she mutters under her breath and finally steps out of them. She then throws them at me, and they hit me square in my face.

"Happy?" she asks. "Pervert."

I take the tiny black strip and stand up.

"I am happy, thank you for asking." I move to her, watch her back away as her eyes grow wide. I grip a handful of loose hair not caring if I mess it up. "You throw anything at me again and we'll have another conversation with you across my lap, am I clear?"

She grits her teeth.

"Am I?" I ask with a tug.

"Yes," she hisses through her teeth.

"Good girl," I tell her, releasing her and stepping back. I watch her as I bring her panties to my nose and to her horror, I inhale. "I'm right, aren't I? Our little tête-à-tête got you hot and bothered."

"You're an asshole, Jericho St. James."

"That I am," I say with a chuckle before tucking them into my pocket and taking her arm. "Shall we? We're running late."

20

JERICHO

When I walk into the Red Room with Isabelle on my arm, all heads turn. We do make a striking couple, I have to say. Young, beautiful, fragile Isabelle on the arm of a devil such as me. Two half-breeds in the eyes of The Society, my father having bought our way into the ranks of Sovereign Sons and her mother most likely having been raped by a Bishop.

Carlton is staring daggers from a corner where he is holding court with the cream of Society crop. I smile, tug Isabelle closer.

"Smile, sweetheart, or someone may get the idea you're unhappy to be on my arm."

"I am unhappy," she says, but then someone waves from across the room and I feel Isabelle's excitement as she raises her hand in greeting.

I glance at her, but she's quick to school her

features so I follow her gaze to the woman who is now making her way through the crowd toward us. Julia Bishop. Her cousin and single mom of four-year-old Matthew Bishop. She lives in the Bishop house. Another stray relative Carlton took in.

Her perfume precedes her, the cloying scent turning my stomach. She's a few years older than Isabelle. Twenty-four if I remember correctly. She's attractive, there's no denying that, but there's something calculating about her. Even the way she extends her hand to introduce herself to me has been practiced.

"Hi. I'm Julia, Isabelle's cousin. You must be Jericho St. James."

I look at her extended hand, then to her face. Her smile is wide, radiant. And rehearsed. I can play that game too, so I smile, take her hand.

"Enchanted," I say. I'm not. But I am surprised when in my periphery I see Isabelle turn a curious glance my way.

"I've been trying to get hold of my cousin but just realized her phone is sitting on her nightstand out of charge and since I didn't have your phone number, well, I'm just glad to see you've let her out of the lair tonight."

This one's something. Before I can respond I see Zeke. Beside him is Marco, the right-hand-man of the man I came to meet with. I relax my hold on Isabelle.

"Well, I'm sure you have a lot to catch up on," I say and lean close to Isabelle to whisper in her ear. "Don't disappear or your lesson of earlier will be repeated."

She faces me when I draw back, puts her hands on my shoulders and rises on tiptoe.

"Don't jerk off too hard while sniffing my panties."

I wrap an arm around her lower back and tug her closer.

"I'll let you do the jerking later," I say and lightly bite the shell of her ear.

"In your dreams," she whispers and smiles sweetly.

I smile back because hell, this is fun.

But I glimpse Carlton Bishop's ugly face beyond Isabelle's shoulder and release her. I have business to conduct tonight. I walk away from Isabelle and her cousin, signaling to Dex who is standing subtly in the shadows to keep an eye on Isabelle then walk out into the courtyard where Marco and Zeke are waiting.

Zeke makes a point of checking his watch. "I wasn't sure you would extract yourself."

"Fuck off," I tell him and turn to Marco. "I hope I didn't keep anyone apart from my brother waiting."

"They just got here," Marco says.

Zeke and I follow him through the courtyard to

one of the small private rooms. Once we enter, he closes the door, and the two men stand to greet us.

"Jericho," Lawson Montgomery, also known as Judge, says. He extends his hand.

"Judge." I take his hand, shake it. "It's been a long time." Judge and I crossed paths at Harvard years ago.

"We'll remedy that. It's good to see you again. Ezekiel," he says and the two shake hands.

I turn to the other man whom I only know by name and watch as my brother shakes hands with him, the two exchanging pleasantries. My brother has kept up appearances over the last five years, but I don't know how far his friendships go.

"Santiago, this is my brother, Jericho. Jericho, Santiago De La Rosa. The man I told you about."

"Santiago," I shake his hand as I take him in, the half-skull-face tattoo impressive even though Zeke warned me. "Good to meet you."

"Same," Santiago says. We sit on the leather Chesterfields, and I see the folder on the coffee table.

"I'm sure my brother filled you in on the ugly details," I say to Santiago and Judge.

"Your family history is interesting," Santiago says.

"As interesting as yours." I study Santiago. He is a Sovereign Son and a force to be reckoned with. For years after the explosion that claimed the lives of his brother and father and left him scarred, he lived a life of solitude plotting his revenge. That revenge came in the form of Ivy Moreno, the daughter of the man he believed had orchestrated the killing of so many Sovereign Sons. Things didn't go the way he planned though. She recently gave birth to their second child. Looking at him, I wonder about her. Because she'd have to be something else to have turned this man's head.

"We have a lot in common," he says.

I think about Isabelle, about how right he is. But I can say one thing for sure. I will never let Isabelle become to me what Ivy has become to him.

Santiago grins as if he's reading my mind.

"How are your daughter and mother?" Judge asks. "Zeke tells me they're home."

"Adjusting," I tell him. "My mother, as you know, is recovering."

"I'm glad to hear it."

"Thank you." We had thought for so long that she would die. That the cancer would beat her. But she's in remission and slowly regaining her strength.

"And Angelique?" Judge asks.

"It's going to take her a little longer to call New Orleans home."

"Children are resilient," Santiago says. He's been studying me all along.

I nod although I worry about Angelique. Isabelle wasn't very far off about her. She is a fragile little girl.

Zeke pats me on the shoulder and I realize I've gone off into my own thoughts. "She'll be fine. She just needs a little time."

"I wonder how much having Isabelle Bishop in the house will help," Santiago adds. "I don't think men like us are equipped with the...softer side children need."

I look at him surprise by the comment. "Isabelle?"

He smiles.

"You make a mistake. She isn't there to develop any sort of relationship with my daughter no matter the role she plays."

"Her role as vessel."

I nod.

"Don't be too sure you can control it."

"I will control it. Control her."

"Hm." One corner of Santiago's mouth curves upward as if he's humoring me. I shift my gaze to Judge who is studying me, expression unreadable, and beside me, my brother is doing the same. I'm still not sure he's fully on board with my plans but I push the thought aside because it doesn't matter.

"What did you find?" I ask Santiago.

He touches the sealed folder between us. "Carlton Bishop is not a nice man, but I don't think any of us thought otherwise," Santiago says.

I want to take that folder but hold back. My heart

is beating fast because whatever is in there could damn Bishop, but I also know it will cost me.

Again, as if reading my mind, Santiago speaks. "And although I have uncovered something that may be useful to you, there is no evidence of any involvement on Carlton Bishop's part in your father's death." His gaze momentarily but decidedly rests on Zeke.

"No?" I ask, confused.

He brings his attention back to me and shakes his head. "No."

I'm confused. That's what this meeting is about. "What do you have then?"

"The Bishop girl lost her brother one year after losing her parents."

"Isabelle?" Zeke asks.

"This isn't about Isabelle," I say.

Santiago gestures to the folder and I take it, break the seal. I reach inside to lift out the stack of papers while he speaks.

"The parents' deaths were an accident from the look of things. But the break-in at her brother's house, that was planned."

"What?"

"Attempted rape—"

"What?" I interrupt, dumfounded.

He nods. "Brother walked in, surprised the culprit. Got himself killed."

I glance at him, my brain taking a minute to follow, then shift my attention to look through the pages. Police reports, hospital records. The certificate of death for Christian York. Multiple knife wounds. I keep going, looking at the photos from the crime scene.

And then I get to her.

"There's nothing here about a rape."

"No, there isn't but that doesn't mean there wasn't an attempt. I assure you my sources are infallible." I look at her jeans. How they're undone, shoved halfway down her hips. Or possibly pulled haphazardly up. "In my opinion the whole thing was staged to cover up the real intention which was murder."

I look at the picture, at her face. At the strange angle of her arm, the blood on her chest. She lies on the shards of glass that were once a coffee table.

But rape?

"Christian York was the target?" I ask absently.

"No," he says, catching me off guard. "Isabelle was."

"Why? And how do you know this?"

Santiago reaches over to take the pages from me, flips through and sets one on top. This one is numbers. All kinds of numbers.

"Easy enough. I followed the money. I tracked it from Bishop all the way through," he starts, tracing a group of numbers with his finger that make no sense to me but appear to be a map to him. "To where it ends up here. In Danny Gibson's bank account. A Bishop charity was used to transfer the funds."

"Danny Gibson?"

"The man currently serving a prison sentence for the murder of Christian York."

I'm doing the math but I'm unprepared. Zeke suggested talking to Judge who has access to Santiago De La Rosa. If anyone could dig up what I needed, it was him, so I'd asked Judge for help with finding evidence of wrongdoing on Carlton Bishop's part in the death of my father. I didn't ask about this. Although I'd wondered about the break-in at the York house that killed Isabelle's brother, I didn't care. It didn't matter for my purposes. Still doesn't.

I look from Judge to Santiago to my brother, who takes the pages from me to flip through them.

"You're saying Carlton Bishop had Christian York killed and Isabelle left for dead?"

"I'm saying she was the target. Not him."

"Why?" Zeke asks, clearly having as hard a time as I am understanding why.

"It's in the file." Santiago gestures to the papers Zeke is holding. "She's half-Bishop. They share the same father," he says to me. "If he doesn't produce an heir and she does, he forfeits his inheritance. He loses everything and she gets it all."

"And he hasn't been able to produce an heir." None of Carlton's wives have carried a child to full term. Faulty sperm, I'd guess. Some scum shouldn't

have the capacity to procreate. Carlton Bishop is that
scum.

"Exactly," Santiago says.

"I'm sure he could arrange for his wife to become
pregnant but considering the magic of modern-day
science, well, however you look at it, unless by some
miracle the man produces a child within the next
year, Isabelle Bishop stands to inherit the Bishop
fortune," Judge sums up.

This I know. Carlton trying to kill Isabelle
though when she would have been sixteen years
old? It catches me off guard.

But then again, why would it?

I came to get information on Carlton's involvement in my father's death but this? It may give me
the ammunition I seek but it's unsettling to say the
least.

"What remains of the fortune," Judge adds. "The
land if nothing else. Unless, of course, she's dead."

"You're sure about this?"

"Gibson tried to clear his name telling just that
story but sadly there was no evidence to support it.
Those reports weren't easy to come by."

"How did you come by them?"

He shrugs a shoulder. "Money always leaves a
trail. A map if you know how to read it. And I'm very
good at reading maps."

"Bishop knew no one would believe Gibson if he
told his story."

"Exactly. He is a criminal. Has served time before. He broke into the York house to rob them but happened upon the occupants. He did what he had to do. Or so said the prosecutor who presented the case, and the jury ate it up. Men like Gibson look like they belong in prison. Bishop knew what he was doing when he hired him. When the money Gibson claimed to have been paid vanished without a trace, well, it was his word against Carlton Bishop. Danny Gibson will rot in prison. And quite frankly, he deserves to be there. But so does Bishop."

Zeke puts the stack of papers down on the coffee table, the photo of Isabelle on top. I look at it. At Isabelle passed out on the broken shards of the glass coffee table, face and body bruised, swelling, broken.

Carlton did this. Just like he killed Kimberly, he did this to her.

"Why take her in then?" I ask Santiago. "And why not finish the job in the years she's been living at the Bishop house?"

"Because somehow, and I don't know how, knowledge of who her father is reached IVI. And Society blood, well, I don't need to tell you about how it is revered. Carlton Bishop had no choice but to take her in. Why not kill her in the years she's been under his roof? I don't know. I think he would have if he could have but something stood in his way. As for preventing her from inheriting it seems he's found a workaround. He's arranging a marriage contract as we speak."

"I initiated The Rite. He can't decide for her."

"I think he's going to Hildebrand with a case to get her back," Judge says. "I wonder if he'll use the fact that no heirs will be born to him to argue his case."

"It won't matter," I say, realizing how similar my plan is.

Zeke turns to me. "He's arranged for accidents before. If she were to give birth to the next heir, it would be easy to simply take over guardianship if the parents were gone and ensure his own future."

"What will you do?" Judge asks me.

"The Bishops have always hated the St. James's and that goes both ways. Both families have been brutal, but the Bishops more so."

"They may say the same about you," Santiago adds.

"He can say whatever the hell he wants. My daughter is motherless because Carlton Bishop wanted to eliminate my family to take back land he and all the Bishops before him have always considered theirs. He took her life. He stole from my daughter. From me. I will take everything from him to make him pay. This information doesn't change my plans," I say, standing, wanting to be out of this suddenly stifling room. "I still have everything I need to do what I need to do."

"You won't go to The Tribunal?" Judge asks.

"No. I'll handle this myself."

"As you should," Santiago says.

I study him. We have this in common at least. "Thank you, Santiago. I'm indebted to you."

He stands, extends his hand. "I wish you success. Should you need anything else, my door is open to you."

I nod, turn to Judge. "Judge. Thank you."

He shakes my hand.

The two of them leave the room and I'm alone with my brother, with my thoughts, with those photos, that damning evidence. For three years she has lived in the house of the man who had her brother killed. The man who had arranged to have her killed. And she doesn't have a clue.

"Your plan is the same as his. You'll use her like he would," Zeke says.

"There's a difference. I won't kill her."

"Well, isn't she a lucky girl then."

We study each other. "Do you hate the Bishops?"

"You know I do."

"Then what's your problem?" I ask, stepping toward him.

He doesn't back away. "My problem is that there are better ways to do this. Like what I've been doing."

"Quietly breaking down his fortune."

"It hits him where it hurts."

"But he doesn't see who is doing the hitting."

"He suffers all the same."

"Not enough," I say, shaking my head. I stuff the sheets into the folder and straighten to face Zeke again. "I want him to see it's me. I want him to know."

"No matter the cost."

"She's a Bishop."

"She's a girl."

"Our father would have done no less." I say, knowing I'll get a reaction out of him. His relationship with our father was very different than mine.

"And you idolize that brutal man?" he asks, right on cue. I don't actually know why I bring it up. I didn't agree with much of what my father did when it came to my brother, but I was first-born. I was his heir. And in many ways, I was like him. Zeke and Zoë, not so much. They were different. I wonder if it wasn't Zoë's influence that made Zeke see our father differently than I did. He was a ruthless man and as ruthless as Zeke is, he is fair.

"I don't idolize—"

"Oh, Jericho!" He shakes his head like he's so fucking disappointed in me. It pisses me off.

"If you don't have the stomach for it, look away. Oh and no need to leave flowers on Kimberly's grave. I'm home. I got it covered."

"Fuck you, you asshole." He shoves my chest,

sending me back a step. "You think you are the only one who mourned her loss?"

I chuckle. "That right there is the difference between me and you. You *mourned* her. I still mourn her."

"Because that's what she would want? She would never want the father of her child stuck in the past letting his life be eaten away by revenge, while his daughter grows up not knowing him. Not really anyway, because he's too busy with his vengeance to see what's right in front of his eyes."

I drop the folder on the seat of the chair beside me and shove him back hard. "Don't you dare. Don't you fucking dare! She died in my arms!"

"I know. But you're not the only one who lost her. She's gone. She's been gone. Angelique lives. And that little girl's afraid of her own shadow. Is that what you want? What you think Kim would have wanted?"

"I'm keeping my daughter safe. I will do anything I need to do to keep her safe and you don't get a say in that!"

"And how will you explain Isabelle to her? How will you explain what you're planning? Because she understands more than you think. And she sees everything. Do you really want her growing up afraid of her own father?"

That stops me. "Why would she be afraid of me?

She has no reason to fear me. I protect her. I will always—"

"Yeah, I got it. You'll do anything to protect her even if the path you're choosing will make a monster out of you. No better than our own father. You don't know the half of what that man was capable of."

His words hit me harder than his fist would have and I find myself staring at him like he just knocked the wind out of me. Rage and regret and betrayal burn inside me. I do know the brutality of our father. I've seen the evidence of it on our mother's body.

Zeke looks away, shakes his head. He pushes a hand into his hair. "Fuck. I didn't mean that," he says.

"No, you did." I reach down to take the folder. "But you're not wrong. I do have one thing in common with dad. He never forgot his hatred for his enemies and neither will I." My voice doesn't sound like my own. I walk up to him, look at the man he's become. See the differences between us. "I'm going to do what I have to do. What I swore to do. If you can't handle it, stay out of my way."

I walk past him out the door, through the courtyard and back to the Red Room. I've lost my appetite for dinner. For the show I'd make of having Isabelle Bishop, of having initiated The Rite. I look around the room for her. I want to leave. Except that Isabelle isn't here.

Fuck.

I see her brother in a heated conversation with Councilor Hildebrand at the far corner. Is he already making his case to marry her off right out from under my nose?

Well, he will be too late.

My phone buzzes in my pocket and I dig it out, see a text from Dex. One word.

Chapel.

I shake my head and move toward the chapel. She can pray all she wants, my Bishop girl. No god will save her from me.

21

ISABELLE

J ulia and I slip into the chapel as soon as Jericho is out of sight. She sighs once as the door closes behind us and we're alone.

"Are you okay?" she asks.

I nod. "So far. How are you? How's Matty?"

"We're fine. He misses you though."

"I miss him too."

"Do you think you'll be able to see him soon?"

"I don't know. I—"

"It's fine. Here, before I forget." She opens her bag to retrieve my phone and charger. "So I can get hold of you."

I smile, take both and shove them into my clutch. "Thank you. You're a savior!" I hug her but quickly remember Julia isn't a hugger.

"Paul called to say he moved the lesson to his house by the way. I told him you may not be there."

"I doubt he'll let me attend." Paul Hayes has been giving me violin lessons for the last six months. We have a small group of us who can't afford private lessons and none of us are enrolled in a school so it's what I've been able to do. When I was still in high school my music teacher taught me, but since graduating, Carlton has refused to fund what he calls my little hobby. And since he wouldn't allow me to get a job considering my station in life as a Bishop—I rolled my eyes when he said those actual words—he thought my allowance should be enough to provide for anything he didn't. I've been using that money to pay for lessons. "I'll call him."

"Let me know if you need me to do it."

"Thanks. Carlton told you what Jericho did? Initiating The Rite?"

"Yeah. I heard the details. At least the parts your brother was willing to share. I'm guessing only those that don't cast him in a bad light because if Hildebrand went along with it, then whatever Jericho St. James has on Carlton is big."

"You don't know what it is?"

She shakes her head.

"There's shared history, though. It goes back centuries," I say.

"That I do know. The gruesome story of Nellie Bishop. Her body is buried on stolen land. Bastards."

"Stolen? I thought it was bought."

"Not exactly fair and square but I suppose that's how Jericho St. James would tell it."

"I guess I'm not surprised."

"Do you know what he's planning?"

"To make my life miserable."

"Well, I know Carlton is trying to get you home. He's going to talk to Hildebrand tonight. You'll have to marry though to get you away from St. James."

"Why? What does that have to do with anything?"

Julia studies me for a minute, uses the pad of her thumb to wipe away what I guess is smeared eyeliner on my temple. "You're so innocent, Isabelle. I like that about you. Just keep taking your birth control pills. Please tell me you have them?"

I nod but her comment confuses me. Or maybe it's the way she said it. But before I can ask anything, the chapel door opens and even though I have my back to it, I know it's him. I feel his presence in the shiver that runs along my spine. In the way my body reacts to him like it's on fire.

Julia stiffens but schools her features in a matter of moments. She smiles. It's a smile that shows her to her full advantage. She's beautiful, my cousin. Sophisticated. Polished in a way people who come from money are. I may be a Bishop now, but I don't come from money. The opposite. I'm an imposter here and they all know it.

But there's something in that smile of hers.

Something off. There's a hardness to Julia. Or maybe it's just that her skin is thicker than mine.

"You know you're the talk of the town," she says, stepping around me to walk toward Jericho.

I turn after her and watch. His eyes are on me, and I wish they weren't. They're too hard. Too cruel.

"After your big disappearing act to return like you did. I heard you made quite the entrance the other night. Too bad I missed it."

She stops a few feet from him, and I watch how she does it. How she doesn't shrink away. And I think about what he said. Well, what his brother said. That I'm no match for him. I'm not. But my cousin, she could take him on. She'd have a fighting chance. Is that why he chose me?

Weirdly the thought of them together bothers me.

He shifts his gaze from me to her as if just realizing she's standing there. "Excuse us," he says and steps past her to approach me. Julia turns to watch him, and I see her surprised expression but it's only a blur because he's taking up all the space in the small chapel. All the oxygen there is to breathe.

By the time he reaches me she's gone. I only know from the loud clang of the heavy door closing.

"I told you to stay put." He takes my arm and I see he's holding something in the other. "What were you two talking about?"

"Nothing. My cousin mostly. I'd like to see him."

"Hm." His gaze moves over me, and I clutch my purse tighter. If I can get to the house, I can hide the phone. But only if I get it past him first.

"Where were you?" I ask.

"Meeting." He doesn't sound like himself. Something has him bothered and he's having a hard time hiding it. The way he's looking at me feels different. Like he's trying to glean what is inside me. He searches my face before his gaze lands on my collarbone.

I touch the scar to make sure it's hidden by my hair.

"A meeting at a social event? Is that the whole reason we came? So you could go to some meeting?" I ask to deflect.

"Why do you come in here?" he asks, glancing around the chapel. "It's twice now that I find you here."

I shrug a shoulder, try to dislodge his hand. He eases his grip a little. "My mom used to bring me here when I was little, and she had to clean the compound. It was good money, so she took the jobs, but when my father or brother weren't home, there was no one to leave me with, so she'd bring me here and tell me to stay put."

"How little?"

"I don't know. The first time was my fifth birthday." I remember because she promised we'd go buy a gift with the money she'd earn.

"She left her five-year-old daughter alone in a church?"

"Unlike you and everyone in this place, we didn't grow up with money to spare. We couldn't afford a sitter."

"Did she think Jesus would babysit?"

I narrow my gaze. "I guess she did, pot."

"Pot?"

"Pot calling the kettle black. You know the expression? Or do you need me to explain it?"

"How the hell does that apply to me?"

"You leave your daughter to be watched by strangers."

"I hardly—ah fuck it. I don't answer to you, Isabelle Bishop." He sets the folder he's holding down on the altar and studies me, the look in his eyes stranger than usual.

"What's going on?" I ask.

Instead of answering he shifts his hand to my shoulder and pushes me to my knees.

Panic rises inside me. I'm not sure if it's the look on his face or the weight of his hand that scares me more.

"What are you doing?" I ask.

When my knees hit the floor, he shifts his hand to the top of my head. His touch is gentle. At first.

"Why did you tell me about growing up poor?"

"What?"

"Your story. Why did you tell me?"

"You asked."

He cups the back of my head, then grips a handful of hair and tugs forcing me to look up at him. I drop my clutch to grasp his arm. "Is it so I feel sorry for you?"

"I told you because you asked. That's all. I don't want or expect your pity, so keep it."

"Or is it so I don't see you as a Bishop?" It's as if he doesn't hear me at all. He tightens his grip. I'm not even sure he's aware he's doing it.

"You're hurting me."

"Answer me."

"I think you'll only ever see me as a Bishop."

"Because that's what you are."

"Let go. I mean it."

"Or what? What will you do, little Isabelle Bishop?"

I don't answer his taunt. What can I say? There's nothing I can do. If I scream no one will come. Even if they do, they'll take one look at us and choose a side. His.

He twists a little harder. "Rumor has it the bastard Reginald Bishop put in Mary St. James's womb was conceived here. Right in the spot you're kneeling. A sacrilege to her and to the god you pray to."

I wrap my other hand around his forearm but it's useless. I can't budge him. He crouches down so his face is inches from mine. He watches me as he twists. A tear slides from my eye. He becomes a blur as more follow and I wonder for a minute if he means to do the same to me. To hurt me like my ancestor hurt his.

"Please let go... You're hurting me."

He blinks, eyes becoming slits. I wonder what happened in his meeting to bring on this dark mood. He eases his grip on my hair and brings his other hand to my stomach, then lower to cup my sex.

I gasp with surprise, and he just watches me.

"Please," I manage.

"Please what?" he taunts, fingers working, the only thing between him and me the soft cloud like material of the dress. And it feels good. I hate it, but his touch feels good.

He cups the back of my head while his fingers move over my sex. His eyes burn into mine.

"Please stop or please make you come?" he asks.

"I hate you," I manage even as I suck in a breath when he kneads my clit.

"But you want me to make you come all the same."

I should be repelled by his touch. But like the last time I find myself gasping for air. Find my hands not pressing him away but clinging to him, wrapping around his shoulders.

"I'm not like him," he mutters.

"Who?"

"Reginald Bishop. I'm not like him."

I try to follow.

"Say my name," he says like he did last time.

I shake my head but when his fingers move off their mark, I find myself pushing into his hand.

"Say it. Say it when you come."

Not say it and I'll make you come. Say it *when* you come.

I swallow hard. I want this.

He draws me to him, kisses me. I don't kiss back. I can't. But I don't fight the kiss, either. I don't bite. Because I want to come. I want to come this time.

"I..." I start to say against his mouth, and he just swallows the sound, swallows the words. I don't even know what they were.

"My name, Isabelle. Say it."

My dress must be soaked. Everyone will see. Will know. But right now, I don't care. All I can feel is him, his fingers touching me, on me, inside me, rubbing me and when I can't take anymore, I lean my head into the crook of his neck and I'm panting, breathing in the scent of him.

"Say it," he says again, voice hoarse.

I turn my head, press my open mouth to the skin of his neck and taste him, salt and man. When I do, I feel him shudder. But the instant it happens, his hand is in my hair again, tugging me off.

But his fingers keep doing their work, knowing exactly how to touch me. A moment later, I give myself over to it, to the sensation of his hands on me, to the warmth of him, the smell of him. And when I come, I drop my head back and do as he wants. I say his name. I'm not sure he hears it. It's just a breath. Just the quietest whisper. Because I've never felt this way before. Never felt like I would come undone when my own fingers play over my clit.

"Again. Say it again." His mouth is on my throat, hot and wet.

"Jericho." I blink, seeing him in a blur of sensation, my body jerking against his hand, fingers digging into his shoulders, the smell of incense all around us. Him all around me.

And as I float back to reality, I remember where we are. Kneeling on the chapel floor.

I remember who I'm with. A man who hates me.

But when I look at him, it's not that hate I see in his eyes. It's something else. Something dark and dangerous. An inferno in the depths of those strange, cunning eyes.

He pulls his hand from me slowly, releases his grip on my hair and cups my cheek. His fingers are damp. With his thumb he wipes my face and I think he's wiping away the stain of a tear.

"Tomorrow," he says as he pulls me to stand, my legs wobbling, my knees not quite working. "Tomorrow you'll wear my mark. Tomorrow your blood will stain my sheets. And then you'll be mine. For better or worse. Until death do us part."

22

ISABELLE

F*or better or worse. Until death do us part.*

The strange words circle my brain.

Jericho drapes his jacket over my shoulders and hurries me out of the chapel, out of the compound. No one sees me, at least not the state of my dress, although I catch a glimpse of Julia before we're out of the courtyard. Before he puts me into the car that's idling along the curb, Dex in the driver's seat. He doesn't look at me as we drive back to his house. His face is stone. That folder on his lap.

In the rush of it all and maybe in his distracted state, my clutch doesn't catch his eye. I half expect him to search me, but he doesn't. He sits silent instead. I find myself hugging his jacket closer, trying not to look at him. Is he thinking about what just happened? It's cool in the car, the air-conditioning on high. At least I tell myself it's the air-conditioning that's got me shivering.

When we get into the house, I can hear people talking, their voices lowered. It's his brother and mother. They're standing by the unlit fireplace in the living room. Jericho stops when he sees them, so I stop too. And they quiet, their eyes on us.

"Go to your room," he says and walks away, leaving me standing in the foyer and disappearing down another corridor. They both watch as he disappears before turning their gazes on me.

I look down at myself, see the darker spot on the dress and hug the jacket closed. I hope they don't see it and hurry up the stairs to my own room.

Once I'm inside I lean my back against the door wishing I could lock it. Although I don't know if I want to lock it to keep him out any more, so I tell myself that even if I could, my devil has another way in. The one that leads to his room. What had he said? It's for when he requires access to me? I can't remember the exact words, but I can't shake that feeling of being a possession. Being his.

I shudder, the jacket too big on my shoulders. I smell him on it. Smell him on me. And I shrug out of it, let it fall to the floor. I don't look at the spot on my dress where my own arousal, my own pleasure, broadcasts my shame.

I came.

I let him make me come on the floor of the chapel.

I wanted it. God. What is wrong with me?

I set the clutch on my desk and walk into the bathroom, stripping off the dress as I go, dropping it right into the trash can. I don't think that stain would come out anyway. I switch on the shower as hot as I can stand it, step into the glass enclosure, and think about his words.

Did Reginald Bishop really rape Mary St. James? And in a church? Is anyone capable of that? Yes. Of course, they are. That's a stupid question. Julia is right. I'm naïve. She used the word innocent, but she was being kind.

But he could be lying. What's to stop him? He can make up any story he wants. It's not like I can Google it. Fact-check him.

But that's not all that has me so upset and I know it. It's the fact that I wanted it. That I wanted *him*. That I clung to his shoulders and didn't want to let go.

It's the fact that I came.

"Shit!"

The cuts from our game of chase burn in the flow of hot water but I embrace the pain. I deserve it. I pull out the pins that hold my hair in place and let them drop to the shower floor, tugging out strands in the process. More pain. Once I've freed my hair, I pour shampoo onto my palm and wash vigorously then repeat before scrubbing my body wanting to erase his touch from me. Wanting to erase my shame.

I fucking came. I let him do it. Didn't put up anything remotely resembling resistance. What is wrong with me?

I stay in the shower until my skin is pink and raw. Once I'm out and drying myself off I remember my phone inside the clutch. I need to hide it before he finds it. So I hurry out of the bathroom, water dripping from me as I rush to my bedroom, half-expecting to find him standing there holding the evidence of my deceit. But he's not here. No one is. I'm alone and the clutch is where I'd left it.

From inside, I take my phone in hand and press the power button, but it doesn't turn on. The battery must be drained so I push the nightstand away from the wall and plug it in behind the bed, hiding the phone as it charges. As I dry off, I think about what Julia said about me having to marry to get out of here. Get away from Jericho St. James.

For better or worse. Until death do us part.

Her even stranger comment about my birth control pills. How does she know I'm on them? Did Carlton discuss putting me on birth control with her? The humiliations never end.

I open a dresser drawer to find pajamas and my

T-shirt inside. Christian's T-shirt. It's an unexpected boon especially on this night of nights. It's been laundered and returned just as Jericho said it would be. It's a small comfort and I slip it on. I don't recognize the smell. Well, I do, from Jericho's clothes, but it's not the same as it used to be. Although the shirt had lost its scent years ago and I've washed it many times since Christian's death. Still, I'm glad to have it.

I return to the bathroom to double check the little plastic package of pills is still there inside my make up bag. It is. Everything is as I left it.

Okay. I set my hands on the edge of the sink and meet my reflection. I'm being paranoid.

My skin is flushed from my too hot shower, the mirror still a little foggy but I can see enough to know the heavy liner the make-up artist used hasn't washed off completely. In my too-hot shower it has smeared to make me look more like a raccoon than anything else. I switch on the faucet to wash off the remaining makeup then brush my teeth like it's a normal night and I'm going to bed. Although, it's barely nine o'clock and I haven't had anything to eat since earlier today.

As if on cue when I return to the bedroom there's a knock on the door.

"Just a minute," I say, and double check my phone is out of sight before I pull on a pair of jeans and open the door.

Jericho's mother stands there smiling. She's

holding a plate with a sandwich and a bottle of water.

"I understand you never made it to dinner," she says.

I smile at her and move aside so she can enter. She sets the dish and bottle down on the vanity then sits on one of the chairs, so I close the door because I guess she's staying.

"Nope, didn't make dinner," I say and glance at the food.

"I'm sure you're hungry," she says, gesturing to the plate. "Please eat."

"Thanks." I sit down and set the plate on my lap so I can face her. I open the bottle of water first and drink while she watches me. I wonder about her. How much does she know about her son? How much does she know about what he wants with me? More than I do, I'm sure. And how much on his side is she? Would she help me against her own flesh and blood? I doubt it.

"He comes from a place of hurt," she offers as if reading my mind.

It takes me a minute. "Am I supposed to feel sorry for him then?" Because I don't.

"No, I just want you to understand. To hear it from someone other than Jericho. He's too emotional when it comes to this. To you and what he needs to do."

"What does he need to do?"

"What he thinks he has to do," she continues as if she hasn't heard me.

"Which is what exactly?"

She sighs deeply. "Angelique likes you, Isabelle. Very much."

"I like her. She's sweet. Unlike her father," I add that last part under my breath as I take a bite of my sandwich.

She chuckles. "Well, if there's one thing my son has never been and will be it's sweet."

"What is he planning? What's going to happen to me?"

She studies me, then stands, paces for a moment. "His fiancée, Angelique's mother, died in his arms. Did you know that?"

God. No. I shake my head, putting the sandwich down, the bite in my mouth feeling too big, like it will choke me if I swallow.

"He was the target," she adds.

"I didn't know." Goosebumps cover my flesh and I set the plate aside.

"Your brother hired the men who did it."

I blink. "What?" Is it the words themselves, their meaning or the casual way she says it?

She doesn't repeat herself. Just gives me a few minutes to hear her. It's going to take me a hell of a lot longer than that to process.

"The feud between our families has been going on for generations. It started when we bought this land. *Legitimately* bought the land that was once Bishop land. The Bishops have always had money for as long as their history has been recorded. But as often happens with generation after generation of money, the less one has to work for it, the more entitled one feels, the more quickly a fortune is squandered."

Entitled. There's that word again. Reginald Bishop had felt entitled to Mary St. James. At least how Jericho told it.

"And of course, they were a founding family of The Society. How much do you know about IVI?"

"Not much. I never really was all that interested honestly. I only learned that my father, the man who was my biological father at least, was a Bishop a few years ago. I've never considered myself a Bishop. Never considered anyone but the man who raised me with love to be my father. I've never thought about anything else."

"But you changed your name," she says, and I can't tell if her tone is accusatory or what.

"I was sixteen. I had just lost my brother in a brutal attack." My eyes mist. "I had been beaten. I would have died if our neighbor hadn't called the police. So, when Carlton came for me telling me the news of my parentage, taking me in, having me sign page after page of legal documents, I can't say I really cared much about a name or any of the rest of it. I was numb." No one bothers to remember how this all happened. How Christian, who wasn't even supposed to be at the apartment but had come home to check on me, died. I stand up, wipe the tears that fall with the heels of my hands. "I'm tired," I tell her.

"I know your story, Isabelle," she says. She walks toward me, closes her hands over my arms. "And I'm sorry for your loss. Very sorry. We've all lost. But what Jericho is doing now, he's doing to protect Angelique."

"What does my being here have to do with Angelique? Because from what I understand, it's all about revenge. What am I? Collateral damage?"

"There's much more at play behind the scenes. Things you don't know." She drops my arms and walks away.

"Then tell me. Tell me and maybe I'll understand and maybe I can help."

She walks to the door. "I need to go check on Angelique. She still wakes up asking if her daddy is home. If he's coming to see her. That child has lived a life like a fugitive on the run. And this, what he's doing with you, it's all to keep her safe. She's our only concern. We'll all do whatever we need to do for her."

"And what does that mean for me? What's he going to do to me?"

"*To* you?"

"What's he going to do *with* me then?" I ask, my

voice harder. "What does he think he needs to do with me to keep her safe?"

"We've all sacrificed. Keep that in mind. And you will be looked after. Kept safe."

"Safe from who? Because from where I'm standing, the one person I need to be kept safe from is your son."

"That's not—"

"Tell me what he's planning, Leontine." There's no softness to muster up.

"He'll explain it to you tomorrow." She bends to pick up her son's suit jacket and folds it over her arm, putting her hand on the doorknob.

I rush to her, grab her other arm.

"No. Tell me now." She looks down at where I'm holding her, and I follow her gaze. See how hard my grip is. I let her go. "Please."

"Tomorrow you'll marry my son."

"What?" I take a step back, feeling like the wind has been knocked out of me.

"He'll be gentler than most," she says, one hand moving to the back of her neck. "Trust me, Isabelle, it's better than the alternative." She opens the door.

"Alternative? What alternative? That you let me go? That he lets me go?" My voice sounds hectic, panicked. Desperate.

She stops, turns back to me and I can't read her eyes. They're burning, like his burn, but there is a gentleness there. I'm just not sure it's meant for me.

"Go where?" she asks. "Where would you go? Do you have any idea the things your brother has done? What he has planned for you? Did your cousin tell you any of that when she met you in the chapel?"

I'm taken aback. "How did you know about that?"

"You're never truly alone at the compound. Keep that in mind." She steps back into the room and closes the door. "You'll marry my son tomorrow. Then you'll be safe, and he'll do what he needs to do. That's all."

"That's all? That's my life!"

"Your life was forfeit before my son entered it. Your brother saw to that."

"What does that mean?"

"What was Carlton Bishop doing the night you met my son? Wasn't he parading you around under the noses of eligible Sovereign Sons in that ridiculous dress? Do you know how old some are? Do you know the one he'd chosen for you? Maybe you'll recognize the name. Joseph Manson."

"Joseph Manson?" the horrible man Carlton had me dance with at the masquerade ball? Surely not. He was old enough to be my grandfather. But then I remember the way he looked at me, how his hands roamed a little too low on my back. How his rancid breath brushed my neck as he held me closer than necessary. I shudder at the visceral memory and wish I could shower again.

"You know the name," she says. "Three wives came before you. Ask your cousin about that next time you talk to her." She opens the door, steps out then turns back to look at me. "You'll have my son's protection. Remember that. And you need it, Isabelle Bishop. More than you know."

23

JERICHO

I spend that night locked in my study as my brother's words repeat in my head. As her face floats into memory. As the photograph of the crime scene I can't stop looking at stares back at me.

She's no match for me. Zeke's right. She's not meant for our world. But she's in it. He means to strike up a bargain with Joseph Manson? How old is that fuck? Sixty? More? She's fucking nineteen years old.

There's the vision of her face again. Her face when she came. How her eyes closed. How she tilted her head back baring her throat to me. How the vulnerable flesh of her neck tasted.

No match.

How my name sounded on the breath of her whisper as she came on my fingers.

My dick is hard. Fuck. I don't know what's wrong

with me. How many women have I fucked over my lifetime? Countless. How many times have I given any of them, apart from Kimberly, a second thought? How many do I remember the name of? The face? The way they sounded when they called out my name?

All that was to have died after Kimberly. It had for a very long time. Fucking was release. That's all. But now, with her—with *her* of all people—I can't stop myself from remembering. From bringing my fingers to my nose to catch the fading scent of her.

Fuck. Maybe it's been too long. I can't remember the last time I fucked a woman. At the penthouse maybe? That woman in the short maid's uniform shaking her ass at me. Can't even remember her face much less her name. Just a fuck. But Isabelle Bishop? I've memorized every single detail.

I already jerked off when I got home. Twice. My hair is still wet from my shower. I should just go up to her room, help myself to what's mine. Why I'm not, I don't fucking understand. What do I care if she's a virgin on our wedding night? I can bleed her now. Blood on the sheets is blood on the sheets.

But for some reason I don't, and I tell myself it's because there's too much to be done. And there is.

I put the photographs back into the folder and take the single sheet that traces the transfer of funds from Carlton Bishop to Danny Gibson and back. I snap a picture of it with my phone. It's all I need. And I type out a text:

You are cordially not invited to the wedding of Isabelle Bishop and Jericho St. James...

I attach the photo I just took. Because The Rite does offer Isabelle some protections. In order for a guardian to not overstep or take more than his due, any man who has been granted The Rite over a woman cannot marry that woman or form any bond without either her father, brother, uncle giving his blessing. Or, in the case there is no father, brother, or uncle, then The Tribunal gives their blessing. It's to protect the woman from exactly what I'm doing. And I can say I'm glad the safety is in place for the sake of my own daughter. I know well what men are capable of.

But with this little nudge, Carlton Bishop will bless our union.

I send another text. *Tribunal building. Nine o'clock tomorrow morning or I hand all the evidence over to The Tribunal to deal with.*

I have no doubt he'll come. His cowardice will bring him.

The clock in the hall sounds midnight. A knock comes on my door. The touch is too light to be Zeke.

"Come in," I say, scrubbing my face.

My mother enters looking more tired than I feel.

"Why are you still awake?" I ask her.

"Why are you?"

I gesture to the liquor cabinet to offer her a drink. She shakes her head and we both sit on the couch in my office.

"The Bishops have none of my love," she says.

"But…" I start for her, because that's why she's here.

"I expect you to treat her as I expect my son would treat a woman. Any woman."

"Not like dad you mean?" I ask before I can catch myself.

She winces and instantly I feel guilty. I look away.

"I think you'll do better than him," she says, her voice hard. "I hope so at least."

What Santiago said about my father's death plays back in my mind. And not just what he said but the look on his face. The moment his gaze purposely settled on Zeke.

Our father died six years ago. He was not a gentle man. I knew that growing up. He wasn't physically abusive with us, not overly so, but he wasn't exactly the one you'd run to when you scraped a knee either. As much as he wanted to belong to the upper echelon of The Society, he also harbored a special hatred for IVI. I wonder if that longing wasn't what fueled the hate. He had to work for every scrap they gave him. Buying into the rank of Sovereign Son was his *fuck you* to them. Because one thing our family has always excelled at is making money. A lot of it.

Enough that even a secret society like IVI cannot turn their noses up at no matter the source of it.

He had mistresses. Many. I'm not even sure he loved our mother. But their marriage was beneficial to both. It meant funds for her father, and status for mine. Her father's agreement to give my mother to my father was essentially no different than a sale of goods.

I didn't know how brutal he was to her until after she lost her hair from the chemo. I wonder if Zeke knew. I think he did. And I know now that was just one indicator of what my mother endured over the years they were married.

For Sovereign Sons of The Society, the marking ceremony after the wedding is just as important a ritual as the wedding itself, as the bloody sheets, as obtaining the blessing of The Tribunal. It's just the way it is within The Society. The marking is the physical placement of the Sovereign Son's seal, in our case the two-headed dragon, on the back of the woman's neck. It's a show of ownership and has become, for the women—once placement has been endured—a show of rank.

There are two acceptable methods of marking a woman in this modern day. Fire and ink. That wasn't the case in the early days when there was only one.

Both are still offered ritualistically during the ceremony although the old method is just that, ritual. Only a handful of men have chosen it even though the fires burn in their pits and the irons are heated through. Ritual. That's all.

Our father, however, chose the old method.

I glance at the scarf my mother wears around her neck. The branding was to show her and all those present, a member from every sovereign family, that although her family was above his in rank, she would be beneath him in marriage. She would know her place from the first moment the glowing iron sank its searing metal into her flesh, and he burned his mark onto her body.

The thought of my mother kneeling before our father and enduring the pain, the humiliation, makes me sick.

She watches me. She knows what I'm thinking. It's all I think about when I see one of her scarves around her neck. She's never without one.

"The marking," she starts and stops. That's all she needs to say.

"Ink," I tell her.

She nods, a visible relief to her features. Which only makes me wonder at my brother's words of earlier. How much a monster do they think me?

"Everything is ready." She stands. "And I will sleep now."

I stand too. "I'll walk you up." I haven't looked in on Angelique since I got home. We go upstairs together and part ways at Angelique's door. I look after her, wondering about our mother. She is one of the strongest women I know. And she understands what Bishop did, the role he played in Kimberly's death. And she does want her death avenged but she, like Zeke, has softened at the sight of Isabelle Bishop.

Fucking Isabelle Bishop.

Because at the thought of her name, her face floats before me, head thrown back, eyes closed, throat bared, coming on my hand.

24

ISABELLE

The door between my room and his is unlocked. But his room is empty. I don't hear him or anyone else after his mother leaves. I pace my room trying to wrap my brain around what's happening. What I've learned. All that I don't know.

His fiancée died in his arms? That's terrible. And Carlton was the cause of her death? No, that doesn't make any sense. Carlton may be capable of many things but he's not a murderer. Why does Jericho St. James think he is?

I think about what Julia said. How what Jericho has on Carlton must be bad if Councilor Hildebrand allowed him to initiate The Rite. Could Carlton have committed such a thing as murder? No. Just no.

And what she said about him protecting me?

That's laughable. I need protecting *from* him. But she's his mother. She's not going to take my side.

I check my phone and finally I'm able to switch it on. It's an older model and temperamental. I scroll down my short list of contacts and find Julia but her phone rings and rings and finally goes to voice mail.

Should I call Carlton? Warn him? Beg him to help me? But what was he planning for me? To marry me off to that disgusting old man? He couldn't really do that to me, could he?

I pace some more, my gaze landing on the sandwich I barely ate three bites of. I should eat but can't. I need to find him. Understand what the hell is going on. Although will he tell me?

Leontine's words circle in my head.

"You'll have my son's protection. Remember that. And you need it, Isabelle Bishop. More than you know."

What protection do I need? From whom? The only face that swims before me is Jericho St. James's.

But then I see us on that chapel floor, me with my head thrown back, his mouth locked on my throat. Me coming.

Crap.

I decide I need to find him. Find out what the hell is going on. I half-expect the door to be locked when I turn the doorknob but it's not, so I step out into the hallway. And the moment I do, I see him. And I freeze.

He's just coming out of Angelique's room. He

pauses when he sees me. Her bedroom at the opposite end of the hallway so I can't quite see his face, but I clear my throat and close my door behind me to wait for him. I won't cower. I can't.

I watch as he walks toward me, his face its usual stony mask as he comes closer, and I can see his expression. I clear my throat when he's a few feet from me and I open my mouth to speak but hesitate when his gaze shifts to my shirt. I'm very aware I'm not wearing a bra underneath but like he's already said, it's nothing he hasn't seen before. Not that he can see anything. It's not like he has x-ray vision. One eyebrow is raised when he looks back at me.

"You don't have T-shirts without holes in them? Ones that fit you?"

"It's my brother's. Or it was."

"Ah." He studies me. "What are you doing outside of your room?"

"Your mother came to see me."

"I know."

"She told me something strange I wanted to confirm," I say, one hand on my doorknob.

"Confirm?" he asks. "She wasn't clear?"

I falter. It's true. But why would I think it wasn't?

"But... Carlton won't agree to it. And you can't force me. The Society won't allow it. The Rite protects me."

"Hm. Well, Carlton will agree. He'll give us his

blessing, I'm sure. If you don't mind, I'm tired." He steps past me.

"Do I get a say?" I ask, turning to watch him move toward his room.

He stops. Pivots back to me. And I feel small and so completely out of my element. Out of my league. I think of Julia. How she approached him, so confident. And I just feel like a little girl as I stand in my T-shirt with all its holes, a pair of jeans, barefoot as he stands there looking perfect in his suit minus the jacket. Looking elegant and in control. Because he is in control. Of everything.

As if reading my mind he steps even closer and I have to crane my neck to look up at him.

"You weren't complaining at the chapel."

I blink away, embarrassed. But it's what he wants. My shame. More ways to humiliate me.

"I don't want to marry you," I tell him outright.

"You prefer Joseph Manson?"

"No. I don't want to marry anyone. I just want to go to my violin lessons and maybe school and I don't know, just live a normal life. And not be someone's pawn. Yours or my brother's." I feel my eyes fill up and I hate myself a little for my weakness.

"You're a Bishop, Isabelle. And you are a pawn. Mine. You were your brother's before and now you're mine. If you had any delusion about that, about being free before I came into your life, let me dispel it here and now. Carlton Bishop has no brotherly love for you. He never did."

"I don't—"

"As for school, we'll see. I'm not opposed."

I stop at that, bite my lip. "You're not?"

"I'm a modern man. If you want to go to school, by all means."

"What about my lessons?"

"Isn't that the same thing?"

"Violin. I study with a small group one night a week."

"We'll see."

I'm surprised and confused and then irritated all over again. Why does he have to give me permission to do something as normal as going to school or taking violin lessons.

"I already missed some lessons. I need to call Paul and—"

"Who's Paul?"

"Paul Hayes. My teacher."

"Hm."

"Maybe I can go next week. Maybe—"

"We'll see. Don't push your luck."

"Luck." I snort.

"Yes, luck."

"I want a job," I say, standing up a little taller, one hand still on the doorknob behind me.

He chuckles. "You already have one. Don't you remember?"

Oh, I remember. To please him.

"Go to bed, Isabelle. Tomorrow will be a taxing day for you. In." He takes a ring of keys out of his pocket, and I know he means to lock me in.

"I'm not fucking you."

"No? Because you came pretty hard earlier, and I barely had my hands on you. Imagine what I can do with my dick inside you. Imagine how hard you'll come."

"Stop it." I push against his chest, but he doesn't budge.

"Are you imagining it?" he taunts.

I fumble for the doorknob at my back and finally get the door open.

"Good girl. In you go. I don't want you running off anywhere before the big day."

"I hate you."

He shrugs a shoulder. "I'll wait until tomorrow to prove just how much you don't, Isabelle. My mark on your back. Your blood on my sheets. Sleep well tonight, my virgin bride."

With that he's gone, the sound of the lock turning loud, and me left wondering about his words. Knowing the only chance I have is for Carlton to somehow stop this. But then what? Even if he was able to stop Jericho St. James, what then? Let him sell me off to that old man? No. I can't do that, either. My options are limited.

No, that's not true. My options are non-existent.

25

JERICHO

arlton Bishop is disheveled, to say the least, when he walks into the courtroom of The Tribunal building at a few minutes past our arranged meeting time. Actually, he looks like he hasn't slept for a week. It puts a smile on my face seeing him like this.

Hildebrand makes a point of checking his watch. "Mr. Bishop," he starts as he and his two counterparts glare down at the offender. "It is highly inappropriate to arrive at a Tribunal proceeding after we've been seated. Your disregard will be taken into consideration as we make our decision regarding this highly unusual matter."

The courtroom has been modified from its usual setup. The three Councilors still sit on the highest-level looming over us in their wigs and robes. The gallery is empty but for Judge, who serves as advisor to me. Not that I need one. And the dais where the defendant would stand trial has been replaced by a single, rectangular table that must be several hundred years old. I wonder of the fates that were decided upon it as I glance at the many markings where deals were made, promises broken, betrayals avenged.

"Yes, well, it could not be helped," Bishop dares to say as he adjusts his cloak and glances at me with an evil look in his eye. He forces a smile when he turns back to the councilors. "It is my dear sister's wedding day and there was much to do."

It irks me that he can pull it off. That he can sound so fucking casual when I know he's anything but.

I shouldn't care, though. I've won. My victory is in the words he just spoke.

The Councilors glance at one another and it's Hildebrand who raises an eyebrow. "You will not refuse Mr. St. James's request for your sister's hand? Considering our conversations, I assumed, well, why don't you explain it to me."

"Yes, Councilors, my apologies. I admit, I had other plans for dear Isabelle, but it is true that Mr. Manson is quite advanced in age and, well, given her nature," he pauses, looks to me. "She may require a more firm hand than the poor old man could wield."

"Hm," Hildebrand mutters. "It is highly unusual."

I clear my throat and speak. "Unusual or not, as both parties agree, it only remains for The Tribunal to give my betrothed and I their blessing."

Hildebrand studies me. He then drags his gaze to Carlton Bishop who is seething beside me. Do they sense the animosity coming off him?

"Carlton. This is what you want?"

"Yes, Councilor," Bishop says through clenched teeth.

"You give your blessing?"

"I think he said he does," I interject and earn a disapproving look.

"I give my blessing," Bishop says.

I face him and he faces me. He tried to have his half-sister murdered and he now knows that I know. That I have proof. It's why he's here doing what he's doing.

Blackmail. I smile. It never gets old.

An attendant carries down the decree that the Councilors sign. They set it in front of Bishop first. He signs. It's then passed to me. I, too, sign and once the seal is placed, Isabelle's future is secured. By the end of the day, she will be mine and I will be hers. For better or for worse. Until death do us part.

The Councilors leave first and once they're gone, I turn to Carlton who is watching me, his mind no doubt calculating the next move.

"It will destroy her if it comes out," he says.

"You mean it will destroy you."

Hate flattens the blue of his eyes. "Also her."

He's right. I know that. Guilt will destroy her. Her brother died when she was the mark.

How much she and I have in common and she doesn't have a clue.

I gather my things to go.

"I didn't realize she was such a whore, my sister. And in a sacred place no less."

My jaw tightens.

"You know what they say," he leans closer to me. "There are eyes everywhere here. Every dark corner. I wonder who else watched—"

I grasp him by the throat and slam him back on the table. The Tribunal guard are on me in an instant, two sets of hands trying to pry me off.

"Did I hit a nerve?" Bishop chokes out.

I ease my grip. Shove the men off me and straighten. "You're sick, you know that?"

His grin vanishes.

I gather my things and walk away.

"Tell my sister I said to take care. She's quite accident prone."

I narrow my gaze and it takes effort to keep walking. I wonder if he can see that effort in my gait.

"Just don't leave any wells uncovered. You don't want another Bishop girl falling in," he adds as I let the door slam shut behind me.

26

ISABELLE

I spend the whole of the next day locked in my room. I guess he wasn't taking any chances I'd run. Where I'd go is anyone's guess.

I tried to get in touch with Julia but have had no luck. My texts go unread, my voicemails unanswered. Although between the makeup artist, the hairdresser, and the seamstress, I didn't have as much time alone as I hoped.

Now I'm dressed and watching as Leontine directs the woman who did my hair to raise it higher and pick up the tendrils left along my nape. When she's satisfied, I stand and she looks me over, walking a circle around me. I'm wearing her wedding dress altered to fit me. She's a few inches taller than me and apart from it having to be made shorter, it is a near perfect fit. It's simple and pretty, a white, floor-length sheath that is held together by a single pearl for a button at the back of my neck. It's not a tight fit for which I'm grateful. I didn't want a repeat of the feather dress my brother made me wear to that masquerade.

"Do you know the words you must say?" she asks.

"You mean the wedding vows?" She doesn't think I'll be writing vows, does she?

"After the marking. Dominus et Deus. My lord and my god."

"What are you talking about?"

There's a knock on the door and she doesn't get a chance to answer. Instead, Leontine tells whoever it is to enter which annoys me since it's my room, but when Angelique rushes past her, in her own pretty, yellow princess dress, her hair done with ribbons that match and I see her smiling, happy face, I can't help but smile myself. I've seen her once since the incident at the pool which feels like ages ago but it's not.

"Oh, Belle!" she exclaims, stopping just short. "You look so pretty."

I crouch down to hug her and take what I guess is my bouquet from her. "Thank you, Angelique. Wow, I love your dress!"

She spins. "Do you think I look like a princess?"

"I think you look prettier than any princess I've ever seen." I wink.

Jericho's brother, Ezekiel, clears his throat. He's

standing in the doorway in his formal black cloak with a tux underneath. I'm glad he's not wearing that menacing hood. I've only seen him a handful of times for as many minutes and as I look at him now, I think how much like Jericho he looks. The difference is in his eyes. His are both silver. Like a wolf.

"I've been instructed to bring the bride to the car," he says. "Shall we?"

"Yes!" Angelique skips to his side. She's so excited and happy and I wonder if they didn't include her in this bringing of the bride because they know I won't put up a fight with her here. I wouldn't put it past Jericho or his mother. I don't know Ezekiel, but I doubt he'd be on my side in any of this. So, I follow Angelique out and she chats to me and her uncle all the way to the car.

She's easy with him, I see. And he's easy with her as they talk about a world of make believe while Leontine and I watch. It's good to see her like this. The way little girls should be. Not afraid or cautious of everything. Carefree.

I find myself smiling as we ride along, so when Ezekiel sees that smile, he winks at me, and I blink myself back to reality. I fix my features just as the Rolls Royce turns into the IVI compound and our door is opened. Ezekiel exits first, then Angelique. He helps his mother out and reaches a hand in for me to take. I am considering if I can hijack the car when he dips his head inside.

"My brother enjoys a chase," he says casually enough that if Angelique is listening, she won't understand. "But he definitely doesn't like to be kept waiting."

He extends his hand to me again. I wonder if he wants to give the impression that this is somehow my choice. It doesn't matter though. There's only one way this is going to go.

I slip my hand into it and let him help me out. When he tucks my arm into his, I glance up at him, surprised, but don't pull away. He only pauses for a moment to lift Angelique up on his other arm and we make our way across the courtyard and toward that small chapel where Jericho had me on my knees last night.

The courtyard is lit by what seems to be a hundred candles. Fires burn in various pits. Only men are gathered, I notice, and all of them formally dressed in their cloaks, hoods up, masked, drinking drinks.

I glimpse Angelique as she sees them and watch how she hugs her arms around her uncle's neck.

"They're just playing dress up," Ezekiel tells her.

"I don't like their dress up."

Neither do I.

"Then don't look, silly. Look at how pretty Isabelle looks instead," he says with a glance toward me that I can't quite read.

Once we're past the men Angelique wriggles free

of her uncle and comes to my side. She takes my hand and in the same moment, I hear a familiar voice behind me.

"Well, there's the blushing bride." It's Carlton.

I stiffen at the sound of his voice. I don't know why. He's my brother, half-brother, whatever. It's not like I'm afraid of him. And between him and the St. James family, I should know which side I'm safer on.

Leontine casts a wary glance in his direction, but Ezekiel's look is dark. I turn to find Carlton is wearing his cloak and thankfully his mask is pushed to the top of his head.

Angelique stares at him wide-eyed and not without fear.

"Take Angelique inside," Zeke tells his mother in a tone much like his brother's.

"Come, Angelique, we'll wait inside, and Uncle Zeke can walk Isabelle in," says Leontine.

But the little girl shakes her head, drags her gaze from my brother and looks up at me. She tugs at my hand.

"Go on," her uncle tells her. "You have to toss rose petals at the bride's feet. Don't you remember?" he asks but this time I hear the strain in his tone.

"Oh," she says, gaze warily landing on my brother. "I forgot." She looks up at me again.

"Will you come home afterwards? To live with us?" she asks me.

"Home?" Carlton asks and I see him watching with some amusement.

"Of course, she will," Leontine answers, stepping in to take her hand and lead her away, but again, the child tugs to remain in place.

"Promise?" she asks. "You and daddy will come home? I'm not allowed to stay after the wedding."

"I'm sure it won't take that long," I say, thinking her bedtime is eight o'clock. It's only a little after six now.

Leontine gives me a disapproving look but Ezekiel steps in. "There's a second ceremony. Then they'll both be home," he says, that second part spoken in Angelique's direction.

"Come on now," Leontine says to Angelique.

"Promise?" she asks me again. There's something earnest in her tone and I remember what Leontine said. How she's been living like a fugitive. I wonder what that does to someone's trust, especially someone so young. And I think about how they think Carlton had a hand in her mother's murder. But it makes no sense. Why would they allow him here, near her, if that's true?

"I promise. I'll kiss you goodnight when I'm home...when I'm back," I add, just catching myself, thinking of what her father is doing. Of how it could hurt his daughter when it's over. When I'm gone.

The image of the well followed by the one of

Nellie Bishop's grave seem to call up a sudden chilly breeze.

When I'm gone.

A gong sounds then and I'm so grateful for the intrusion.

"You'll kiss her goodnight?" my brother asks as we watch Leontine lead Angelique away.

Once Angelique is safely inside the chapel, Ezekiel steps up to Carlton. Like right up to him, his chest butting up against my brother's.

"You're not welcome, Bishop," he says. Extending his arm to me, he nudges me away from Carlton and behind him.

"No, I suppose I'm not. But she is my sister. And I wanted to wish her happiness and a long life and all that crap."

"How thoughtful of you," Ezekiel deadpans. "You come that close to my niece one more time and I'll break both your legs, you understand?"

"What are you? Your brother's bloodhound?"

"No, I'm my own. Disappear, Bishop, before I make you disappear."

"It's what the St. James's are good at, isn't it? Nellie and who knows how many others?"

Others?

Carlton glances at me. "I just hope you don't plan on adding my sister to that list of disappeared Bishop girls."

Before Ezekiel can answer the chapel door bursts

opens and Jericho is in the courtyard, face ablaze, eyes darker than I've ever seen them. He stalks toward us, taking a look at me, half-pausing when he does before resuming his progress toward my brother.

"What the hell do you think you're doing?" Jericho asks, taking Carlton by the collar and shoving him backward into the wall. I hope Carlton is smart enough to realize he is no match for this man in size and brute strength, much less in rage.

Carlton holds up his hands in mock surrender. "I came to see my sister wed but I see I'm not welcome."

Councilor Hildebrand approaches, two guards following, and it takes one lift of his finger for those guards to pick up their pace and take Jericho's arms. They can't budge him though.

"Go wait by the chapel door," Ezekiel tells me, never taking his eyes off the scene.

"Call your dogs off!" Jericho tells Hildebrand in a voice that's almost unrecognizable without ever taking his eyes off my brother.

"This is not the time!" Hildebrand hisses.

"You stay the hell away from my family," Jericho tells Carlton, shifting one of his hands to wrap around Carlton's neck.

"She's not your family just yet," Carlton taunts stupidly. "And since she will still have Bishop blood running through her veins, I don't assume she'll become that anytime soon." I swear he's trying to egg Jericho on. Even as he begins to choke trying to catch his breath.

"You god damned piece of shit," Jericho starts.

"Get him off!" Hildebrand orders and two more guards arrive but before they can grab hold of Jericho, Ezekiel moves toward him, shoving one of the men who has hold of his brother away.

"Brother," he says. "He's right. Now is not the time."

Jericho's nostrils flare and I can see the effort it's taking him to not kill Carlton.

"Jericho," Ezekiel says more forcefully. Jericho closes his eyes, loosens his grip.

But Carlton doesn't get it. "Not that being family would keep her safe. I mean, look at Zoë. Or your father." Carlton's grin is a hateful, ugly thing as he shifts his gaze to Ezekiel.

When Jericho closes his fist this time, he squeezes. I watch Carlton's face go red. His eyes bulge. I scream, stumbling backward, my flowers falling to the floor.

"Go," Ezekiel commands urging me in the direction of the chapel.

"You don't know anything about my family," Jericho growls.

I can't move, and the moment seems to play out in slow motion. Jericho choking Carlton, Carlton's face, his eyes looking so wrong.

"Enough!" Hildebrand calls out and it takes four of them to drag Jericho off. Four men the size of Jericho to free Carlton. They keep hold of Jericho as Carlton slumps against the wall, sputtering, choking, hand around his throat where I can see Jericho's fingerprints. It takes him long minutes to stand upright but he does it and stupidly he steps toward Jericho who lunges like some trapped animal.

I scream again but the men have him and Carlton grins. Just grins. "Violence is all your family knows, isn't it? Your father taught you well," he taunts.

Around us a crowd has gathered. I look at all the faces, many masked, staring at us, enjoying the spectacle. Certainly no one is stopping it.

"Gentlemen!" Hildebrand says through clenched teeth as he tries to take control of the situation. "This is not a zoo. We are not animals. You'll both be reprimanded for this spectacle but now is not the time." He turns to Carlton. "Bishop!"

Carlton's gaze snaps to Hildebrand.

"Out!" he spits.

"I just came to—"

"Out!" Hildebrand orders and his men move toward my brother who puts his hands up, making a show of backing away. When my brother is gone, he takes one look at me then turns to Jericho. "Are you ready? I need to bear witness, as you know, and I don't have all night."

Bear witness. Something about the way he says it makes my skin crawl.

Jericho takes a deep breath in, grits his teeth, and pulls free of the men holding him. He locks eyes with Ezekiel. "I need a word with my brother."

Hildebrand studies them, then lets it go. When he's gone, I'm left with the brothers and, beyond them, the collection of onlookers who are pretending not to watch.

"What the hell are you thinking bringing Angelique here?" Jericho demands.

Ezekiel may be the only man on earth who isn't cowed by that tone. By the menace in it. By the energy crackling off Jericho's body. And where I would have backed away, he steps toward his brother, the challenge clear. "It's your wedding day. Don't you think your daughter should be a part of it?"

Jericho didn't want his own daughter here? It makes sense, doesn't it? Considering.

"You don't decide those things. And now you leave me with a mess to clean up."

The brothers study one another for a long, long moment before Jericho finally turns to me, expression strained as he looks me over. Without a word he takes hold of my arm and walks me unceremoniously toward the chapel.

I wonder about my brother's visit. His ability to cause so much disruption, wreak such havoc. That was his intention, wasn't it? He knows how to get under Jericho's skin. Just get near his family. His daughter. She is his weakness. Carlton wouldn't hurt her to punish him, would he? No. I can't believe that. But what about the disappeared Bishop girls? And the comment about not being safe even if you are family? And mostly, what of Jericho's rage? I think he could have murdered my brother today and that terrifies me.

But before I can consider any of that, Ezekiel opens the chapel door and Jericho marches me to the altar. No walk down the aisle for me. No soft music. Nothing but the once comforting smell of incense overwhelming my senses as I'm pushed once again to my knees before the altar, this time a cushion softening the impact as I speak the words that will bind me to Jericho St. James forever.

However long my forever will be.

27

JERICHO

I watch her throughout the brief ceremony. I have Hildebrand to thank for the brief part. Father John wanted a full mass said. Good for the soul, I believe was his argument. He can go fuck himself. And so can Hildebrand and so can every other man out there who witnessed the spectacle Carlton Bishop orchestrated so perfectly. Even recruiting my brother and myself as unlikely actors.

Fucking asshole.

And what the hell did he mean mentioning Zoë and my father. I should have broken his nose just for speaking my sister's name.

As far as my father's *accident*, it wasn't one. I'm sure of it. Bishop had a hand in killing him. I know he did. Even if Santiago De La Rosa finds no evidence, I know it in my gut. My father was murdered. His car skidding off the edge of a mountain road like it did? It's too fucking convenient. All evidence lost. Car and man burnt to a fucking crisp.

No. I don't buy it. He was murdered. And the whole thing stinks of Carlton Bishop.

Isabelle's low voice murmuring the Lord's prayer along with Father John brings me back to the here and now.

I glance at her. My beautiful, innocent bride. She's simply dressed in the gown my mother wore for her wedding to our father. The gown is a white silk that is designed with the marking ceremony in mind with the single button closure on the neck holding the silk in place.

That brings me to thoughts of my mother. Did she know what my father would do? Did she know he meant to open the dress and brand her publicly? Did she then bow her head of her own accord, tears drowning her as she touched her lips to his shoe to say the words required of her? To make her pledge and bestow upon him the power of lord and god.

Isabelle glances at me, her lips ceasing their mutterings. The prayer has ended. In her eyes I read her questions but there is a stillness to her. A quiet. She had it that first night too, when she sought shelter in this very chapel before those men entered. Before I stepped out of the shadows where I'd been sitting watching her. Was it a stroke of fate that carried her in here that night? That let me observe her before she even knew of my existence.

Beauty and her devil. She, innocent in that feather dress. Me, cloaked and masked, horns curling to high heaven. A terror to behold.

She watches me and finally blinks, lowers her gaze. She makes the sign of the cross as Father John brings the crucifix to her lips.

I can't take my eyes off her. Will she be so calm in the moments that will follow this ceremony to the next one?

The priest clears his throat and we both look up at him. Time for the vows to be said. The promise to love, honor and obey. It's a sacrilege, this sham.

Love. Useless.

Honor. I could give a fuck.

It's only her obedience I'm interested in, and I listen to her repeat the words. Do they have any meaning to her? Her eyes give nothing away.

When it's my turn, I say my part, then take her hand and slip a simple gold band onto her finger. She looks down at it as if surprised. Did she expect diamonds? A big, fat ring?

I hold the band she'll slide onto my finger out to her.

She glances at the ring of gold on my palm then at the small gathering of people she doesn't know. None will help her out of this one.

I wait for her to look back at me and gesture for her to go on.

She takes the ring and pushes it onto my finger

and a few moments later, the priest declares us husband and wife and gives me permission to kiss my bride.

I close my hand over the back of her bare neck to pull her to me and, eyes open, I kiss my bride. A symbolic gesture. And then it's over.

I rise to my feet, thank Father John, and help my bride stand. I keep hold of her hand as we turn to the company gathered, the only women my mother and daughter. Even they shouldn't be here according to custom.

Angelique slips her hand free of my mother's and runs toward us. She's the only one in this whole room who is smiling. I scoop her up with one arm to hold her and think about how her life depends on mine. Of how much she needs me.

"Daddy!" she hugs my neck and leans her slight weight toward Isabelle so I have no choice but to let her hug Isabelle into our little circle that has been two for all her life. Now made three.

I consider this as I feel her little arms squeeze us tight. What will she expect now? What does she think this makes Isabelle?

I hadn't wanted to bring Angelique tonight. Hadn't wanted to mention a wedding at all. It has nothing to do with her. This marriage is a means to an end. And when that end comes...

I look at Isabelle once Angelique releases us.

When that end comes, I'll deal with the consequences. I'll rearrange the pieces for Angelique then.

I set Angelique down as my mother steps toward us and, after kissing her on the top of her head, I hand her over to my mother.

"You'll come home. You promised," she says to Isabelle.

Isabelle crouches down to kiss her cheek. "I promised and I always keep my promises."

My mother takes her as Isabelle straightens and the two of them exchange a look. Two generations of women given to Society men. One knows what is coming. The other is still innocent. But not for long.

My mother gives Isabelle an almost imperceptible nod. I'm confused by this and glance at Isabelle whose expression is unreadable.

Courage I think she's saying.

I won't use the irons. My mother suffered more than Isabelle will.

Isabelle gazes softly down once more to my daughter but when her eyes land on me, she adjusts her features as if putting on armor. I've done that, I remind myself. Made her terrified of me within a few days of knowing me.

I tug her toward me. "What did you promise Angelique?"

"Only to kiss her goodnight," she says.

"Take care with your promises to my daughter."

Her eyes search mine as she takes this in.

The procession of guests makes their way toward us, and I turn my attention to them. I paste a neutral look on my face as the men, all upper echelon members who, I'm sure would rather not have been in attendance considering I'm not like them. Not blood. They line up to congratulate me. I shake hands as the thought circles. I am not one of them. I will never be one of them. My father may have bought our entry tickets, but you can't fake blood.

I don't give a fuck, though. My father used to, and I saw what it did to him, that wanting to belong where you don't belong. Wanting to be where you're simply not wanted.

Once that majority of witnesses has gone, the only men left are Zeke, Santiago De La Rosa, Judge and Hildebrand along with his two personal guards.

Isabelle moves closer to me as Santiago approaches, and I realize it's her first time seeing the man with the half-skull face tattoo. Judge, no less menacing with his height and build, stands at his side. Judge acknowledges Isabelle with a nod while Santiago studies her a moment longer.

"Congratulations," he says to her.

"Thank you," she mutters. I think it's automatic. And I am not sure she's blinked as she tries hard not to stare at death staring back at her. He enjoys this, I think. Relishes the discomfort people must feel at the sight of him. I respect him more for it.

"Shall we move downstairs, gentlemen? I believe this is our entourage," Hildebrand mutters.

"What's downstairs?" Isabelle asks once everyone files out toward a door at the opposite end of the one that leads to the courtyard.

It's not really downstairs. More a space between the chapel and the Tribunal building carved from stone that leads to a tunnel connecting chapel, Tribunal and the main compound buildings. It also leads to the cells housed beneath the Councilors chambers. It is said this was done because due to the design, sound carries up to their quarters. And the Councilors of The Tribunal have a bloody history.

"It's where the marking ceremony will take place."

"Marking?" she asks, not moving when I mean to follow the others as Hildebrand's guards hold the door open.

I turn to face her. "I told you last night. You'll wear my mark."

"What does that mean exactly?" she asks, pulling back.

"You'll see in a minute."

"I don't want to see," she says when I take a step. I look back at her and see her tremble. See her wrap her free arm around her stomach.

"We could do it in the courtyard with all the gawkers. Would you prefer that?"

"I just want to know what you're going to do to me."

"Your brother really hasn't educated you in the ways of The Society, has he? I'm going to tattoo my mark onto your neck and back."

"You... What?"

"Or alternatively I could brand you with it."

Her face loses all color.

"Your preference?" I'm running out of patience. Bishop showing up saying those things, Zeke bringing my daughter, it's all fucked with me. "My preference is ink. Less...screaming."

A choked sound comes from her throat, and I tug her forward, moving her toward the heavy door and through the windowless passages lit only by torches of fire.

"Jericho?" she starts, stumbling, arms wrapping around me in an effort to stop our progress as I half-carry her through. We just need to get through this next part. And as much as I wish it were just she and I, there are rules that we all have to abide by and this is one. Witnesses are necessary. At least it's just the handful I've chosen.

The cavern where the ceremony will take place is large, the ceilings low, this circular room also lit by fire, with a single barred window letting in fresh air, the night a cooler one than we've had.

The room itself is as medieval as it comes. Chairs have been arranged for my guests to relax as they bear witness. Refreshments are served by two waiters who stand in the shadows. At the farthest corner beneath the window stands the iron pit inside which burns a fire. I recognize the handle of the poker sticking out of it. Ceremony, I remind myself. I don't let myself dwell on what my father did with that poker.

Judge and Zeke speak quietly in one corner, although their eyes follow us. Hildebrand sits in his throne-like chair, his soldiers standing behind him. Santiago stands alone.

"What is this?" Isabelle asks in a full panic, stopping dead when her eyes land on the makeshift dais where she'll be the guest of honor.

"Your marking ceremony," I tell her. "Take off your shoes."

"What?"

"Your shoes. Take them off."

She's confused but she does it, and, leaving them at the door, I walk her toward the dais upon which lays a silk cushion for her knees. My chair and the equipment I'll need to mark her stand just behind that cushion. Before it stands an intricately carved wooden pillory that must be hundreds of years old. Made especially for the marking ceremony, it's low to the ground, designed with the purpose of having the woman it hosts on her knees. Another form of supplication. The thought of it, of Isabelle bound by it, is more erotic than anything else and a part of me wishes I could make these witnesses disappear.

"Jericho?" she asks, her voice a choked whisper as she resists.

I walk her to the center. Hildebrand dispatches his soldiers and when Isabelle sees them, she turns to run, except that I have her arm and she just runs herself into my chest.

I wrap one arm around her and hold the other up to halt the soldiers.

Isabelle's breaths are pants against me, her face hidden in my shirt. She's not making a move to get around me or out of my grasp. I don't know if that's because she knows there's no getting out of here or if she's simply seeking protection against the soldiers.

I dip my head down to her ear.

"Ink. Just ink. Not fire," I tell her.

She shakes her head, buries her face deeper against my chest.

"You just relax, and it won't hurt." Well, I'm not quite sure that's true. To me, a tattoo is not painful. It's almost meditative, in fact. But to her, I don't know how she'll take it.

"I don't want to do this," she says, dragging her gaze up to mine. Her face is wet, eyeliner smeared. "Please don't make me do this."

"That's not a choice you can make. Your choice is how we proceed. Do I ask these men to put you in the pillory or do you kneel and submit to it? To me?"

She just stares up at me with her watery eyes.

I take her wrists because there is something so sexually charged about this ritual. Something darkly arousing. "Kneel, Isabelle. Face your witnesses and kneel."

She glances over her shoulder at them, at the wooden device and I turn her, walking her toward that silk cushion. She resists all along as Santiago approaches and lifts the heavy top of the pillory.

"On your knees," I tell her as she looks at him.

She's shaking, pulling into me as she drags her gaze to mine. "You'll do it?"

Is she taking comfort in the thought that it will be my hand doing the marking?

"You?" she asks again. "Not him? Not them?"

"Yes," I tell her, confused.

Two tears slide down her face, one on each cheek. She nods. She's steeling herself.

"Then you're finished? It's over?"

I don't reply.

She studies me, a wrinkle between her eyebrows. "It's not, is it?"

I wait.

"You'll bleed me," she says, forcing herself to stand tall in this show of resistance. She and I both know she will submit. It's the only choice she can make. "My blood will stain your sheets."

I don't reply, just keep my gaze locked on hers. She's right.

"I won't forgive you any of it, Jericho St. James. Ever."

We remain like that for a long moment, silence between us, but so much to say. I only speak one word though. The only one that matters for now.

"Kneel."

She lowers her lashes, then turns from me and kneels on the cushion.

She leans forward, she sets her wrists into their holes then extends her neck and bows her head, settling into place like a condemned prisoner offering her head to the executioner's block.

Santiago lowers the heavy wooden bar, the sound of him locking it reverberates off the stone walls. He steps behind her to my side.

I look down at her, my supplicant bride. I glance around the room at the men watching the display, no whispers now, everyone is riveted. And I want to clear the room, but I can't. This has to happen, and it has to happen this way. The fact that she won't forgive me can't matter. And she has accepted her fate with more grace than I expected.

But it's not over yet. It's barely begun.

Santiago extends his hand, and someone places a leather folder in it. His wedding gift to me.

I draw my chair closer and take my seat behind her, noting how her bare feet show from beneath the dress, how strangely complete the sight makes this. With two fingers I slip the pearl button from its loop and spread the dress open, baring the entirety of her back. The dress is especially made for a Society wedding by a Society dressmaker. They know what is expected. But it's not quite enough and I take the two sides in each hand and rip the dress a little farther.

Isabelle gasps and I see her hands clench and un-clench.

"Lift up," I tell her and remarkably she does so I can tuck the top of her panties underneath her to expose the cleft of her ass.

Santiago crouches down, runs two fingers over the scar along her spine.

Isabelle stiffens. Can she tell the hand is not mine? And can he feel my aggression as he touches her?

He then lays the flat of his hand on her back. I know what he's doing. He's measuring. And a moment later, once he's satisfied, he nods and steps away.

I clean her back, feeling her shudder at the cold press of alcohol.

"Relax," I whisper.

"Go to hell," she whispers back.

I'll forgive her that. It's where I belong for this act alone.

Santiago opens the folder and holds it out to me. Inside is the stencil sketch. The twin dragons that are the emblem of the St. James house. Created by

Draca St. James, they represent power, might and in some cases, chaos. Wickedness.

I think about the mangled mess that is my mother's neck but only momentarily because as I press the stencil onto Isabelle's back, I know what I'll make is something beautiful. Twin dragons to overwrite the scar her brother put on her back. Maybe not with his own hands but it may as well have been. Twin dragons to match my own tattoo albeit smaller.

Twin dragons to make her mine.

I take off my jacket and roll up my sleeves. A moment later, the tattoo machine buzzes and I begin.

28

ISABELLE

Humiliation comes first. Then pain.

Crap.

The tattoo gun buzzes as needles press into my neck, down along my spine. It hurts.

I grit my teeth so as not to cry out, but I can't help it, not at first, and I'm glad I can't see their faces. Can't see them watching me, watching this. My submission. My very public humiliation.

I don't know for how long this goes on. I'm cold and hot at once and watch as a droplet of sweat falls from my forehead onto the stone until finally, an eternity later, I'm lulled into a sort of dream like state, a quiet at the needle's point. I feel Jericho at my back. He whispers to me telling me I'm doing well. I want to tell him to go fuck himself but as soon as I open my mouth, he starts again, the needles drilling art on my back.

Art? No. Not art. Ownership. His mark on me. His fucking *mark*.

And it's not just my neck. I remember vague talk of this when Julia would tell me the dark secrets of The Society. I'm not sure I believed her then. It was all too archaic. Too impossible.

They're supposed to mark the back of the neck. Fire or ink. Julia always got a glint in her eye at the fire. I wonder how she'd feel at the receiving end of that brand, bound like this in a pillory. I don't think she'd be grinning then.

But what he's doing, it spans to my lower back and farther. And it's when I think it will never end that finally, what feels like hours later, he stops. The sound of buzzing is gone. And I think he must be exhausted. I am.

The men gather around me, Hildebrand standing, his brother and the others coming to see the mark. To congratulate my husband.

"Let's finish this," Hildebrand says. "I'm sure we're all tired."

Finish it? There's more?

But I can't lift my head to see their faces, to know what more is coming. I see them part though, the shoes of the others moving away as Jericho comes to stand before me. He crouches down but I still don't look up. He pets my head, running his hand gently over my skull with the very hand that wielded the terrible machine. How is it a comfort to me?

"The words, Isabelle," he says as he cups my cheek and tilts my face up a little, just enough so I can look at him.

I wonder what I look like, makeup smeared. Eye liner now black streaks down my cheeks. I probably need my nose wiped too. But I don't care.

"Let me out of this," I manage.

He studies me, smears his thumb across my cheekbone, then brings his ring to my mouth and I remember. The insignia is on his ring. The dual dragons. His mark. His fucking mark.

"The words."

Dominus et Deus. My lord and my god. Just like Leontine instructed me.

"The words?" I ask, rage giving me strength. "You want the words?"

His eyes narrow.

I look beyond him at the others, not their faces. I can't see that high. But I bring my focus back to my husband.

He wants me to say the words. To tell him he is my lord and my god.

He can go fuck himself.

So instead of saying any words, I smile up to him, all hate in that curving of the lips, and I spit on his shoe.

Well, at the ground beside his shoe because I miss.

We both look at it. It's not the quantity I hoped for, but the message is clear.

A moment goes by. Another. My heart thuds against my chest. Then he straightens all false calm.

"Gentlemen, if you'll clear the room. I need a few moments with my bride."

I shift from knee to knee, try to free myself even though I know I can't. And as grateful as I am that they're leaving, when that door closes and Jericho moves behind me, my heart thuds and I stare straight down at the ground, at the little bit of white silk I can see beneath me.

"That's no way to start a marriage," he says from behind me.

He takes hold of my hips and draws them up so my ass is in the air putting pressure on my wrists and neck locked in this damned, medieval pillory. With one flip of his hand, he tugs the dress up to my lower back, exposing my thighs and ass.

"What are you doing?" I ask, waiting. Waiting. It's all I can do.

"I could have you taken out to the courtyard for your disrespect. Have you bound to the post. Stripped naked. Whipped."

"Wh... What?"

His fingers slide into the waistband of my white silk panties, and he pushes them roughly down to pool at my knees.

"It would be within my rights."

I try to turn my head to look at him but can't move. "Jericho?"

He doesn't speak but I hear another sound. The clank of the unbuckling of a belt. The whoosh of it being pulled through the hoops.

"No!" I try to wriggle free, to sit on my heels but he grips one hip, fingers digging in hard.

"Stay," he commands.

"I..."

"You prefer a public whipping? Because it will be public. And I won't be the one wielding the whip."

"No. No, please."

"Then stay up. Knees spread."

I stay as he instructs and a moment later, I hear the sound of it, the belt against flesh, the unforgiving, burning sound. I squeeze my eyes shut and scream in anticipation.

Except there's no pain.

I turn my head a little when he moves, and he does it again. The belt doubled over slapping against his own thigh.

I scream anyway. I can't help it.

It's silent for a moment after that and I wait. I wait for him to whip me with that belt. Tears and sweat drop from me onto the ground.

"I'm sorry," I mutter in those moments of silence.

"Are you?" He adjusts my dress higher, exposing more of me, but I think he's taking care with the tattoo.

"You're very pretty to look at like this. I think I'll have a pillory made for you. So you always remember."

He moves behind me and I hear it again, the whoosh, the thud of leather against skin and I sob as if he had struck me.

"Stop, please! I'll say it! I'll say the words!"

"Go on then."

"Do..." I start but have to stop when his fingernails dig into my butt, scratch their way up along my cheek.

He leans over me, face close to mine. "I don't hear you," he says and straightens, bringing the leather of the belt to my hip, testing it softly.

"Dominus et Deus. Dominus et Deus." I blurt out.

"Again. I'll hear it again."

"Dominus et Deus."

"Good girl. Again."

"Dominus et Deus."

"And what does it mean?"

"My lord and my god."

"Had you forgotten the words earlier?" he asks, coming around to stand in front of me so I'm looking down at his shoes again.

I shake my head as best I can and a moment later, he bends and unlocks the contraption and I feel an instant relief. He lifts the heavy wooden top and I draw out slowly, my body stiff and tense. I sit on my heels, the dress falling to cover me, and I look up at him.

He watches me as he loops his belt through his pants.

"Guard," he calls, never taking his eyes from me.

The man who must be standing on the other side of the door must hear him because the door opens and in comes Councilor Hildebrand. But none of the others. He looks at me like he'd like me on that post in the courtyard, stripped and humiliated.

I look back up to my husband who still has not moved his gaze from mine.

"You know what comes next," he says with all the authority in the world, without any doubt that I'll do what I am supposed to do.

My borrowed dress slides off one shoulder as I bring my gaze to his shoes, and I set my hands to the ground on either side, and I try to remember that he whipped himself rather than whipping me. That Hildebrand was standing outside listening all that time. I wonder if he's hard beneath his robe at the thought of me having my ass whipped. I feel disgust at the man.

I lift my gaze once more to Jericho before lowering my head, bringing my lips to his shoe.

"Words," he mutters.

"Dominus et Deus. My lord and my god," I say so

quietly I'm not sure either of them hear it and I remain as I am, head bowed, tears falling, and wait.

Hildebrand and his men leave. When they're gone, Jericho's hand wraps around my upper arm and he pulls me to my feet. My breast is exposed where the dress had already slid from my shoulder and my panties which were at my knees slide to my feet.

He looks down at my breast, tugs the dress up but is careful to leave it open at the back. He then walks me to the door.

"Wait," I say, glancing back my panties on the floor.

"You won't be needing those," he says and pulls me to the door. He bends to pick up my shoes but proceeds to walk me barefoot through the chapel then out into the courtyard where all sound seems to stop at the sight of us.

I wonder what I look like. Not a bride happily emerging from her own wedding. No. I feel how my hair has come out of its tight style only realizing now why Leontine was so specific about how it needed to be off my neck and back. I wonder what they make of the makeup streaking my face. As Jericho moves me through the crowd that parts for us, I can hear the gasps as we pass when they see the ink on my back that leaves no doubt as to what I am.

His.

29

JERICHO

I need to fuck this woman. I need to do it now.

Dex drives us home. I step out of the car, lifting her and carrying her into the house. Once inside I set her down and drop her shoes to the floor. I turn her to me as she adjusts the dress to keep it up. With the button undone it wants to slide to her waist, as it is designed.

I wrap one arm around her lower back and tug her to me while with the other I free the confines of her hair, weaving my fingers into it and tugging her head back to kiss her mouth.

She presses her hands to my chest, making a sound before I swallow it, her mouth open to me, her tongue warm. I grind my cock against her belly, hard against soft, and lift her. I'm aware of the tattoo that runs the length of her spine, so I haul her over my shoulder to carry her to my bed. Once in my room, I lock the door and set her on her feet.

Isabelle stumbles backward two steps.

I watch her as I unbutton my shirt and drag it off. Her gaze shifts to my chest, my shoulders. I stalk toward her, and she looks around for her escape.

There is none.

Pushing my hand into the neck of the dress I tug, tearing it enough that the silk slips to the floor. She's naked beneath. I look her over, take in the small, rounded breasts, nipples puckered, see the slit of her shaved sex.

I walk to the bed, pull the covers off to expose the pristine white sheets all the better to collect her virgin blood. Tucked beneath the mattress are the restraints I draw out, ready to use.

"Come here," I tell her.

Her eyes are on those leather restraints on the four corners of the bed and with a wary glance, she walks toward me.

"Kneel in the middle of the bed facing the headboard."

"Jericho—"

"Do as I say."

She hesitates, then climbs up. I don't help her. I just watch. And once she's there, I take the wrist closest to me, stretch it to the first restraint and bind her, leaving her to rest on her elbow as she waits for me to bind the other wrist.

I move behind her to look at her on her knees, arms spread wide, and I draw the first ankle restraint toward the middle of the bed and bind one ankle, then the other, stretching her legs wide but keeping her on her knees.

"Head down and keep your ass up."

She cranes her neck to look back at me.

"Do it, Isabelle."

Her face burns red, and she turns away before raising her ass high, back deeply arched, knees spread wide by the restraints so all of her is on display.

It's lewd. Filthy. And before my eyes her pussy begins to glisten and leak down the inside of one thigh.

I'm tempted to take a seat and watch, just watch but I'm so fucking hard I can barely control myself.

"Stay just like that," I tell her. Standing behind her to strip off the rest of my clothes before closing my hands around her thighs and bringing my nose to her.

She gasps as I draw in a deep inhale, taking in her scent, then lick her pussy to ass and back.

Isabelle whimpers and I settle on my knees behind her, looking at my mark on her arched back, the single tail of the twin serpents disappearing inside the crease of her ass. And fuck it's the hottest thing I've ever seen. I should extend it to her asshole, I think. Maybe I will yet.

"You want this," I tell her, dipping two fingers of one hand inside her before sliding them to her clit.

"No, I…"

I lean over her, touch my cheek to hers and listen to her intake of breath as I twirl my fingers around the hard, swollen nub.

"No?" I ask.

She closes her eyes. She doesn't want to want this. Doesn't want to want me.

"Do you want to come?" I run my fingers over her clit.

She moans, and a moment later, nods.

"Say it. Tell me."

"Please."

"Please what?" I straighten, slide my cock through her folds. "Please what, Isabelle?"

"Please…. I want…"

I keep two fingers on her clit and slip my cock to her entrance. It's tight and I watch her tense as I begin to stretch her to accommodate me.

"Too much," she starts, drawing away, but my fingers are on her clit again and she stills, arching her back deeper.

"Say it," I demand, my voice hoarse with the need to thrust into virgin territory. To bleed her.

"Make me come!" she cries out and I reward her, turning my fingers over her clit and sliding my cock deeper. When I hear her choked intake of breath and feel her walls pulse around me, I dig the fingers of one hand into her hip and splay her wide. I drive into her, tearing through her barrier, relishing her cry when I do it, feeling the warm gush of blood as I bury myself to the hilt. I savor the tight feel of her as I close my thumb over her asshole and draw back, looking down at her as I do, as I see red staining my cock, her thighs, dropping to my sheets.

I drive in again and again, hearing her pants as I take her, as she buries her face in the sheets and comes around me again, walls pulsing.

My release is thunderous, racking my body, calling an animal sound from my chest and throat as I spill my seed inside her. The knowledge that she's mine now, all mine, only mine more heady than I anticipate. So much more than I imagined.

When I draw out and she collapses beneath me, blood and come spill from her. The white sheets no longer pristine but stained with her virgin blood, the evidence of our raw, primal lust. And all I can think is one word. One word over and over again. The only one that makes any sense.

Mine.

Mine.

Mine.

30

ISABELLE

He cleans me when it's over. When I've collapsed on the bed after multiple orgasms, our bodies and the sheets, stained red.

I lie in his bed spent half-expecting him to send me to my room, half-wanting him to. The shower switches off and a moment later, he returns to the bedroom with a towel tied low around his hips, droplets of water clinging to his chest, torso and arms, his hair wet. He stops as if surprised to see me in his bed and I have to shift my gaze from his eyes.

I'm lying on my side facing him. I'm too exhausted to move when he comes toward me. He drops the towel and before he switches out the lamp, I glimpse the slashes of red on the outside of his thigh. The marks of the belt.

I turn my back to him when he climbs in and

only relax when he draws a silky blanket up over my hips.

It's silent for a long moment. "All right?" he asks.

I feel strangely sad by the question as a tear slides down one cheek. I don't understand this. I should feel hate. Only hate.

But then I think about those red slashes on his thigh. "Why did you do it?" I ask.

"Which part?"

"Why didn't you whip me?"

"Ah."

Moonlight slivers through the part in the curtains. It comes over my shoulder onto the bed and the floor just beyond. When I feel his fingers trace the outside edges of the tattoo, I know he can see it in that silvery light.

"Why?" I ask again.

"I don't know," he says after a long moment passes. "Go to sleep, Isabelle."

"I didn't know it was real," I say, wiping another tear. "I didn't know about the tattoo. The marking. All those men watching."

"Shh. It's over. Go to sleep."

"It's not normal." I sniffle and if he didn't know I was crying before, he does now.

"It is life within The Society and although you and I may be half-breeds to them, we are a part of it, and we must obey certain rules."

I look at him over my shoulder. "I thought you made your own rules."

"I do in many ways but when they serve me, in this case taking you from your brother, I will do as I am expected to."

"You almost killed him."

He doesn't respond but his jaw tightens.

"I don't understand what taking me will achieve. It's not that Carlton will miss me or be upset that I'm sleeping in your bed. He doesn't care about me. We both know that. So what are you planning? What will I be made to endure next?"

A grin curves one corner of his lip but instead of answering he pushes the blanket off my hips and insanely, I find my body reacting. My center warming. Preparing. He rises onto his knees and takes one of my thighs to reposition me, angling me so I'm face down, my stomach on his knees, my legs spread on either side of him.

I set my forearms down and brace myself. I'm sore but there's a part of me that wants this.

He grips my hips and raises them, and, to my surprise, bites my right cheek.

"Ow!"

But when he next spreads me open and licks the length of me, I'm gasping again, waiting, anticipating. When he pushes my legs wider to bury his face between my legs, I fist the sheets in my hands and close my eyes. Clenching my teeth when I feel his on my clit, on my lower lips, his tongue dipping inside me then drawing out, circling the hard nub, licking my length from hole to hole.

"I think I can eat you all night," he says and continues to lick and suck and explore with his tongue. The scruff on his jaw rough and abrasive, so opposite the softness of his tongue and lips. "But I really need to be inside you again," he says, lifting me to a seat on his lap so I'm facing him. Our eyes locked, he slides me onto his length. He's slow, taking care. He's thick and hard and I clutch his shoulders as he moves my hips. My over-sensitive nipples scrape along his chest, sending sensation straight to my core and soon I'm gasping, clinging to him, my head bowed. My body wants more even though my passage is raw, abused from earlier and now this, more of him. I call out his name when I come and he grips a handful of hair to force my head back to watch me.

"Look at me," he says, voice hoarse when I close my eyes, the moment too vulnerable. "I want to see you."

I open my eyes and I watch him too, see how one eye darkens, the other brightens, midnight and silver. I hear his short intakes of breath and feel the thickening inside me just before he drives me down hard and grinds against me, throbbing. His eyes are too beautiful to turn away from as I watch him come undone. As I take more of his seed inside me.

This time when it's over, he doesn't get up to shower. And he doesn't clean me. Instead, he lays me down.

As I feel his seed slide out of me, I rest my head on his pillow and close my eyes, too exhausted to move, too raw and empty. Somehow, my eyes flutter closed even as I watch his on me, even as I know it's dangerous to ever let myself drift to sleep with this man. My husband, it happens. And this, the way he makes me come, the way he makes me want him, drives that point home more than anything else has.

Because even if Leontine was right and I do need protecting from some outside force, I am also right to wonder who will protect me from my own husband.

31

JERICHO

It's not long after we've fallen asleep that I'm awakened by Isabelle's murmurings. Her tossing and turning. I open my eyes and watch. Listen. Her eyes are closed but her lips are moving, some words unclear, others leaving me with a hint of what the nightmare is.

"Christian," she says, forehead wrinkling, the skin around her eyes growing wet. Her arm reaches out and she tries to grasp something then it drops to her side.

For a moment, she seems to settle back into sleep but then it starts again. This time, it's a full panic. A low moan comes from inside her throat. It's the sound of someone trying to scream but that scream is trapped. I know those nightmares. The terror of them.

"Isabelle," I say softly. I don't touch her yet.

"No. No." Her arms flail at air. "Don't touch me!"

Don't touch me.

A flash of the image of her lying on the shards of glass, bleeding, plays before my eyes. I see how the jeans are open. See the shred of panties beneath.

She hadn't been sexually assaulted according to the police report.

Isabelle whimpers like a frightened child.

"Isabelle. Wake up." I place a hand on her stomach. It's gentle but I hope reassuring. But it's the wrong thing to do because it triggers her. She grabs my forearm with both hands nails digging into flesh.

"No! No! No!"

I sit up and she starts slapping at my chest, my face.

"Wake up, Isabelle. It's a dream. Wake up!"

When she draws her nails down my chest drawing blood, I grip her wrists, holding them in one hand and hugging her to me tight.

"Wake up, Isabelle. It's a dream. Just a dream."

"Christian?" she blurts, drawing back, eyelids flying open, blue eyes wide and frantic and searching. "Christian!"

I hold onto her, watching her. She's calling for her brother.

"You're having a dream, Isabelle. A bad dream. You're safe."

She watches me as I speak, eyes coming into focus on my face, then around me, taking in the surroundings. Her body goes limp as she remembers.

"Let me go."

I nod. Slowly release her. "Are you all right?"

"Fine." She looks away, wipes her eyes. She pushes the blanket off her legs.

"Where are you going?"

"My room."

When she moves to stand, I set a hand on her arm to stop her. "You need a glass of water."

"I'm fine. Let me go." She won't look at me.

I get up. "Stay," I tell her and go into the bathroom to get her a glass of water.

Remarkably when I return, she's still sitting there. Her eyes are red and she's trying to hide the fact she was crying.

"Here," I say, holding out the water.

She takes it, drinks one sip and hands it back. I set it aside.

"Can I go now?" she asks not quite looking at me.

"You'll sleep in my bed tonight."

She glares up at me. "I thought you weren't interested in sleep."

Ah. She has a good memory. I smile. "Lie down."

She does, careful to lie on her side. She lays her cheek on her hands and closes her eyes.

I tuck the blanket around her and climb in on my side, setting one arm over her waist hoping to anchor her.

"Is it the night of the break in?" I ask a few moments later.

"I don't remember."

Lie.

"Do you have it often?" I ask after a minute. "The nightmare?"

"Please don't pretend to care." She tries to tug free, but I draw her closer.

"Do you?"

"Why? Are you worried it'll disrupt your sleep cycle?"

"I know how terrifying it can be to feel helpless in sleep."

"Do you?"

"I do."

"I'm sure proximity to you brought it on so if you're really concerned—"

"Right." I shake my head. "Goodnight, Isabelle. If you need me—"

"I won't."

"Right."

———

ISABELLE IS STILL SLEEPING WHEN I WAKE THE NEXT morning. Her back is to me, the silhouette of her soft and curving, her hands still tucked beneath her cheek, hair a long, black river spilling over the pillow, the blanket covering her hip, long legs exposed and beautiful.

I don't move just yet. I take her in. Then I study the tattoo. My work. My mark on her. Santiago's design. He's very good. The twin dragons face one another, mouths open, locked in battle and embracing at once. It's in their eyes, that connection. Their powerful bodies split and spiral her spine erasing the scar, the devil's tail dipping into the curve of her lower back and disappearing into the cleft of her ass.

Fuck.

I'm hard at the sight of it. At the thought of her last night. Of how she looked on her knees, ass offered to me. How she felt, how warm and wet and tight she was.

Fuck.

But then later, that nightmare, her thrashing about. I make a mental note to find out more details of that night. Learn if the police report left anything out.

But now is not the time. I have things to do, and they don't involve fucking my wife. Not until after.

She doesn't stir as I slip out of the bed but even after my shower, she hasn't moved. Her body must be exhausted after what it was made to endure, not to mention her mind. Her emotions.

I watch her as I dress, study her face in sleep. Soft and relaxed, eyelashes thick and heavy, lips parted just a little, her breathing deep. I scribble a note for her on a piece of paper and leave it on the nightstand. I go downstairs and find Angelique eating breakfast with my mother.

"Daddy," she says with a big smile on her face when she sees me.

"Good morning, sweetheart," I tell her realizing last night I never kissed her goodnight. Neither did Isabelle. Broke her promise. Broke my own. Not a night has gone by that I haven't kissed my daughter goodnight when I've been home.

I walk toward her, kiss her forehead when she turns her face up to mine.

"Where is Belle?" she asks sweetly.

I'm irritated at her nickname of Isabelle but remind myself she's a little girl infatuated by the idea of the princesses in her storybooks. That's all. "She's still sleeping. She's tired after yesterday."

"Can I wake her up after breakfast?"

I glance to my mother. "After your lessons, all right? We should give Isabelle time to sleep but you can spend time with her this afternoon."

Angelique's shoulders slump. "I don't need lessons. Not with mean Mrs. Strand," she says under her breath.

"Now, that's not nice," my mother says.

"I want Belle to teach me music," Angelique says.

"What?" I ask.

"It looks so pretty in her notebooks, daddy. And she's going to play her violin for me."

"Is she?"

Angelique nods. "Can she teach me?"

"We'll see."

She sighs. She already knows what those words mean but now I'm curious what Isabelle has told my daughter.

"Are you going to work?" she asks me. I often wonder what she thinks it is I do. And if other five-year-olds are so attentive. But she's not like other five-year-olds I remind myself. Her life is so very different from theirs.

"I have a few meetings."

"Will you teach me how to swim later? You said you would."

I did that afternoon I'd found Isabelle and her in the water and lost my shit. "Yes," I say. "When I'm home."

"Really?"

"Really. I promise."

She smiles wide and picks up her stuffed bear to pretend feed him a spoonful of cereal.

I pick up a mug and fill it with coffee.

"Zeke up?" I ask my mom.

"He's in his office."

"You two have a good morning," I tell them before kissing the top of Angelique's head and walking out of the dining room toward Zeke's office. I knock on the door, and he calls out for me to enter.

"Morning, brother," he says, looking me over.

"Good morning," I say, closing the door.

He leans back in his seat and studies me. "How is she?"

Am I irritated he asks about her? Maybe. "Asleep."

Tension is high as I sip my coffee and we study each other.

"You know I don't want Angelique anywhere near IVI," I tell him.

"But you are a part of IVI. She is a part of it whether you like it or not. Did you really think to keep the wedding a secret from her?"

I take a deep breath in and move to sit down in one of the chairs across his desk. I set my coffee down.

"I don't know what the fuck I thought," I admit. I shake my head. "Maybe it was too soon to bring her home."

"No, not too soon. If anything, you're five years too late. She should have been here from the start. But she's here now. And she's safe, brother. You need to start loosening your grip. You can't control everything."

"Fuck if I can't."

"She asked about school. She's been having her

afternoon snack with Nina, Catherine's granddaughter. Nina's her age and she was telling Angelique all about her kindergarten class. Has she asked you about it yet?"

I look at my brother because no, she has not.

"She asked me," he says. "Asked when she would start school."

I pick up my coffee mug and drink. "Why is Catherine's granddaughter coming here in the afternoons? Is it a regular thing?"

"Really?" Zeke looks at me. "You may be the older brother, but I've been running things here while you've been gone. Catherine has her routine and if her granddaughter comes over every day after school until her mother can pick her up after work, that's fine by me. You know Angelique will meet people. You can't keep her locked away in a tower forever."

"I'm not planning on forever. Just until Bishop is no longer a threat." I drink another sip of coffee and study my brother who clearly does not agree with my plan. I set my mug down. "Bishop looked at you last night. When he made that comment about Zoë and dad."

"Did he?" Zeke asks but I see the momentarily flicker of tension before he schools his features. "Your point?"

"Why did he look at you? Because Santiago gave you the same knowing look when he told me he had no evidence that Bishop was involved in our father's accident."

"I didn't realize."

We sit in silence for a long, long minute. "Is there anything I don't know, brother?"

"Like what?"

I shrug a shoulder and wait.

"I have to get to the office," he says, standing.

I remain seated, watch him. When our father was killed Zeke took over the management of the investment firm our great-grandfather founded. It's one of the family businesses.

"Brother?" he says it like a question but it's my invitation to leave.

I get to my feet. "I'll see you later," I say, taking my coffee mug and walking out into the corridor where Dex is casually waiting. "Find out for me if Carlton Bishop is having his breakfast in the usual spot, will you?"

"Sure thing."

"And bring my car."

He nods and when I go into the dining room to set my mug down, I find it empty. Angelique and my mother have finished breakfast and their plates are being cleared. I walk into the kitchen to find Catherine pouring pink batter into a cake form.

"Well, good morning, Jericho," she says, stopping. She wipes her hands on her apron.

"Is that color natural?" I ask of the pink.

She smiles proudly. "Not completely. Did you get breakfast?"

"I'm not hungry. Zeke tells me your grand-daughter comes by after school."

She is taken aback. I'm not one to get involved in the personal lives of the staff. "She does. Her mother has a new job and only finishes work at five, so she spends two hours with me in the kitchen. She's no trouble and I still do my work."

I shake my head. "No, that's not why I'm asking. It's fine. She and Angelique get along?"

The older woman smiles. "They do." Her fore-head wrinkles and I get the feeling there's more she wants to say but won't.

"I'm glad," I say. "It's good for Angelique to have a friend her own age. But if they play outside, you send someone with them?"

"They don't go where they're not supposed to. Angelique knows the rules."

"Send a man with them anyway. Just to be on the safe side."

She hesitates, then nods. "Yes, sir."

I nod and walk out of the kitchen, the exchange feeling awkward. I've known Catherine since I was a kid but now, so much has changed. I've been gone so long, and it all feels different. Like it's not my house. Like they're not my staff.

But I remind myself why I'm here and why things are the way they are. When I get to the front door and see Dex standing beside the Lamborghini, I focus on what I must do today. Because there was something in the look Carlton gave my brother yesterday. It's no coincidence that Santiago De La Rosa exchanged a similar look with him during the same topic of discussion. And I mean to understand what it's about.

32

ISABELLE

I'm not surprised when I wake up sore all over the following morning. I am careful not to roll onto my back, afraid it will be tender but when I sit up, I wince, tender in other, more intimate places.

Jericho is gone. His pillow is cold. And on the nightstand is a note, brief and to the point telling me he hopes I'm feeling better, that we'll discuss the dream later and not to shower so as not to get the tattoo wet just yet.

I roll my eyes. I won't be discussing that nightmare with him. I won't discuss Christian with him. Or that night. Ever.

But then I remember how he held me. How gentle he was when I scratched bloody lines down his chest. Then again, maybe he deserved that considering what he's done to my skin.

I get up and walk into the bathroom to look at the mark. Turning my back to the mirror, I crane my neck to see the reflection and gasp. The colorful tattoo spans the length of my spine. It's narrow and more slender than the one on his back. Somehow more feminine. And although I can't study the details just yet, it is beautiful. I can see that much. It's still covered in plastic, so I leave it alone, wrapping a towel around myself and walk back into the bedroom to go to my own room. I use the adjoining door since I'm only wearing this towel. I don't need Angelique to catch me taking my walk of shame.

But my gaze finds the once-white sheets and blanket covering the bed. I gasp. It's stained with my blood, not to mention the other things. At the sight I feel sticky between my legs and hurry to take the bedding off the bed. Just as I'm rolling it into a ball a knock comes on the door before it opens. The housekeeper I'd met the other morning smiles after her surprise at finding me here.

"Good morning, Miss," she says and shifts her gaze to what I'm doing.

"Good morning, Catherine, right?" I say, leaving the sheets and trying to stand there like I haven't just been caught in the act of trying to hide my shame of last night.

"That's right. And you don't need to worry about that. I'll take care of the washing. You just leave your things to me, too, all right?"

I hadn't even thought of laundry. The day-to-day tasks of living. "Um, okay. Thanks. Is... Jericho home?"

"No, miss. He left a few hours ago."

"Okay. Thanks. And please call me Isabelle."

She smiles sweetly. "All right, Isabelle."

"I'm going to go get dressed," I say awkwardly and quickly head to my own room, feeling my face burn at the thought of what she'll find when she unrolls those sheets.

Back in my room I wash myself carefully without getting the tattoo wet. Then dress in a pair of shorts and a loose-fitting top that will hide the tattoo but not irritate it. As I come out of the bathroom, I hear the buzzing of my phone. I hurry to where I have it hidden beneath my pillow. It's silenced but the buzzing is enough to alert me and when I see who it is, I answer quickly.

"Hello? Julia?"

"Sleeping beauty. I've been calling you for hours."

I check the time. It's almost noon. I never sleep in but last night took its toll on me in so many ways.

"It was a long night," I say, sitting on the edge of the bed.

"I bet."

"Not like that. I mean the whole thing." The marriage, the marking. Jericho almost killing Carlton.

"Carlton told me he came to congratulate you, but your husband wouldn't let him near you."

"It wasn't about me. He just gets very protective when it comes to his daughter," I find myself saying. Am I defending Jericho St. James?

"You should see the bruises on Carlton's neck! You can't think what Jericho did was okay."

"I don't," I tell her, picking a piece of lint off the bed.

"Are you okay this morning?" she asks seriously.

"Yeah. I'll be fine."

"I want to come see you. Matty does too."

"I don't know that they'll let you past the gates. What did you tell Matty?"

"That you got married. I wouldn't have said anything, but Carlton brought it up."

I sigh. "Was he okay?"

"I don't think he thought much of it honestly. He's only four. All he knows is he misses you."

"I miss him too."

"Tell me about the marking. The ceremony is always such a secret since no women are allowed to witness except the one being marked."

"You have a creepy fascination with it, Julia."

"I have to live vicariously through you."

"You do know it's not that I want this," I say when she sounds too eager.

"Tell me."

"It's a dragon tattoo all the way down my back."

"Not just your neck? That's strange. I wonder why he did that. They didn't do it in the courtyard either, which is tradition."

"How did you know?"

"Grapevine. News travels fast especially news of the mysterious Jericho St. James and his young bride."

I groan.

"I wonder why Hildebrand allowed it to be so private."

"It wasn't exactly private, Julia." I love my cousin but sometimes she gets in her head about things, and she has this fascination with all things IVI. If she knew the reality of it, I wonder if she still would. "There were witnesses and..." I trail off, too embarrassed to mention the pillory, grateful suddenly that I can't see her just now. That I won't have to show her the tattoo. His mark.

"And what? Don't keep me in suspense."

"Nothing."

"You had sex with him, didn't you?" she asks so abruptly I feel myself flush. When I don't answer quickly enough, she sighs. "See if you can get to the compound. We can meet there. You're the wife of Jericho St. James now. Surely you're allowed to lunch at the compound."

"I'm not so sure of anything, honestly. I'm especially not sure what he means to do with me."

"I've been thinking about that." She pauses and I

realize she must be out somewhere because I hear the distant buzz of voices.

"Where are you?"

"Oh, just at breakfast. But on what he wants, there's only one thing that makes sense."

"What's that?"

"Do you know how the Bishop inheritance works?"

"Bishop inheritance? Why would that matter?"

"Do you know?"

"You mean like a will?"

"I mean the way the rules have been written from as far back as there was a fortune to inherit."

"Not really, no." I've never thought about it. Never really thought it applied to me anyway.

"Right now, Carlton is the sole inheritor of the estate. And as the only direct descendent of the inheriting line, apart from you that is, he'll remain so until his fortieth birthday."

"Next year?"

"Yep."

"What does his age have to do with anything apart from him being first-born?"

"There's a catch."

"What catch?" I ask, amazed at the extent of her knowledge.

"He needs an heir to keep hold of the fortune."

"What?"

"Or it goes to you. If you were to produce an heir that is."

"What are you talking about?"

"You and Carlton are the direct descendants of Marius Bishop. You are the *sole* descendants."

"But an heir?"

"It's the rule and a male heir is preferable as you know. They hate to give their fortune to a woman, but they'll have no choice if Carlton doesn't get busy."

"But he and Monique are separated."

"Exactly."

"And she's in France."

"M-hm."

I consider this and have a question of my own. "So, if I hadn't come into the picture, if no one had figured out who my biological father was, and Carlton failed to produce an heir, then what?"

"Well, then the fortune changes lines."

"To?"

"Leonardo, his younger brother."

Something clicks into place then. "Your father."

"M-hm," she says again.

"Which in turn means you. You'd inherit if Carlton or I failed to produce an heir?"

"Well, you're only nineteen. Your biological clock has barely begun ticking."

"Is that why you mentioned birth control pills? Because you think this is what Jericho's planning?"

"What else makes sense, cousin?"

"So, what, he'll get me pregnant then take the Bishop fortune from Carlton?"

"From all the Bishops."

"No, I can't imagine that."

"He is the Head of your Household. It all falls to him even if you're the one with Bishop blood and you're the one carrying the child."

"I have my pills, though. Three months' worth. And I'm sure he'd have taken them away if this was his plan. He is the one who had my things brought over."

"True. Still."

I am silent as I absorb the weight of this. Could it be true? No. No way. He'd have taken the pills for sure.

"Anyway, I have to go. Try to meet Matty and me for lunch soon. We can talk some more."

"I'll try."

"And in the meantime, take your birth control pills and enjoy the sex because honestly you could have done worse! Speaking of," she starts, lowering her voice. "I didn't ask you about the sex. How was it?"

Bloody, I want to say but don't. "Goodbye, Julia."

"You're no fun."

"I'm hanging up."

"Fine. Bye, Isabelle. Take care in that house."

33

JERICHO

I pull up to the entrance of the Savoy Hotel and Dex and I step out of the car. I toss the keys to the valet who stands looking at the car with his mouth agape.

"Don't hit anything," Dex tells him.

"No sir!" he says, and I almost expect a salute.

"You'll make the kid nervous," I tell Dex as we step through the double front doors of the posh hotel and head toward the breakfast room. We pause at the hostess stand and I scan the large room where they manage, even for the size, to make the tables seem private.

"Sir, can I help you?" the hostess asks just as I spot the back of Bishop's balding head. I wonder if he's aware he's losing his hair.

"No, thank you. I found who I'm looking for."

Dex stands just inside the entrance, and I weave

my way around elaborately set tables and waiters carrying trays of mimosas and silver carafes of coffee to Bishop's table. I'm surprised he's got his back to the door but as I near, his companion tucks her phone away and I wonder if she saw me before I even glimpsed them.

Julia Bishop. Isabelle's cousin.

Carlton stands and makes a show of ducking a punch. "Whoa, big man, here to finish the job? Do I need to call security?"

"Sit down, Bishop, you're making a spectacle of yourself."

"Wouldn't want that," he says.

I don't get him. He's a fool but too much so. It's not real and I know enough to keep my guard up.

Julia meanwhile watches me with hawk-like eyes. When I turn my gaze to her, she gives me a wide smile and I get the feeling she's used to men looking at her. Tripping over themselves to please her. I glance at Carlton and wonder if he's one of those men. Kissing cousins. Wouldn't be the first time.

"I hear coffee's good here," I say taking an empty chair from the next table and setting it at theirs. Not bothering to wait for an invitation, I sit down, and Bishop watches me with incredulity, then resumes his seat. He raises a hand and snaps his fingers, actually snaps his fingers, all the while his flat eyes are locked on me.

"Coffee," he says when a waiter approaches.

"Congratulations on your nuptials," Julia says, picking up her fork to spear a strawberry and pop it into her over-rouged mouth.

"Thank you," I tell her and turn to Bishop. "I'd like a word."

"Why ask permission now? Just make yourself comfortable." He pushes his half-eaten breakfast plate away. "Your presence has ruined my appetite."

"Well, I'm sure skipping a link of sausage won't do you any harm." He looks a little like a sausage, I think. A raw one. Pink and soft. "I'd like a word *alone*."

He narrows his gaze as if trying to glean what I'm thinking then turns to gesture to Julia with a dismissive nod of his head.

"I haven't finished," she says.

"You have. Go," he tells her, and I watch this dynamic between them. I can't say they like each other exactly but there is something there.

Julia sulks but stands, tucking her designer bag under her arm and shaking her ass as she walks away in her sky-high heels.

"You seem to take in all the Bishop strays," I say.

"I'm generous like that."

"M-hm. What about your wife?"

"My wife is none of your business."

The coffee comes and the waiter leaves. I pick it up and take a sip.

"What do you want, St. James?" he asks.

"I want to know why you said what you said about my father and sister."

He picks his napkin off his lap and wipes the corners of his mouth which have curved upward. I don't like this. I don't like having to ask. Don't like being at a disadvantage.

"Why not ask Ezekiel? Which by the way," he starts, setting his elbow on the table and leaning toward me. "Who the hell named you three?"

"Why did you say it, Bishop?"

He sits back again, makes a point of studying me, head cocked to the side. "You know, I'd thought you two were in cahoots. Just assumed it."

My jaw tenses but I keep myself perfectly still.

"To defend your sister's honor and all that shit," he adds.

I pounce, picking the knife off his dish and stabbing it into the polished wood of the table a millimeter from his little finger. "Be. Careful."

He looks down and I can see he's visibly shaken. For all the hurt he's caused he's just a coward. Aren't most men like him, though? Giving the orders but unwilling to carry out the violence. Or maybe they think that excuses them somehow. Makes them less culpable.

Carlton picks the knife out of the table with a strange little giggle and holds it in his hand. He turns it over, examining the edge which is too sharp for sausage and eggs.

"You and I may have more in common than either of us cares to admit," he says.

"I doubt that."

He studies me for a long minute. "Did you fuck her yet?"

I'm not sure if it's the question itself or the way he phrases it that gets my hackles up.

"That's none of your business, is it?"

"Her mother was a whore, you know. Like mother like—"

"That's my wife you're talking about. Be. Very. Careful."

His expression darkens but he doesn't finish the insult. He changes gears. "How much are you willing to sacrifice to avenge your dead fiancée?"

My hands fist, my heart hammers against my chest. I'm going to kill this man.

"It would be a shame if your pretty little girl became an orphan, wouldn't it? Wait. Would that make Isabelle her mommy?"

"Why did you say it?" I repeat, fingers digging into the arms of the chair as I tell myself to keep calm. To remember why I'm here. To not let this man rattle me. Because it's what he wants. It's all he wants.

He throws his napkin onto his plate and pushes his chair back but instead of standing, he leans close to me. "Sometimes it's better to hide in a corner and lick your wounds. Admit the better man won. And walk away while you still have something to lose."

I lean toward him, too, but he doesn't back away. "Why did you fucking say it?"

He grins. "You want to know about daddy dearest and your dead sister? Let me ask you this. How badly do you want to know? What are you willing to give up for that knowledge? What do they say? Ignorance is bliss, did I get that right?"

He stands.

"Are you so anxious to know the stock you come from? Because you're just like him, aren't you? Even the fucked-up eyes. A carbon copy of dad. I just hope you don't commit the sins he did. Recycle an ugly past." He takes a step away but stops, turns. "Just ask Zeke if you're not sure what I'm talking about."

34

ISABELLE

I walk out into the hallway and remember my promise to Angelique to kiss her goodnight when I returned last night. Feeling guilty, I walk toward her bedroom, not sure she'll be in there. I'm surprised to find her door open a crack and Angelique inside with Leontine and an older woman I've not yet met.

"Good morning. Or afternoon," Leontine says, making a point of checking her watch.

I blush. "Good afternoon," I say in a quiet voice as Angelique looks up from her small desk and waves. I realize this must be her teacher. "I can come back if it's a bad time."

"It's all right," she says. "Come in and meet Mrs. Strand, Angelique's teacher."

I extend my hand and shake hers. She smiles but her lips are more pursed than anything else and I wonder if they couldn't have found a friendlier looking teacher for the little girl. But I stop myself. I'm judging and it's not fair.

"Good morning," Mrs. Strand says. "It's nice to meet you and although I don't expect interruptions daily, I understand last night was a special night."

"Well, I don't mean to interrupt. Just wanted to check in on Angelique. How are you doing, sweetheart?" I ask as I walk around the desk and look at the book they're studying. "Oh, that has pretty pictures," I say, crouching down beside Angelique's chair.

"I like my princess books better," she says. "This one's too easy."

"Memorizing is not the same as reading, child," Mrs. Strand says in a tone that bothers me.

"I didn't memorize," Angelique says, casting her eyes down.

I rub the little girl's back. "We can read a princess book later, okay?" I whisper in her ear.

She nods but I see how her eyes glisten when they meet mine and I wonder how sensitive she is. And how a comment like this dour old woman's could hurt her tender feelings. I make a funny face to show her I'm on her side and she giggles.

"Daddy's going to teach me how to swim this afternoon," she says.

"He is? That's great."

"But we can read after that."

"That sounds good to me," I say and straighten when Mrs. Strand clears her throat, her not so subtle signal. "I'll see you after your lessons, okay?"

Angelique nods reluctantly and I walk out of the room, leaving the three of them in the room.

I go downstairs to find coffee and something to eat, making my way into the kitchen where May, the woman who had carried in my dinner the other night, is washing dishes. The smell of cake wafts from the oven.

"That smells delicious," I say with a smile.

"That's Catherine's cake." May switches off the water and turns to me, wiping her hands on a towel. "Can I help you, ma'am?"

Ma'am. "Isabelle," I say. It feels weird to be called ma'am.

She smiles and nods. "Can I get you something?"

"I can get it myself if you don't mind. I'm just looking for coffee and maybe a piece of toast or something."

"Of course," she says and walks over to a restaurant style espresso machine. "What would you like?" she asks.

"A cappuccino if it's easy enough."

She nods and gets busy making me a gorgeous cappuccino. She then goes to a bread box and opens it to reveal a loaf of homemade bread. She picks up the knife and slices two thick pieces for me. Setting them on a dish and adding them to a tray loaded with jams, butter, and various cheeses.

"That's fine," I tell her when she starts grabbing for more jars. "More than enough."

"I'm sure Mr. St. James wants his bride well fed," she says just as Catherine walks into the kitchen.

"That he does," she agrees. "Come on now, we'll set you up in the dining room."

"I don't want to be any trouble. I can just take the tray and eat outside."

"It's already quite warm and there will be rain later."

"I don't mind the heat and if it's going to rain I'd better get out when I can."

"All right then." The younger woman carries the tray out and I follow her, still feeling guilty about being waited on. I take the seat at a table near the pool with an umbrella to shield me from the sun. I'm glad when she leaves me alone and I can eat my breakfast, thinking about what Angelique said about Jericho teaching her how to swim. I can't picture it. At all.

I'm at a loss for what to do when I've finished breakfast and confirmed Angelique will be in her lessons for the next few hours. It seems a bit much for such a young girl but what do I know. After spending some time walking around the house and peering into rooms all of which are empty but immaculately clean and richly decorated, I change into running clothes and decide to go for a jog. I want to get my bearings around the property and get some exercise while I'm at it.

The sun is hot and I'm grateful for the cloud cover as I jog into the woods using the same path Jericho had taken me that night he played his stupid game of chase. Running feels good. Makes me feel like myself. Or maybe it's just making me feel a little in control. Whatever it is, I like it and thirty minutes in, I feel rejuvenated, albeit a little sweaty.

I keep going until I come to the edge of the property where the wall that divides Bishop and St. James lands stands, impenetrable like the men on either side of it. Ivy grows along the wall and in some places, I see blooms of soft yellow flowers, the same that bloom on the other side. I think about Angelique then. I think she'd like to see this and make a mental note to bring her. If I'm allowed to, that is.

The wall encompasses the entirety of the property and I remember many a time standing on the other side of it. Running my fingers over the cool stone. I think about my life before and after Jericho St. James, this wall the physical divider between the past and my new present. My future.

My mind wanders to what Julia said. To Jericho's intention. It's too harsh to process though. Having a child for the purpose of revenge. Of taking something that doesn't belong to you. Has he given thought to the child? To that little life he would bring into the world in the name of his vengeance? A child for a pawn. It's unthinkable.

No, he can't. Julia can't be right. It's too horrible. Too monstrous even for him. And I'm not sure how monstrous he is because my brain keeps taking me back to that moment in the cavern. How he hurt himself rather than hurt me. No monster would have done that. Not with his enemy bound and bared to endure his punishment.

Thunder crashes overhead. I look up to see how the sky has darkened and not a moment later, that sky opens up and a heavy rain rushes down. It will break the heat and humidity, but I have to hurry to take shelter and only realize where I am when I see the top of the stone building come into view from just beyond the trees.

The chapel.

The graveyard.

Lighting followed by thunder rock the ground beneath my feet. I don't make a conscious decision but run as fast as I can through rain and toward the shelter of the little church. I don't stop to think as I open the cemetery gate, the creaking dulled by the sound of a soaking rain. I hurry to climb the chapel stairs then push the heavy door open and slip inside. Closing the door behind me, I lean my back against it as my chest heaves with my breaths. I'm soaked through and hug my arms around myself.

It's only slightly less eerie in here during the day and I try to remind myself there's no such thing as ghosts, even though I know that's not true. I walk to the altar, finding matches, and light some candles there for illumination. They're dusty, I notice, but I realize something else. I smell incense. And it's fresh. The other night when he brought me here the air smelled stale, the chapel closed up. Like no one had been here for a long time.

Someone's been here since that night. I wonder if it's Jericho.

Lightning brightens the stained-glass window over the altar catching the ornately carved wooden cover of what at first glance looks to be a bible. I touch the silver etched into it as I lift the heavy tome to have a closer look, but it's too dark to read by the light of the few candles. I open it, see the fancy script remembering how Jericho had looked at it so reverently that night he'd brought me here. I wonder if it's handwritten or just made to look that way. As I turn the pages, I realize it's the former. When lightning next strikes, my gaze lands on the grave of the author himself and I find myself jumping away, as if warned.

My breath catches and I tell myself to relax. No ghosts. Not here.

I take a seat in the first pew to wait out the storm. And I find that same peace settling over me as did when I'd be in the chapel at the IVI compound all those years ago when I was a little girl. Jericho made fun of my mother thinking Jesus would babysit me. Maybe God was watching out for me, though.

Whatever it is, I find myself leaning my back against the wooden pew and just listening to the silence inside as the rain pours outside. I don't know how much time goes by but when the rain stops and the sun shines, I get up to blow out the candles, noticing the tabernacle lamp burning still, and open the door to walk outside.

It's bright enough that I have to squint and stop for a moment to take in the beauty all around me. The raindrops have made the green somehow brighter while droplets reflecting the bright gold of the sun drop from trees.

I glance around, seeing how the cemetery is well maintained. Mostly.

My eyes land on Nellie Bishop's grave and I walk toward it, open the rusting gate surrounding it. She was Mary's friend, he'd said. Both girls were innocent. I know that in my heart. And as I kneel in the overgrown grass of her grave and brush off the mud caking her stone, I feel a tug at my heart for her. For Mary, and even for Draca St. James. Not for Reginald Bishop, though. There I only feel a chill. The same chill I always felt when I passed his portrait hanging over the fireplace in the living room of the Bishop house.

The *Bishop* house.

I need to remember I am a Bishop, too. And that house has been my home for the last three years.

But for now, I don't think about those things. I think of Nellie. Of how she was punished to punish the truly guilty. And I think we have at least that in common.

A chill makes me shudder at that thought. Will he put me in the ground beside her when he's finished with me? Will he let me be forgotten just as the St. James's before him have let her be forgotten? No, worse. Let her serve as an example of what happens to Bishops who cross St. James's.

I find myself pulling at the weeds then, clearing her grave as best I can. And when I'm done, I get up, wipe the mud off my knees and shins and I go back to that wall where the yellow flowers grew. I pick as many as I can carry and take them back to lay at Nellie's grave. Because I'll remember Nellie Bishop. I won't remember what happened to her. At least the horror story Jericho told. I'll just remember the girl who didn't deserve her fate. And as I spread the flowers over her grave, I think how beautiful it is now, a memorial to a life.

35

JERICHO

Why did I let that bastard get to me? What did I expect going to him anyway? Asking him a question my brother should be answering.

Are you so anxious to know the stock you come from? Because you're just like him, aren't you? Even the fucked-up eyes. A carbon copy of dad. I just hope you don't commit the sins he did. Recycle an ugly past.

I step onto soft grass and bring the bottle of whiskey to my lips. I don't remember when I stopped pouring it out. Don't remember when Dex drove me home from the bar I found myself in too early in the day.

The house is dark, and the rain of the afternoon only seems to have made the air muggier, more humid. I make my way to the path that will lead to the cemetery, grateful for the moonlight. Although I know this path. Even though I haven't lived here for five years I'll never forget it.

Dad's funeral was the last one. Six years since then. I didn't come back to bury Kimberly. I sent her body back for Zeke to take care of while I looked after my daughter. The fact that Angelique survived is still astonishing to me. She's a miracle. Or she would be if I believed in them.

Before dad's funeral it was Zoë's. That was a bad one. I guess all funerals are bad, though. But when at barely eighteen you bury your sixteen-year-old sister I think that ranks pretty high on the fucked-up scale.

She never left a note. Don't all suicides leave a note? I think that is part of why it's hard. The not knowing. Not understanding. We were close, the three of us. At least I thought so.

I wonder if her death was worse for Zeke, though. They were twins. He took it badly, but how does one take something like that well? And mom. Fuck. She almost died herself. Dad kept it together. He never spoke of it, but I'd sometimes hear him go down to that cellar after he installed the steel door to keep the rest of us out. He wasn't taking any chances after Zoë. Maybe someone should have shut off access after Mary all those centuries ago, though, because Zoë hanged herself in the same place. From the same beam. The hanging beam.

Fuck.

Just ask Zeke if you're not sure what I'm talking about.

I take another swallow of whiskey and round the corner to the graveyard. Before I can ruminate on Bishop's words, I see something that at first surprises me, then, after that moment, enrages me.

I let the bottle drop from my hand as I stalk toward Nellie Bishop's grave. It's been cleaned up. Mud and moss that had obscured the woman's name removed and wiped up. Weeds pulled. Grass looks like it was ripped out. And lying in a rectangle that would cover the rotted corpse beneath are flowers. Yellow flowers. Some whole, most just petals but bright, somehow holding on to their color as if mocking me as they glow in the moonlight.

Fury burns inside me. Only one person would have done this.

An enemy in my own home.

An enemy I brought into my home. My bed.

I don't think as I stalk back to the house. I barely recall the walk. Don't remember climbing the stairs to my room. I do remember my irritation at finding it empty. Although I don't think I instructed her to be in my bed.

I push through the connecting door and when I see her comfortably asleep on the bed, I lose my shit. The growl that comes from the cavern of my chest startles her awake, putting her instantly on alert. I'm not sure if she can see my face, but she must feel the rage rolling off me and the danger it presents to her.

When I take one step toward the bed, she lets out a little scream and stumbles off the other side, falling to the floor as her legs tangle in the sheets.

"What did you do?" I ask, taking a step with each word.

She scrambles back on hands and feet like a crab. She can't get away from me fast enough. But she won't be getting away. Not tonight.

I reach down, grab hold of her arm, and haul her to her feet. When she opens her mouth to scream, I pull her to my chest and clamp my hand over it.

"Shut. Up."

She struggles, shaking her head, the sounds she's making muffled. When she bites my finger, I pinch her nose with thumb and forefinger, keeping my palm over her mouth. Her fingernails draw blood as she scratches my forearm when she can't get air and I tighten the arm I have across her stomach.

"Shut. Up. Do you hear me?"

She nods, whimpers. Drops her hold on my forearm. That may not be a conscious choice, though. She needs air.

I let go of her nose, loosen my hand over her mouth. She sucks a breath in, and I lift her off her feet to walk her to the door. There, I let her down and push her against it. I make a fist in her hair and turn her face, pressing her cheek to the wood.

"You make a sound, a single fucking sound, and you'll be sorry. You get me?"

She doesn't open her mouth. Just nods frantically, eyes all wide horror.

I draw her back by her hair, open the door and march her to the stairs and down. She's got hold of my hand and is quiet as she can be although she's a sniffling, crying mess. I'm sure my hand pulling her hair hurts as I navigate her by that fistful to the bottom of the stairs where remarkably she doesn't fall. I walk her toward the kitchen, through it and out the door I'd left open in my hurry. I make sure to close it now.

The night is damp, as usual, but it isn't raining. All I hear are the sounds of insects and night creatures and Isabelle's labored breathing as I shift my grip to her arm, walking her to the cemetery. She's muttering something, maybe begging me to slow down. I don't know. I can't hear her. Blood rings in my ears and the closer we get the angrier I become.

How dare she?

How dare she betray me in my own house?

She knows where we're going. She knows what this is about and when we get to that flowerbed over the Bishop grave, I drop her to her knees.

She lands on all fours and takes a minute to sit on her heels. She looks around her then up at me. She's shivering. Wearing that goddamn T-shirt again.

But it's not the shirt that ignites the anger inside me into a red-hot flame. It's the look in her eyes. Her resistance.

"What. Did. You. Do?" I demand.

She gets up, feet sinking into the muddy mess, yellow petals and blades of green grass she'd torn our earlier sticking to her feet, shins and knees.

"I cleaned up Nellie Bishop's grave. It was long overdue, don't you think, you piece of shit?"

She shoves at me. I don't know if she really thinks she'll budge me. When I don't move, she does it again.

"Me, a piece of shit?" I ask her, walking her backwards until her ass hits the grave marker. I lean into her forcing her to bend backwards as her hands come to my chest. "What are you then, Bishop?"

"You're drunk, Jericho. I can smell it on you. Get the hell away from me." She shoves again.

Jericho. It's the first time she's used my name without me having told her to say it and for some reason it makes me stop. I look down at her, blue eyes almost black in this night. Cheeks flushed. I glance farther down to the part of her chest exposed by the too-wide neck of the worn shirt. It must be years old. I look at her thighs, her bare feet. I wrap an arm around her and with the other reach under her shirt to take hold of her panties and pull them down her legs.

"What are you doing?" she cries out.

I ignore her, step on the white silk that slips off her feet when I lift her to sit on the top of the wide stone marker.

"I'm teaching you what a Bishop means in this house," I tell her as I unbuckle my belt, undo the button of my pants, the zipper. "I'm teaching you what you're good for," I say as I keep one hand around her back and use the other to lift her thigh. I bend my knees just a little, just enough, and wedge myself between her legs. She gasps when I push into her and I swear that first moment, that warm, tight passage is like a fucking homecoming when it should be anything but.

She's just a vessel. A Bishop. Something to fuck. To use. A means to an end.

But those aren't the thoughts I'm thinking as I hold her tight and thrust into her.

"What... I..." she stutters.

My next thrust cuts off her words and her hands come to my shoulders, gripping tight to me.

"You're getting wet, Isabelle," I tell her with a smirk and another hard thrust that makes her head bounce on her neck. "Don't tell me you like my dick inside you." Another thrust, and her breath catches. I lean her back, using the stone to hold her upright and fist a handful of hair with my free hand. I tug her head back and watch as I fuck her. I listen to her pants as her eyes go darker and her cheeks flush with blood. Her mouth is open, lips glistening as her pussy tightens around my cock, gripping it, dripping around it.

"You have to... Stop..." she gasps, words cut off as she takes my thrusts.

"Say my name. Say it when you come."

"I hate you," she tries as her eyes close, and I feel her squeeze around me.

"Say it!"

Her eyelids fly open. She's coming and fuck, I'm getting harder watching her.

"I hate you, Jericho St. James," she tells me as her head drops back into my hand which isn't a fist anymore. When her pussy next squeezes my dick and she cries out, I come. I come so fucking hard that for a minute all I see are her eyes, her open mouth, her face. The rest of the world is a blur as I release, empty inside her, an ecstasy I can't remember ever feeling before this. Before her.

And when it's done, when it's over, her legs dangle, arms barely holding on to me as I step back, carrying her with me. When I pull out of her, I feel the gush of come spill down her thighs. Her feet touch the ground, but her knees buckle, and I have to hold her up.

We stay like this for a minute just looking at each other. Each watching the other.

Enemies.

Lovers.

But that word, it draws my rage to a sharp, dangerous point.

No. Not lovers. Never lovers. It is a betrayal to my own name to ever think of her as lover.

I push her to her knees. She drops easily enough. I grip a handful of hair and she whines but hasn't the strength to pull me off.

"Clean me," I tell her.

She just looks up at me and I tighten my hold on her.

"With your mouth. Clean my dick while my come runs out of your pussy and onto your ancestors grave."

She closes her mouth, pushes against my thighs.

I bend closer to her, force her head back. "Do it or I'll bend you over and show you what a lashing from my belt feels like. It's what I should have done the other night. Clearly I've been too easy on you."

She blinks, wipes the back of her hand across her eyes.

"Do it, Isabelle."

"I hate you."

"I could give a fuck." I grin as I straighten. "You bite and I'll whip your ass. Am I clear?"

"Fuck you."

"Am I fucking clear?"

"Yes!"

I draw her mouth to my dick which is still not quite soft after that rutting, still covered in our combined come. Her lips part and fuck. Fuck me when that warm, wet tongue licks the length of my shaft. Fuck me if I'm not going to get hard again at the feel of her on me, at the look of her kneeling before me, licking me clean. I watch her as I move her over my dick and she watches me, eyes huge, wet, growing wetter when I push into her. She chokes before I let her draw breath.

She's clearly inexperienced but I'll manage. I move her over me and I'm hard again. I guide her, going deeper, feeling her throat constrict, and in no time, I'm coming. My dick throbs inside her mouth as I hold her steady and watch her take me. Watch her swallow.

When it's over, I release her and she drops to her hands, panting, spitting.

I crouch down and grip her jaw to close her mouth and make her look at me.

"Don't waste that, Isabelle. Swallow it down. All of it."

I hold onto her as she does, tears streaming down her cheeks. She wipes at her face with muddy hands when I release her and I look down at her as I straighten to tuck my dick into my pants. She looks so small. So fucking small and vulnerable as she hugs herself, searching behind her for her ruined panties. And something about the sight of her like this, here and now, sniffling, more than a little lost, it sobers me. Or maybe it was the fucking that sobered me. Whatever it is, I don't like it. Because it also softens something inside me.

And that is a weakness.

But when she turns huge, wet eyes up to me, I'm undone.

"Can I go now? Are you finished humiliating me for the night?" she asks, trying to sound indignant but only sounding hurt.

Fuck.

I don't answer. I don't know how. Don't have a clue what to say.

I take a step back and find the bottle I'd dropped here earlier. It's on its side and I pick it up, drink the last of what's left, a dirty mouthful. I turn away from the girl on her knees in the middle of a fucking cemetery. The girl I'm breaking inch by inch.

"Get out of here," I tell her hoarsely and walk toward the chapel. I can't look at her.

"She waited for you, you know that?" she calls out as I get to the stairs.

I pause.

"All afternoon. Did you know? Did you even think about her?"

I turn to see her. She steps toward me but hesitates, stops.

"What are you talking about?" I ask, going to her as she scrambles backward.

"Angelique. She put on her favorite bathing suit and gathered up her toys and waited for you. She fell asleep on the floor behind the front door, you jerk. You fucking selfish jerk."

Fuck.

"You promised you'd teach her how to swim. Or did you forget while you were drinking yourself into oblivion?" she asks, gesturing to the bottle, her voice surer as she takes strength from my silence. "I get it that you hate me. No, I actually don't. You hate my brother and I'm a means to an end in your twisted mind, but your own daughter? You're damaging her. Have you even thought about that? Thought about her rather than yourself? I doubt you have!" she turns to walk away, stops and steps toward me. "You know what? She'd be better off without you."

The words hit me like a fist, and my brain rattles in my head. I stumble backward, drop down onto the step, let the empty bottle fall to the ground.

I expect Isabelle to go on. Tell me all the ways I'm failing my daughter. Because she's right. I am. And she's right that Angelique would be better off without me. Hell, I know that myself. Always have.

But she doesn't go on. She stops. Pivots. Rubs her face with both hands.

"Shit," she mutters into her hands. "I didn't... I didn't mean that."

I don't reply. I'm still stuck on one of the words she used. Damage. Stuck on the fact that my daughter would be better off without me. It's true. But no one's ever been brave enough to say it to my face. Even when Kimberly was pregnant, I just thought she'd be a good enough mom to make up for my lack. But now? All these years with only me as a parent? My daughter deserves better.

"Jericho?"

She deserves so much better than me.

"Jericho, I'm really cold," Isabelle says. She has her arms wrapped around herself and is shivering hard.

I look at her. "Go."

She studies me, hesitates. "Come with me."

I shake my head, look at the empty bottle on the ground wishing it was full.

"I need you," she says.

I watch her face, try to read her. "You don't need me."

"Please."

I look at her standing there in that threadbare shirt, ruined panties clutched in her hand, her feet bare. I'm sure they're cut up. I did that. Damaged her too. It's what I do.

I leave the bottle where it is and get up.

She's still afraid of me, though, because she takes one step back then stops herself. When I reach her, I look her over, wet and muddy and waiting here for me when she could have gone. When I told her to go.

And I find I can't meet her eyes, so I pick her up, hold her cold and shivering against my chest and carry her back to the house. I leave a muddy trail to my bedroom and into the bathroom where I set her on the edge of the tub and look at her feet, the mud caked on her legs, the ruined shirt, the panties she's still holding.

"Take off your shirt," I tell her and shift my attention to the large tub. I run a bath, checking the water temperature as she takes off the shirt. When I look at her, she's standing naked, one arm across her breasts, the other to cover the V between her legs. I don't comment. "Get in the tub."

I feel exactly like a jerk. The selfish jerk she accused me of being. I watch her climb into the tub and sit in the middle of it. She hugs her knees as the water fills up.

Without a word, I use the handheld to wash the mud off her, drain the dirty water and fill the tub until it's almost to her shoulders. I switch off the water.

She only steals glances at me, but I can't look away from her. I pull my shirt off and sit at the edge of the tub at her back. I don't want her to see my face. Not right now. With the handheld I rinse her hair as she hugs her knees to her chest.

"You're right," I tell her. I lift her hair off her back and set it over her shoulder. I look at the tattoo. It looks good. It looks like she's mine. And I wonder about karma. About why she's been placed in my hands.

She turns her head to meet my eyes and I force myself to meet hers.

"Kimberly would have been a good mother to her," I say, a sort of confession. "A better mother than I am a father. I know that. I've always known that."

"I didn't mean what I said. That she'd be better off—"

I put up a hand to stop her. "She would." I've never said this out loud. Not in five years. Even though I've known.

She turns so she's facing me. "Fix it," she says.

"It's too late."

"It's not. Just fix it."

It's too late. Isn't it? "How?"

"Just be here for her. That's all she wants. Just be her dad who is here for her."

"I can't—"

"You can. It's a choice, Jericho. Like you said to me once. Everything is a choice. You just have to choose her."

I lock my jaw. She's right. I get up, grab the bottles of shampoo and conditioner, something new I guess Catherine put in here, and return to the tub. "Turn around," I tell her. She looks at the bottle and turns and we sit in silence as I shampoo her hair, the only sound that of water dripping now and again into the full tub, that of me rinsing her hair, washing it again, massaging conditioner into her scalp careful of where I pulled her along by that mass not an hour ago.

And I think about what I'm going to do to her. Think about her fate.

She doesn't deserve it either. Doesn't deserve me or Carlton Bishop or any of the shit that's happened to her. The shit she doesn't know the half of. But here I am. And here she is. And when I'm finished bathing her, I lift her out of the tub and dry her and carry her back into the bedroom.

"Get on your knees," I tell her as I set her on the bed. "Your back to me."

She watches me suspiciously as I open the night-stand drawer and take out a tube of salve. When she sees what I intend to do she sits on her heels with her back to me and tugs her hair over one shoulder to expose her back.

I look at her for a long minute. She's beautiful. So beautiful. And young. And she doesn't deserve this.

I rub salve into the ink on her back. And this time when I turn her over and fuck her, I do it slowly, tasting every inch of her before sliding my length into her, taking my time to feel everything. Watching her face, memorizing the look of her, the feel of her. Tasting how she tastes when I kiss her mouth.

My thrusts are deep but measured, not meant to hurt, not this time. And as she comes, I draw back just enough to watch her because I know this moment is fleeting. I know it will be gone before either of us blinks. And I know the look in her eyes now, the hope inside them, I'll extinguish it when she sees what I have planned next. Because it's what I have to do. Because I wasn't quite right about all things being a choice.

Some things aren't choices at all.

Some are destiny.

And my destiny is to ruin hers.

36

ISABELLE

I'm alone in his bed when I wake up. I glance at the clock. It's a little after nine in the morning. I wonder when he slipped out. You'd think I'd notice it, feel the movement of the bed or something. Feel the loss of warmth. Because he held me last night. I fell asleep with my head against his chest.

I sit up, rub my face. What is wrong with me? What he did last night was terrifying. *He* was terrifying. And when I said what I said to him, when I slung my words to damage him, I almost didn't recognize myself. That's not who I am. I don't try to hurt people no matter who they are.

But in this case, it wasn't to hurt him. Not wholly, at least. It's true what I said. I watched that sweet little girl fall asleep half leaning against the front door waiting for her daddy to come home and teach her how to swim like he promised he would.

She wore her yellow bathing suit again with all those ruffles. It twists my heart even now to think of it.

She was quick to hide her tears when I asked her if she was all right before she went to bed. I can still hear myself making up an excuse for him. Telling her he must have been delayed at work.

What a messed-up situation this is. But I do know one thing. A parent, even one as little available to his daughter as Jericho St. James, is better than no parent.

I get up and go to my room to shower. I make a point of taking my birth control pill before I leave the bathroom to put on a loose-fitting dress because even though the nights are cooler, the days are still warm. I go downstairs and find Ezekiel sitting in the dining room reading a paper while drinking a cup of coffee. I haven't seen him since the wedding. The marking.

I feel my face heat up at the memory of what he witnessed, me made to kneel, locked in that pillory, my dress torn to expose my back fully to be marked.

He puts his paper away and studies me.

I try for a smile and break eye contact as I move around the table to the one place still left untouched, mine I guess, and pick up the mug.

"Coffee or tea?" he asks, standing.

"Coffee please."

He nods, picks up a carafe and pours for me. "Sit

down and eat something," he says before I can scurry back upstairs to hide in my room.

I bite my lip.

"Sit, Isabelle. I won't bite."

"Your brother said that once too," I say, I don't know why. I don't wait for him to comment but pick up my bowl and load it with fruit and yogurt.

"I'm not my brother but you are right about him. He definitely bites," he says and when I look at him, I find him smiling.

I can't return that smile. I'm unsure what is going on.

He walks around my chair, and I find myself sitting very still when I feel the brush of his fingers on my shoulder.

"May I?"

I turn to look up at him.

"The mark. I'd like to see it."

I hesitate. I'm pretty sure Jericho won't want me to bare my back to his brother. I'm not sure I like it myself, the idea of anyone but Jericho seeing me, seeing it. But it feels awkward, so I lift my hair and set it over my shoulder. My back is bare just to my shoulder blades.

He whistles, traces one of the dragons and for a moment I wonder if he's going to unzip the dress to see more of it. Then I realize what he's touching isn't so much the tattoo but the top of the scar along my spine.

"He did it to hide that scar. I don't imagine he mentioned that."

"What?"

"That's why it runs all the way down your back."

I'm confused. But then I realize why, and I shake my head at my own stupidity. "What, did he think the scar was ugly? Couldn't stand to look at it?" It is ugly but fuck him.

He sets a hand on the table and leans a little closer. "If he hurts you, you can come to me," he says, the whispered words making me shudder, his fingers feather light along my spine.

"Brother." The sound comes from the hallway. It's a rumble, like the rattle of a snake. A warning.

I gasp and turn and for as surprised as I am to see Jericho standing there, Ezekiel casually smiles as if he already knew.

"Brother," Ezekiel repeats.

Jericho is holding Angelique in one arm. She has her bathing suit on, and one arm wrapped around her father's neck. In the other she's holding her stuffed bear. Jericho is dressed more casually than I've ever seen him in swim trunks and a T-shirt. But his expression is as fierce as ever and I get the feeling if Angelique wasn't here, he'd have grabbed his brother by the throat.

"Uncle Zeke, will you swim with us too?" Angelique asks Ezekiel.

"Wish I could sweetheart, but I have a meeting this morning. I'll see you later though."

"Just a minute," Jericho says, putting a hand on his brother's chest to stop him from passing. He sets Angelique down. "Go into the kitchen and ask Catherine to make us some lemonade. I'll be right there."

Angelique pauses, looks up at her father.

He smiles but I see how tense it is.

"I'll help you," I say, standing.

Jericho looks at me. "You sit."

I sit.

"Daddy?"

"Go on, Angelique, I need to have a word with Uncle Zeke. I'll just be a minute."

"Promise?"

"I promise."

"Okay," she says reluctantly.

Jericho watches her walk away. I watch Jericho because when he turns back to Ezekiel a moment later, the look on his face is murderous.

"Did I interrupt something?" he asks his brother, stepping just a little too close to him.

"Just having a look at the mark."

"Didn't get enough of an eyeful the night I put it on her?" Jericho asks, cocking his head to the side.

"You know the rules. I had to be present."

"But you didn't look away, did you?"

"Why would I?"

They're well matched. Same height, built about the same. Jericho's angrier, though. But Ezekiel, in his casual manner, leans toward his brother in a way that says he's not afraid of him.

"Relax, brother. She's yours," Ezekiel finally says.

"Remember it."

A moment passes between them, and I wonder at this exchange. It's charged, wrought with tension, and my mind wanders to Angelique's mother.

"I never forgot it. I don't forget much, in fact." Ezekiel turns to me. Smiles. "What I said stands, Isabelle."

He leaves before I have to respond, thank goodness because I have no idea what I'd say.

Jericho comes to stand behind my chair and in response, every hair on my body rises on end.

"What did he say?"

"I don't remember."

"No?"

I keep my eyes on the table and shake my head.

He leans down, bringing his face to the crook of my neck, sending a shudder down my spine.

"Did he touch you?" he asks, words a whisper.

"No."

"Are you sure?"

"Yes." My voice is a squeak.

"Because you're mine. Do you understand that Isabelle?"

I turn my head just enough to see his eyes.

"Do you?"

"Yes."

"Good." He turns his face, closes his mouth over my pulse. When he draws away, I shiver. "Because if anyone touches you, I will cut off their hands."

I gasp and he pulls back. I look at him, shocked at his words, at the violence of them.

"Finish eating and then go put on your bikini," he says. "I want you at the pool."

"He didn't mean anything."

"Didn't he?" He reaches over me to snag a piece of bacon from one of the serving dishes. "You don't know our history, Isabelle. You just stay away from him."

"We have lemonade!" Angelique announces from around the corner and holds up a thermos.

Jericho doesn't take his eyes from mine. "Good. I'm thirsty," he says. He sticks the bacon into his mouth, picks up my napkin to wipe his fingers and drops it on the table before turning to his daughter and walking out of the dining room like a whole different man. Not the one who just threatened to cut off his brother's hands. Not the one who did what he did to me last night.

The sight of it leaves me wondering which of them is the real Jericho St. James.

37

ISABELLE

He is a different man with her. I watch them in the pool but keep to the side, dipping my feet in and looking after Baby Bear. They're splashing and laughing. He pretends to be a shark and she squeals with laughter when he bites her toes. He teaches her to float on her back. Teaches her to doggy paddle. Tells her she's never allowed in the pool alone.

They're having fun. It's the strangest thing to see. And the sweetest. So at odds with the man of just moments ago. The one who threatened violence to anyone who laid a hand on me. I can't reconcile the two very different sides of this man.

Angelique adores her father. Shines under his attention.

"Isabelle," Jericho calls from across the pool.

I raise my eyebrows.

"Get in the water."

Setting Baby Bear aside, I slip into the pool and swim toward them.

"Watch, Isabelle!" Angelique says and I stop a few feet from her. Jericho reluctantly releases her and for a moment, she goes under, but her head pops back up in a heartbeat and she's smiling and paddling toward me.

"Wow!" I clap my hands and reach out my arms to catch her. She can only manage a couple of moments but it's a great start. We send her back and forth between us a few times until she tires out just as Leontine walks out toward us, a warm smile on her face.

"Well, look at you," she says to Angelique who is beaming.

"I can swim, Nana!"

"I see that," Leontine says, unwrapping the little yellow towel that matches Angelique's bathing suit. "Maybe your daddy will take you swimming again later but for now, we need to get you bathed and ready for your lesson. Mrs. Strand will be here soon."

Angelique deflates at the mention of the woman's name. "I don't want her."

"She's your teacher. Don't be silly," Leontine says.

"Why can't I go to school like Nina?"

Jericho's expression darkens but before he has to answer, Leontine does.

"Come Angelique. Catherine made you a snack and there's going to be cake for you and Nina later. We'd better hurry."

She pouts but Jericho carries her to the stairs where he climbs out and hands her over to be wrapped up in her towel and lifted up by Leontine.

"I don't like her," Angelique mumbles. "She's not nice."

"Now, she's fine. You just have to get used to each other," Leontine says as Jericho wraps a towel around his hips and watches them.

I walk to the edge of the pool and haul myself up. "Don't forget Baby Bear," I tell Angelique.

"Will you come too?" she asks me, taking the bear.

Although I'm not sure Mrs. Strand will like that I nod because from my brief meeting with the woman, I am on Angelique's side. I don't like her much either. "I'll come after I shower."

"Okay," she says and lets Leontine walk her away. I don't miss the look Leontine gives me.

Jericho turns to me, eyes sweeping over me. I'm wearing one of the bikinis I found in the dresser. I wonder if he chose it for me. I pick up a towel and wrap it around myself, flushing when his eyes meet mine again.

"You saw the woman?"

"Briefly."

"How is she?"

"I don't know."

"First impression."

"You're asking my opinion?"

"I think you have my daughter's best interest at heart regardless of how you feel about me."

Well, that is true. "I really only spent a few minutes in the lesson."

"And?"

"Angelique is very sensitive, and Mrs. Strand may not be used to that."

"You don't like her."

"I didn't say that."

"You didn't have to. She thinks you're going to give her music lessons."

I smile nervously.

"Did you tell her that?"

"I guess. Maybe I told her I'd show her."

"Hm. If I need to hire a music teacher—"

"I can do it. Teach her some basics."

"I haven't heard you play."

I study him for a moment. "I'm not in the right headspace I guess. Considering."

He draws in a long breath and exhales. But when he opens his mouth to say something, Dex walks out, and he stops. He glances at me then to Jericho. "I have that information you wanted."

Jericho holds his gaze and nods. "Let me get showered."

Dex returns to the house and Jericho puts a hand at my back to walk me upstairs. "If you want me to consider resuming your violin lessons, you'll teach my daughter. You figure out your headspace whatever the fuck that means," he tells me as we head to his bedroom.

"You mean that? You'll let me resume my lessons?"

"I don't waste words, Isabelle."

"Okay."

He nods, then closes and locks the door and turns back to me. "If she wants to swim later, take her. Just don't take your eyes off her."

"I know that. I know not to take my eyes off a child in the pool."

"Remember what my brother said yet?" he asks, eyes boring like lasers into mine.

I'm caught off guard and hesitate. "No," I finally say.

"Nothing at all?"

I shake my head.

"Liar."

His gaze moves over me, and he reaches a hand around my neck. The next moment the top of my suit drops to the floor as the backs of my knees hit the foot of the bed. He looks at me, reaches one hand to cup the back of my head, fingers weaving into my hair as with his other hand he weighs one breast, thumb flicking over the hardening nipple. He dips his head and licks that nipple, then sucks. I gasp when his teeth close around it and he draws it out, the sensation just on this side of pain, sending heat between my legs.

He watches my reaction, releases my nipple and straightens to kiss me hard, the hand that was just at my breast sliding down over my back to push the bikini bottoms to the floor.

Cupping my ass, he draws back. His pupils are dilated, and his breathing is uneven. I feel him against my stomach, skin cool, cock hard through the still damp swim trunks.

He moves the hand that's got my ass around to my belly and gives me a nudge. It's all it takes for him to have me on my back and he stands over me, spreading my legs with his as he strips off his suit.

I've seen him before. Or more I've felt him. But now to see him like this fully naked in broad daylight, it's different. New. I'm greedy as I search his body, broad shoulders, muscular chest, ink wrapping around powerful arms. He grips his cock and I feel it in my core when he pumps in his hand. He's big. I've felt that already.

He bends, nudging my legs up, opening me to his sight as he sets one knee on the bed while still pumping his cock. And I think I'd like to see him come. I'd like to watch him make himself come.

The thought sends a flush of heat to my cheeks. I glance away before he sees. But then his free hand wraps around my thigh and he's pushing me wide, his cock at my entrance. I'm ready for him. Hungry for him.

I let out a moan when he enters me. It feels good. So good. But I try to cover my mouth, afraid to make too much noise.

"Sound proofed," he says, leaning down to lick my nipple, the one he neglected last time. "You can scream, and no one will hear you."

He looks at me when he says that part and his grin is wolfish. His words have a double meaning. I hear that. But when he draws out fully to thrust into me again, I don't think about them. I don't think about anything. I can't, not when he's moving inside me like this, his weight partially on me, our bodies falling into a rhythm, everything fading but this, him inside me, my legs winding around him as I lift myself toward him for more because I want more. Deeper. Closer.

I want to come.

My arms wrap around his neck.

"Look at me," he says.

It takes me a minute.

"Isabelle."

When he says my name, I do it. I look at him.

"What do you say when you come?" he asks and just as he says it, he slips a hand between us and slides his fingers from my pussy to my other hole. I don't have time to react, don't have time to put up any resistance. When he presses the moistened finger to my ass it only takes once, twice for him to push inside me and then I'm lost. "What do you say?" he asks as he thrusts one more time and I come.

I say it. I say what he wants to hear. His name. Because it's all I can do as I feel him thrust one last time before he stills, pressing deep against me, inside me. The sensation of having him inside me like this, having his weight on me so different than anything I've ever felt. All I can do is cling to him, nails digging into flesh, moans that sound foreign to me coming from my chest, and him so close, so close.

He pulls out slowly when it's over and I come back to reality as I feel his seed slide from inside me. I feel embarrassed as he lays on his side and splays one hand on the flat of my stomach.

I watch him as his gaze moves to my belly and I wonder what he's thinking. Wonder again at the different sides of this man. One brutal, an unforgiving devil. The other this. A gentler beast.

But still a devil.

He must feel me watching him and when he shifts his gaze to mine, I feel my cheeks burn.

"Always say my name when you come. I want to hear it every time. Understand?"

I swallow, nod. What do you say to that?

He gets up, looks at me, then goes into the bathroom. I'm not sure what to do when I hear the water go on but a moment later, he's back with a washcloth. He sits beside me, opens my legs to clean me.

"I can do that," I say quickly, grabbing his hand, embarrassed again.

He moves my hand away and makes a point of opening my legs to look at me. He meets my eyes and watches me as he thoroughly cleans me. I can't look away even though I want to, and I feel my cheeks burn with embarrassment.

"I will take care of you, Isabelle. You're mine," he says when he's finished. "And even if you can't remember what Zeke said to you, remember this. If anyone touches you, I will cut off their hands. That includes him."

He gets up and casually walks back to the bathroom where I hear the shower switch on. I don't hesitate to get up, gather up the scraps of my bikini, grateful for that door between our rooms. I scurry to mine like a little mouse, not sure how to react to him, to how he is, unable to meld the two sides of this man together. The brutality and rage versus the gentle father. The sometimes lover. The man who would cut off his brother's hands should he touch me.

I don't know and the hardest part of all is that I can't make sense of my own feelings. Last night at the cemetery, I hated him. But then when I said what I said, when I saw his face, I don't know what happened. Like my feelings got all twisted up inside. Then him carrying me back, washing me gently, asking me how he can fix the damage he's doing to his daughter? It shifted something inside me and all I'm left with is confusion.

38

JERICHO

I pull through the gates of De La Rosa Manor, Santiago De La Rosa's family home, park my car and walk toward the front door which is already open. A woman is standing just inside.

"Mr. St. James," she says. "Good morning. This way."

I walk in and I take in the place. It's huge and old but very well maintained if a bit dark. I've heard rumors about Santiago De La Rosa though. The dark is on purpose. Or it was for many years. After the explosion that killed his father and brother and ruined his face, he became a sort of recluse. Although he wasn't hiding away licking his wounds. He was, like any good Sovereign Son, plotting his revenge against the Moreno family.

"Elena!" a woman calls out and I see a flash of a little girl running, giggling as the woman comes into view behind her. She doesn't see me. Her attention is on the baby she's carrying in one arm as she chases the runaway who can barely be two.

This must be Ivy Moreno. Ivy De La Rosa now. The face of the vengeance Santiago sought against her family. My mind wanders back to my first meeting with Santiago back at the IVI compound. How I'd wondered about the type of woman who could make a proper husband and father out of a man like Santiago De La Rosa.

"Daddy's working, you naughty girl," she tells the little girl, catching up with her and hugging her.

The child giggles as Ivy nuzzles her neck.

"Daddy has a few minutes," Santiago says, stepping out of the shadows. His eyes are on me as he lifts the toddler in one arm and wraps the other possessively around his wife. He kisses the top of the baby's head and pulls Ivy close.

"I didn't know anyone was here," Ivy says, startled at seeing me.

"You had your hands full," he tells her as I walk toward the family and wonder again at this woman. At how she was able to domesticate a man like him. Because I can see his devotion to her. He didn't give up his vengeance entirely, though. Did she forgive him for what he did?

"Jericho," Santiago says once we're only a few feet away. "Welcome."

I need to find out more about what happened

between the De La Rosa and Moreno families. I want to learn how these two came from hating each other to having a family together. To very clearly loving one another.

I smile to Ivy. "Good morning. I didn't mean to intrude." I didn't. Actually, seeing his family like this has got me off my game. "I'm Jericho St. James," I tell her, extending a hand.

She looks to her husband who watches me but gives her an almost imperceptible nod. She extends her hand, slipping it into mine.

"Ivy De La Rosa. This is Elena and little Santi," she says, and I can hear her love for these children in her voice.

The little girl openly studies me, her eyes just like her father's. There's nothing shy about this child and I get the feeling she has her daddy wrapped around her little finger. It makes me think of my own daughter. How she's so opposite. So quiet and shy. I think about what Isabelle said and wonder if she's shy because she's afraid. If she's afraid because in trying to protect her, I've made her that way.

"Nice to meet all of you," I say, and turn to Santiago. "I realize you're busy, but I'd appreciate a minute of your time."

He nods, turns to his little girl. "Go help your mommy with your brother," he tells her. "And when I'm finished we'll play."

The little girl gives me a look and sighs. "Santi is

no fun. All he does is sleep and poop. Poop and sleep."

Santiago chuckles, crouches to set her down and whispers something in her ear which makes the girl clap her hands in excitement.

"Promise?"

He winks at her. "Promise."

"Okay." She turns to Ivy and takes her hand. "Come on, mommy," she says and leads her away.

Ivy just shrugs a shoulder. "Nice to meet you, Mr. St. James," she says to me and the two disappear down a corridor.

Santiago is studying me when I turn back to him. "Looks like you have your hands full," I tell him.

"In the best way," he says and glances to where his family just disappeared.

"I won't keep you from them for too long."

He nods. "This way." I follow him down a corridor to his office where he closes the door and takes his seat behind the large desk. I note the computer screens in the room, see the flashes of numbers, see him glance at them. I wonder how his brain works. How he makes sense of it all. He's made the members of IVI, my family included, a lot of money over the years. The man is a genius. And a force to be reckoned with.

He gestures to the seat in front of the desk that I take.

"How can I help you?"

I study him as he steeples his fingers, gaze unwavering, the half-skull tattoo as if showcasing the darker, dangerous side of this husband and father. We have that in common, though. I have killed to keep my family safe. He has done the same.

"What is your business with my brother?" I ask outright, deciding straightforward is the way to go with this man.

He grins. He was expecting this. Probably anticipating my visit.

"My business with Ezekiel is my business with Ezekiel. Just as my business with you is my business with you."

"I thought you might say that, but I'm here because I have a feeling that business overlaps."

"As brothers that may always be the case." His gaze doesn't waver.

Mine doesn't either. "Carlton Bishop made a comment that has piqued my curiosity."

"Did he?"

"Well, not so much the comment itself as the way he looked at my brother when he said what he said. It's similar to how you looked at him during our meeting at the compound. When you mentioned my father's accident."

"Hmm."

"Except that Bishop went a little farther to give the impression that his death and my sister's death were somehow related."

Santiago leans back in his seat, and it takes him a moment to answer. I can tell he's trying to decide something in that moment. "They died years apart."

"That doesn't mean anything."

He glances down, forehead furrowing, jaw tightening. He looks at me again, leans his elbows on the desk. "Leave it, Jericho," he says, tone different.

My jaw tenses, my throat tightening. "Leave what?"

"I won't tell you my business with your brother."

"And yet clearly that business has something to do with me."

"But I will give you some advice," he adds, ignoring me.

"It's not advice I want. It's the truth."

"I don't believe Ezekiel has lied to you."

"He hasn't told me the whole truth though, has he?"

Santiago stands up, walks to the window, and pushes the curtain aside to look out. Over his shoulder I can see his family outside. Ivy pushing the little girl in a swing while the baby sleeps in the stroller at her side.

He turns back to me. "I'm going to give you that advice anyway. Leave it alone. It has nothing to do with Carlton Bishop. With what he did to you or to the mother of your child. If it did, I would tell you."

"Are they related?" I start, I don't know why because something is telling me to heed his advice.

To leave it alone. Let the dead lie. "My sister's death." Her suicide. I can't quite bring myself to say the word though. "My father's."

He doesn't answer me. Just studies me for a very long time. Too long. "Your brother is not your enemy. That's all I can tell you. Now, if you don't mind, I made my daughter a promise and I don't break promises."

I get to my feet his words cutting in a way I know he had no intention to cut. I think about Angelique. About her falling asleep on the floor while waiting for me to keep my promise. I have to shove that image aside though. So, I remind myself of Isabelle's words telling me to fix it, to choose. I choose my family. This is all about my family. Always has been.

But I've been focused on Angelique, on Kimberly's murder, on vengeance for so long that I've neglected the rest of the family. Has my brother come to terms with his twin's suicide? What kind of life has he lived all these years?

"Will you be at the auction?" Santiago asks me, bringing me back to the present.

The auction. It's set to take place in a few weeks at IVI. I have my eye on something that will be auctioned off. "Yes," I tell him.

"You'll bring your wife?"

I nod.

"Introduce her to Ivy. I think they may have a thing or two in common."

I nod, my mind still wrapped up in my reason for coming here. In what Santiago didn't say and what that tells me. It was my own question that triggered it. If my sister's and my father's deaths are related. Zeke knows something I don't. And whether or not it has to do with Carlton Bishop, I mean to find out what it is.

39

ISABELLE

Jericho is gone a lot over the next several weeks and when he's home, he's distant. Something is going on between him and his brother and whatever it is has them both in a foul mood.

I spend my days with Angelique and my nights in his bed. That's one area he's consistent, his appetite never waning. And something is growing between us. At least in those moments. A strange connection. But maybe I'm reading too much into it. I mean, it's sex. And although I sleep better in his arms than I have on my own in three years, I need to remember that.

Just sex. That's it. No matter how good it feels when he holds me after.

I talk to Julia regularly now although I haven't seen her since our brief visit at the compound. I wonder how things are at the house. How Carlton is. How he is with her. I've never really understood their relationship. She moved into the Bishop house before I did. Monique, his wife, left soon after that although she has returned to attend certain IVI events. I know he still pays her monthly living allowance and in the arguments I've overheard, I wonder if that allowance is contingent on her showing up. On them giving the impression they're still together.

I was surprised at the extent of Monique's dislike of Julia and even Matty. Who can dislike a child? I wonder, though, if it's envy more than anything else. Monique and Carlton don't have children.

But if what Julia said is true of the inheritance, I wonder why Carlton keeps up appearances as far as his marriage goes. They don't love each other. That's obvious. So why not divorce her and find someone else? And have children to ensure the inheritance remains his? Although I guess he's tried. Monique is not his first wife.

I'm just considering this when my phone rings. It's Julia.

I slip into my bathroom to answer even though I'm feeling relaxed about taking the call since Jericho is out of the house. But I won't take a chance I'm wrong because I'm pretty sure if he finds the phone, he'll take it from me and punish me for having had it in the first place.

"I have a very interesting story about your husband and his brother," Julia says, sounding excited. Ever since I told her about Jericho threatening to cut off the hands of any man who touched me, including his brother, she's been like a dog with a bone.

"What is it?" I ask.

"I managed to get hold of a woman who used to work at the St. James house. Rose Smithson."

"Okay. I don't know the name."

"No, you wouldn't. She was let go years ago. About six years ago. Less than that. She and almost the whole of the household except for a woman named Catherine."

"I know Catherine. She's in charge of things and I get the feeling she's been around since Jericho was little."

"Yep, that's right."

"So, what happened that the whole household was let go?"

I can almost hear her grin when she next speaks. "Well, there was a scandal involving the brothers and a certain woman."

"Kimberly?"

"That's the one."

"What happened?"

"Did you know Kimberly and Ezekiel were a couple? They apparently met at some event he was attending and she was working."

"Working?"

"As a waitress. It was a work event so nothing at IVI. They dated for a few months, and he brought her home to meet his family and I guess things went a little sideways then." She sounds almost gleeful.

"You mean she met Jericho and the two of them..."

"Ended up in bed together."

"What? While she was with his brother?"

"That's when Leontine started to let some of the staff go although Rose wasn't one of them. She stayed on until Kimberly started to show."

"Wait. Back up. So, Ezekiel and Kimberly were dating, and Jericho stole her from him and got her pregnant?"

"That's what I'm hearing."

"And Leontine fired the staff to cover it up?"

"She sounds like a witch."

"She's not though. Not as far as I can tell. But that was years ago and maybe she's changed. I know she's been sick."

"Breast cancer. It was touch and go for a while from what Carlton told me, but she is in remission."

"I guess something like that will change a person," I say.

"Back to the juicy stuff though. So once Kimberly got pregnant, Jericho proposed marriage. I guess he's old-fashioned that way."

I can almost see her rolling her eyes.

"And according to Rose anytime the brothers were in the same room for a while there it felt like a bomb went off. They'd fight, I'm talking physically fight. Ezekiel was in bad shape according to Rose and I'm honestly not sure if Leontine even liked Kimberly. Probably thought her beneath them. And when she came between the brothers, well that was that."

"That's a lot to take in. And you're sure she's telling you the truth?"

"I mean, it's not like I can fact check her."

"How did you find her?"

"That wasn't hard. It was finding one who'd talk to me, and she was it. The others have been hush-hush. Rose, though, answered to cash. She also hates Leontine so maybe this was her version of payback."

"Why does she hate Leontine?"

"Said she was a bitch to her."

I feel the beginnings of a headache coming on and press my hand to my forehead.

"Listen, I have to run," Julia says and honestly, I'm grateful. "I'm getting Matty before dinner and we're going to the toy store for his birthday. Carlton's letting him pick out his own gift."

"Carlton's going to a toy store?"

"I know. Shocker. But if he's buying, I'm in."

Julia hasn't worked since she moved into the Bishop house. She's told me how much she hates having to depend on others to pay her way but hasn't done much about it. Although with a four-year-old, I'm not sure how much you can do.

"Well, have fun. And thanks for the gossip I guess."

"Are you doing okay?"

"I'm fine. Settling in."

"You're not pregnant or anything are you?" she asks, her tone worried.

"No. I'm still taking my pills. I won't get pregnant. I don't think it's what he wants, Julia. I'm pretty sure he'd have taken the pills away if it was. He controls everything."

"I hope you're right," she says. "I'll talk to you soon, okay?"

"Tell Matty to pick something expensive," I say. "And tell him happy birthday from me." I hate that I'll miss his birthday. It'll be the first time since I moved into the Bishop house.

We hang up and I tuck the phone back into its hiding place behind my bed. I then walk out into the hallway where from the landing, I see Zeke with Angelique. They're talking animatedly and I watch them together. He's sweet with her. He loves her, it's obvious. And she loves him.

A moment later he turns his gaze up to meet mine and I'm startled at being caught.

"Belle," Angelique says, following her uncle's line of vision. "Uncle Zeke just took me on an adventure. Look what I collected!" she holds up a bunch of yellow flowers. The same ones I'd used to decorate Nellie Bishop's grave.

I clear my throat and walk downstairs, hoping the heat I feel in my cheeks isn't obvious to them. I wonder if he knew I was up there all along.

"They're so beautiful," I tell her.

"They don't really smell but I like them. I'll take you to get some if you want."

"Remember what we agreed, Angelique. You're only to go into the woods with your father or me."

"But Belle is a grownup Uncle Zeke."

"Isabelle doesn't know the woods like we do."

Angelique looks over at me and I meet Ezekiel's eyes and nod. "He's right. I would hate for us to get lost."

"There you are," comes Leontine's voice from around the corner. "Nina's here. She'll have dinner with us tonight. What do you think about that?"

"Oh! I bet she'll like these too. I'll give her some," Angelique says and takes her grandmother's hand.

Leontine studies us for a moment. "You two coming?"

When I turn to Ezekiel, he's watching me. "In a minute," he says, reading my mind.

"A minute," Leontine says and walks away. I wonder if she's closer to one brother over the other. I wonder what she thought of Jericho stealing Kimberly away from Ezekiel.

"Can I ask you a question?" I ask before I lose my nerve.

"Has your husband given you permission to talk to me?" I'm caught off guard by his question but a moment later, he grins. "All the better if he hasn't," he says and opens his office door to invite me in.

40

ISABELLE

I haven't been inside this office since that first night. I stand just inside the door and look around at the space. It's different now with the waning evening light.

Ezekiel takes his seat behind the desk and watches me as I make my way to a chair in front of his desk. He leans forward, setting his elbows on the desk and steepling his fingers.

"Why did you say what you said the other day?"

He raises his eyebrows and I wonder if he's forgotten.

"That if he hurts me, I can come to you."

He shrugs his shoulders and leans back in his seat. "You looked like you might need a friend."

I study him, try to figure out the dynamic between him and his brother. Try to figure out if he's playing me. Using me somehow.

"Is it true you were with Kimberly before Jericho was?" I blurt out.

"Where did you hear that?"

I shrug my shoulder and wait for him to answer.

He grins, gets up and comes to the front of his desk. He leans against it, looking down at me. This is when I see the true similarity of the brothers. They have some physical things in common, yes, but it's not so much that as their presence. All alpha male and power.

"What if I told you we shared her for a time."

It takes me a minute to follow but when I do, I feel my throat go dry.

"She was with both of us," he clarifies.

I'm not sure what I look like but the expression on my face makes his grin widen.

"Not what you expected to hear?"

"I..."

"Don't worry, I don't think it's his intention to share you."

I start to get up, but he shakes his head.

"Sit back down."

"I should go."

"Sit." He walks to a side table and pours himself a drink. "Would you like something?" When I don't answer, he decides for me and brings me a glass of whiskey. "You may need this considering the evening ahead of you."

"What does that mean?" I ask and take the glass

although the scent of it turns my stomach and I set it aside. I've been nauseous easily lately. Anxiety.

"Tonight is the auction."

I nod.

"Well, I don't want to spoil my brother's surprise."

I'm confused by this, but I'm still stuck on the other thing. "You shared her?"

"I know it's unconventional, but many people do it, Isabelle. You've lived a sheltered existence if this is the first you're hearing about this sort of arrangement. We'd shared women before Kimberly. But this was the first time one of us fell in love. Well two of them fell in love."

Love. Jericho loved her. Of course, he did. It's what this is all about.

"I bowed out at that point. The relationship was no longer appropriate."

"The three of you?"

He nods and there's something in his eyes that makes me pause. Had he loved her too?

"Do you blame him? For her death I mean?"

"Her murder."

"Her murder," I repeat uneasily.

"You're a curious thing, aren't you?"

"I just want to understand."

"What would understanding this do?"

"I don't know. What I do know is that your brother is keeping me here like a prisoner. I'm not allowed to leave. Not allowed to have a phone." It's true technically. "Not allowed anything."

"If you could leave, where would you go?"

"Home."

"The Bishop house?"

"I guess so."

He tilts his head to the side, studies me. "Are you sure you're welcome there?"

"What do you mean?"

He smiles, shakes his head. "And a phone." He gestures to his cell phone on the desk. "Would you like to make a call?"

"That's not... You know he's restricting me."

"And you're here now because of what I said. You've come to me for protection."

I study him now. Wonder at the game he's playing. Wonder if I've made a mistake.

"Have you considered he's protecting you?" he asks.

"From what? He's the one I need protecting from."

"I've seen how he is with you. I'm not sure if what you're saying is correct. Jericho can be harsh but he's loyal."

"He's unpredictable."

"That too, but like I said, he is loyal. And he knows more about you than you realize."

"What do you mean?"

"Just that you may be better off here in this house than your half-brother's."

"I don't understand. Why wouldn't I be safe at my brother's house? That doesn't make any sense."

He folds his arms across his chest. "He loved her very much, you know."

I'm taken aback at this change and hearing him say the words somehow makes my stomach hurt even though I already knew it. Jericho loved Kimberly.

"Back to your earlier question. No one needs to blame him for her death. He does that all on his own."

"Carlton didn't kill her. He's not capable—"

"You don't know what your brother is capable of, Isabelle, and you being here, under our roof, it may be keeping you safer than you realize."

"Your mother said something similar the night before the wedding. She said Jericho would protect me, and that I needed protecting. I'm sure you understand why I wouldn't believe either of you though."

"We're not lying to you."

"Well, you're not telling me the whole truth either, are you?"

"Why are you here, Isabelle? Why have you come to me? You are my brother's wife, not mine."

"You said—"

"I said you could come to me if he hurts you. I didn't say I'd gossip with you."

"I'm not gossiping."

"You should talk to Jericho. Ask him your questions."

"Jericho hates me."

"He may want to hate you, but he doesn't."

I'm confused by this but before I can think what to say, there's a knock and the door opens. It's Leontine. "Dinner's ready. The girls are waiting."

"We certainly don't want that," Ezekiel says and gestures for me to get up, our conversation over.

41

JERICHO

I sabelle's room is empty when I go to get her but when I hear a giggle from down the hall, I find her in my daughter's room dressed in an indigo gown, hair twisted intricately on top of her head, her back fully exposed. Angelique is standing behind her, attention captured wholly by the dragon tattoo she's tracing with her finger.

"It's like daddy's but smaller," she says.

Neither of them has heard me and I stand in the shadow of the door watching.

"Can I have one too?" Angelique asks.

Isabelle closes the book on her lap and draws Angelique around. "If you want one when you're older, that'll be up to you, but you're too young now. Besides, what would happen to it when you grow taller?"

"It would get all weird and stretched out," Angelique says making claws out of her hands.

Isabelle mimics her and they cuddle. My mother has told me about the two growing closer and about Angelique's reliance on Isabelle. Her affection for her. I'm not sure what I think about it, so I stand here and watch them together. Isabelle clearly cares for Angelique and it seems mutual.

"You look very pretty, Belle."

Belle. She thinks Isabelle is one of her princesses. It grates on my nerves although I shouldn't mind. Angelique comes alive around Isabelle in a way she doesn't around anyone else. Her little fingers play over one of the twists of Isabelle's hair.

"Thank you," Isabelle says.

"Is your tummy better? You didn't eat very much at dinner. Nana says you need to eat more."

"I wasn't too hungry," Isabelle says. She reaches for something on the nightstand. When I realize what it is, something I hadn't realized had been unpacked since we moved into the house, I tense up.

"Is this your mother?" Isabelle asks.

Angelique nods. "It's what Nana tells me, but I don't remember her."

Something twists inside me.

"She was very pretty," Isabelle says. "You look like her, you know that?"

Angelique shrugs a shoulder, not interested in the photo. "I want to look like you," she says.

"What?" Isabelle asks.

"You're my mommy now, so I want to look like you."

"Angelique, I—"

"You're married to my daddy. It makes you my mommy, Belle."

I push the door open too hard and it bounces off the wall, startling them both. Isabelle's eyes meet mine and the book on her lap slips to the floor as she stands.

"Oh no!" Angelique cries out and drops to her knees.

Isabelle and I remain staring at one another a moment longer before she, too, is on her knees. It's one of Angelique's many princess books and the pop-up castle has been bent.

I walk inside, take the book from them. The two get up.

"It's broken!" Angelique says.

"I'm so sorry," Isabelle tells her.

Angelique gives me an angry look but takes Isabelle's hand sweetly. "It's not your fault," she says, and turns back to me.

It's my fault then. My daughter has just chosen the side of the enemy over her own flesh and blood.

"I think we can fix it," Isabelle says. "Look, it's just bent. Should we try?"

"I'll get you a new one," I say, feeling strangely defensive and on the outside.

"I don't want a new one. I want mine," she says. This fight is with me, and I get the feeling she's expressing feelings she has subconsciously been holding back.

"Shouldn't you be in bed?" I ask her sharply, too sharply. She's in her pajamas and it's almost nine o'clock.

"That was my fault," Isabelle says when Angelique presses against her leg, both hands around one of Isabelle's now. "I wanted to kiss her goodnight and I woke her up by accident."

I look from my daughter to this invader in my house.

"Everything all right?" We all turn to find my brother standing at the door.

"Fine," I say. Taking Isabelle by the arm, I walk her to the door. "See that Isabelle waits downstairs while I tuck my daughter in."

Isabelle looks at me like she wants to tell me to fuck off but holds her tongue and it's a good thing she does.

"Isabelle?" Zeke says.

"We can fix the book together tomorrow. If your daddy lets us, that is. Goodnight, sweetheart," Isabelle says before spinning on her heel and walking out of the door right past my brother.

My hands fist, my jaw tenses.

"Why don't I tuck Angelique in. I'm overdue reading her a bedtime story anyway," Zeke says.

I nod, bend down to kiss Angelique on top of her head, but she doesn't wrap her arms around my neck like she usually does. Instead, she folds them across her chest and makes a point of turning away, letting me know she's angry.

"Go. You're already late," my brother says.

I gently lift my daughter's chin up. "We'll fix it tomorrow."

She glares at me and I don't know what else to do but leave. But the moment I'm out of her bedroom, anger returns.

I find Isabelle downstairs by the door, arms folded across her chest looking as petulant as Angelique.

"She's five. You're nineteen," I tell her as I take the light wool cloak off the rack and drape it over her shoulders. "Don't pout."

"I'm not pouting. You were a jerk. Did you apologize to her?"

"Apologize for what?"

"For scaring the crap out of us when you barged in like that!"

"Why didn't you eat dinner?"

She rolls her eyes. "How long were you standing there anyway?"

"You mean was I there long enough to hear you

ask about her mother? To hear my daughter ask if you're her mommy?"

I don't realize I've walked her backwards until her back is pressed to the wall and I'm looming over her.

"I never assumed anything like that," she says.

"Yeah? You've been playing house though. Getting comfortable. Too comfortable." I lay a hand against the wall and lean into her. "You forget your place. And I've let you. We'll fix that tonight."

I take her by the arm and walk her out the door and to the back seat of the waiting Rolls Royce. She scoots to the far side as soon as I let her go, folding her arms across her chest and watching out the window as Dex drives toward the compound.

I will teach her tonight. Just like I had planned. Because I have been too soft on her.

42

ISABELLE

The auction is well attended and by the time we arrive, the baroque ballroom is full of elegantly dressed men and women drinking champagne from crystal flutes. Jericho slips the cloak from my shoulders and hands it to the woman checking coats. He pockets the ticket she gives him and sets his hand at my lower back to walk me into the crowd where heads are already turning.

I know why he chose this dress for me. Why he required my hair to be done up, my back fully exposed. I hear it in the gasps and the chatter as we walk past the other guests, and I feel myself shrink a little.

I am a thing. His thing.

That's what Jericho is proving tonight. I guess this is his punishment. Him teaching me my place. Asshole.

"Is this what you wanted? To show them all that you own me?" I ask him as he takes two flutes of champagne and holds one out to me. I'm tempted to throw it in his face but I'm not stupid.

He smiles down to me. No, it's not quite a smile. It's more of a predator's leering grin just before the animal goes in for the kill.

"I don't care about them. I only care that you know who owns you. And I can promise you one thing. You will know without a doubt before the night is out."

"Jericho," comes a voice from behind me.

I stiffen, recognizing it, and turn to find the man with the skull tattooed on half his face standing there with a woman. A beautiful woman with a friendly smile.

Jericho puts a possessive hand around the back of my neck.

"Santiago. Ivy."

Santiago smiles but Ivy's is the one that warms up the room. "Hi," she starts, extending her hand. "I'm Ivy De La Rosa. You met my husband, but I haven't had the pleasure yet."

I take her hand and feel her give me a squeeze. The gesture is conscious, a message of sorts. And I don't want to let go.

"I'm Isabelle Bishop—"

"St. James," Jericho corrects.

We both glance at him and I clear my throat and turn back to Ivy. "It's nice to meet you, Ivy."

A waiter appears with a tray, but Ivy shakes her head. "I'm going to go get some juice," she tells Santiago, keeping hold of my hand when she does.

"Me too," I say, setting my still-full glass on the tray and slipping out of reach of Jericho. "The thought of alcohol turns my stomach," I say, looking back at my husband. "Like so many things seem to tonight."

Jericho's eyes narrow but I hear Santiago chuckle as we walk away. "The tattoo looks beautiful. Perhaps I will extend Ivy's," he says. I don't hear Jericho's response.

"Men," Ivy says with a roll of her eyes although I see her affection for her husband in the quick glance she throws over her shoulder before she turns her full attention to me. "I'm still breastfeeding so I can't have champagne," she says. "It's too bad. I swear these Society events are much easier to bear when I can have a drink or two."

"How long have you been married?" I ask. Ivy is a beautiful, confident woman and I'd guess just a few years older than me. It's strange, maybe it's that we're so close in age that I feel how opposite we are. How my confidence has waned, how I seem to be in survival mode. That isn't since Jericho St. James though. This has been going on since Christian's death.

"About three years now. I met him much the same way you met Jericho," she says once we reach the bar. "Orange juice please," she orders and turns to me. "Same?"

"Yes, please."

She holds up two fingers and the bartender hurries to fill her order, serving us orange juice in the fanciest glasses I've ever seen it served in. We weave through the crowd to a quiet corner where we sit on a deep burgundy velvet couch that is as stiff and uncomfortable as it is beautiful.

"What did you mean? That you met your husband the same way I met Jericho?" I'm not sure who knows what about our situation.

"I mean Santiago took me to punish my father."

"Your father?"

She nods. "He thought my father had done something to his family, but he was wrong." Her expression darkens and I see her force a smile back on. "But the reason I told you is I know how it feels in the beginning and I want you to know you're not alone. You can always talk to me."

"He thinks my brother..." I can't bring myself to say the words. "He thinks Carlton did something that I don't think he could have done. The Bishops and the St. James's have a terrible history. A bloody one. And although Carlton isn't an angel, I just don't think he's capable of what Jericho is accusing him of. And I feel so out of my element. I don't know how to handle this." All of this comes pouring out of me possibly surprising me more than it does Ivy.

"Well, from the way he's watching you I'd guess you're doing something right."

I look up to find Jericho's eyes on me from across the room. "I think he just wants to make sure I don't run off," I say with a shrug and a smile wishing I had a strong drink now as I sip the juice.

"I don't think so. The mark, can I see it?"

I turn just enough so she can have a look.

"Oh, it is gorgeous," she says, tracing the outline of it. "Santiago designed it. Jericho asked him to make sure your scar was covered."

I look at her. "That's what his brother said too. I guess he finds it ugly. I have another one," I touch my collarbone. "I wonder if he'll tattoo me there too. Cover me with ink to hide the ugliness."

"I don't think it's about ugly or beautiful," Ivy says. "From what Santiago told me he wanted to erase it. Put his mark over top of it. Maybe erase the memory of it? I don't know. Santiago wouldn't say exactly."

"Erase the memory? My memory you mean?"

She nods. "That's the impression I had. He said it was an ugly night that shouldn't have happened at all."

"It's the night my brother was killed." I wonder how much Jericho knows about that. Why he cares.

She puts her hand over mine and squeezes.

"Then I understand why Jericho would want you to forget it."

This is a whole other side I haven't yet heard. I've never considered. Did he really make the tattoo what it is to help me forget what happened? No. No way.

The gong sounds then and Ivy and I both look toward the sound. People begin to move toward the chairs set up at the opposite end of the room and I see Jericho and Santiago approach.

"Here we go," Ivy says and stands, keeping my hand in hers. "Remember, if you need anything just call me. Here," she says, slipping a piece of paper and a pen out of her clutch. She scribbles her phone number down and squeezes it into my palm. "That's my cell phone but you can always call the house too."

"Thank you, Ivy. Really."

"Of course," she says and gives me a quick hug before Santiago takes her hand, nods a farewell to me and leads her away.

"How was your tête-à-tête?" Jericho asks as he wraps a possessive hand around the nape of my neck again.

"Much more interesting than any conversation I've had with you," I tell him.

He smiles, gives a squeeze of his hand. "Oh, sweetheart, you are so earning your evening."

I don't get a chance to ask what he means as he

leads us through the crowd to the very front of the room where our seats are located. I'm surprised. He's not one to seek out attention. He's more like the cat who watches from the tree unseen but seeing everything. Waiting to pounce.

It takes a few minutes before everyone is seated and after a welcome and a mention of the charity for which funds will be raised tonight, the auction begins.

A painting opens the auction. It's a beautiful, gold framed landscape from a Dutch artist painted three centuries ago and the amount of money the auctioneer names to start the bidding has me choking.

Jericho doesn't bid on this item. He flips through the booklet instead as the first, second, third and fourth items are set on the stage and taken off the stage once sold.

"Ah," he finally says, sitting back and setting one hand on my knee. He leans toward me as two men carry in whatever is hidden beneath the red velvet blanket. It's clearly heavy. "This one's the one I'm after. It's actually a gift for you."

I only have time to glance at him before the item is placed and the blanket covering it tugged off. And I swear everyone in the room must hear my gasp.

Because there on the stage in the front of the room is a pillory much like the one used during the marking ceremony.

43

JERICHO

I sabelle doesn't speak another word until we're in the car later that evening. I watch her, feeling smug. When we get to the house, she tries to slip free, but I hold on to her wrist.

"Let go. I'm hungry and I'm tired," she says.

I remember what Angelique had asked. If she was feeling better. "Didn't you eat dinner?"

"I didn't feel good so no, not really."

"I'll make you a sandwich." I walk her to the kitchen.

"I can make my own sandwich. You can go to bed or play with your new toy or whatever. Just leave me alone."

"Yeah, no." I switch on the kitchen light and pull out a chair at the counter. "That new toy is *our* toy," I tell her with a wink. "Sit."

"Why would you buy that thing?" she asks as I

gather bread and cheese from the refrigerator. I look at the cold cuts but remember she's a vegetarian.

"I liked how you looked in it," I tell her, returning to the counter and getting a plate.

"I didn't like how I felt in it."

"It'll be different. Just me. No audience." I unwrap one of the cheeses and she makes a face.

"Not that one." She pinches her nose dramatically. "I feel sick at the smell of it."

I study her, smell the cheese which is as neutral as possible. "It smells fine."

"Just butter. Okay? Just butter is fine."

I put the cheese away and butter a thick slice of bread. Once I place it in front of her, she reaches for the saltshaker and sprinkles some on then picks it up and bites into it.

"That's not enough if you're hungry. You need a protein."

She raises her eyebrows as she takes a second bite. "You're concerned about my protein intake?"

"What did you eat today?"

"This. Some juice. An apple."

"That's all?"

"I told you I didn't feel well. Why do you care? Are you upset I'm spoiling your night? You won't be able to lock me in your medieval torture device?"

I butter another two slices as she crams the last piece into her mouth. She doesn't hesitate but picks up a second piece, salts it and starts eating. I get her a glass of orange juice and watch her, thinking. She's been here about two months give or take.

"I talked to your brother today," she says, interrupting my thoughts.

I feel myself tense. She cocks her head and I notice how the pulse at her throat beats wildly. I narrow my gaze and understand why as soon as she speaks again.

"He told me the three of you were an item."

"Pardon?"

She puts her slice of bread down. "You, Ezekiel and Angelique's mom. You were together."

Ah. The silence drags on while she chews, eyes on me. Waiting for my reaction. "Just eat, Isabelle."

Her eyes narrow like she's concentrating. "Is it true?"

"Eat so I can take you out to the pillory."

"I don't want—"

"It doesn't matter what you want. It's what I want. Eat."

Her eyes search mine and she takes a bite then wipes her hands, leaving the final slice untouched. I see the peaks of her nipples pressing against her dress. Notice the flush in her cheeks. It's not the reaction I expected.

"Finished?" I ask.

She nods.

"Let's go then." I gesture to the door.

I don't know if I expect her to run but she

doesn't. Instead, she slips off the stool and walks toward the door. I open it and she steps out and, without speaking, we walk toward the cemetery, the chapel. Her steps slow when I open the gate for her to walk through. I take her hand to lead her around the back of the building because the chapel isn't where I want to be tonight.

She hesitates. It's darker back here, the trees denser.

"Come," I tell her. Not that she has a choice. I unlatch the heavy wooden door around the back of the building and pull it open. Candles are already lit inside, a hundred of them, the scent that of melting wax and abandonment.

"What is this?" she asks, stepping back to me, her eyes landing on the reason I brought her.

I rub my hands over her arms, keep her back against my chest. "Back in the days mass was said here it was the room the priests used to dress. That door connects it to the chapel." I point to the short, narrow door.

At one wall is a leather couch. It's been here since I can remember and the leather is worn, faded. Two large trunks, one containing the moth-eaten ceremonial robes the priests would wear, the other the items I need for tonight. The floor is stone and although it's been swept it's nowhere near clean. The ceiling is high, as high as the chapel ceiling but there is no dirt hill beneath this room. No one is buried underneath. Not that I know of at least. There is a single small window that's boarded from the outside. If it weren't for the candles, the room would be pitch black. Those candles stand on the floor along the walls, in small alcoves carved out as shelves, all around us.

And deeper in the room is the reason she's here. The pillory I purchased tonight stands as the center-piece. It's covered by the red velvet cloth. Dex and the two men who carried it onto the auction floor brought it here and put it in place while the auction went on. It stands open now ready to receive my bride.

"Jericho?" Isabelle asks, turning in my arms to face me.

I look down at her, tug the cloak off her shoulders and let it drop to the dirty floor. Her dress is next. It's easy to strip it off her, unzipping the short zipper at her back, a tug severing the cord holding the wide shoulders together, the silk sliding smoothly down her thighs so she's standing in heels and panties. No bra.

"I want to go back," she says when I take her wrists and walk her backwards.

"We'll go back once we're finished." I bend my head down, draw her closer and kiss her. It's a different kiss than usual. Softer. More sensual. I feel her body relax as our kiss deepens. Hear her quiet moan. I take her lower lip between mine, biting softly before releasing it and dragging the scruff of my jaw across her cheek until my mouth is next to her ear. I tug the cloth off the pillory.

"Are you ready?" I ask her.

She glances at it, shudders, turns back to me.

"Just you and me, Isabelle."

Her throat works as she swallows and she gives a small nod.

I raise her arms and turn her to face the pillory, lean her toward it, bending her because this isn't the exact pillory used during the marking. It's similar but not the same. This one is set on a post and positioned so whoever it holds must bend at the hips. And it's not as old as it's made to look.

I bend her over, setting her wrists in their places, her pretty little neck in its center. I draw back and look at her. Think how perfect she is.

"You're beautiful," I tell her, tracing the ink that glows black in the candlelight.

I heave the heavy top piece in place, securing it and bend to kiss her shoulder. If I were cruel, I'd let her carry the full weight of it, but I'm not that cruel. She'll feel the wood restraining her, feel her submission, but it won't weigh more heavily than necessary.

I step back, listen to the sound of candle flames, to the sound of her breathing. I'm hard. With one hand I draw her panties over her hips and let them drop to the floor. She flexes her hands and I look across to the gold-plated antique mirror set against the wall just across from her. Our eyes meet and hold. I want to have her, to take her now, but we need to settle something between us.

I walk around her once, push a stray hair from her face as she looks up at me through thick lashes. When I'm behind her again I nudge her legs wide and press a hand to her lower back, so she's arched and open for me. Obscenely spread for me. And as I have before I think about how she has this power to make me want. She's no different than many others. She's beautiful but so are others. But it's her I want. This Bishop girl. And I can't understand that.

She watches me in the mirror as I roll up the sleeves of my shirt. She licks her lips, shifting on her feet as a line of arousal slides down the inside of one thigh.

But we aren't just fucking tonight. That's not why I brought her here.

I walk over to the trunk and open it. From inside I take out the black cloak and drape it across my shoulders, closing the clasp, letting the hood hang down my back.

"Jericho?"

I take the mask out next. It's a copy of the one I wore that first night in the chapel, horns and all. I slip it over my face and watch her eyes track me as I return to her.

"You're scaring me," she says when I step behind her.

I place my hands on her ass, spread her open. I close my thumb over her asshole.

"You know if my brother and I wore mask and cloak I doubt you'd be able to tell us apart. His back is inked same as me. Did you know that?"

She shakes her head as I slide one hand to her clit and rub, pushing two fingers into her before dragging that moisture up to her other hole.

"I would know the difference," she says, testing the strength of the lock holding the heavy wooden bar in place. "I would."

"I wonder."

"Are you going to share me?"

I stop, my body tensing.

"Is that why he told me?"

I watch her face as I push my finger into her ass. See her manage a sudden panic.

"Did he touch you?" I ask.

She shakes her head.

"Good. Then I won't have to cut off his hands." I shift my attention to her ass. "Do you remember what I told you the night I brought you up from the cellar?"

She exhales, her muscles tensing around the intrusion, eyes wide in the mirror.

"About Kimberly. Do you remember?" I ask, sliding my finger in and out. I undo my belt and pants and push my cock into her pussy.

She moans, arching her back.

I smile, pull my finger out of her ass, and slap her hip with the flat of my hand.

She gasps and I have her attention again.

"Focus. Do you remember?"

She nods, licks her lips. "You said not to mention her. Ever. You said... you said..."

"And yet you disrespect her memory." I slap her ass again.

"I didn't!"

I draw her cheeks apart, watch her pussy spread to take me.

Her eyes glaze over but after two more thrusts when my shaft is coated in her juices, I draw out and meet her eyes in the reflection of the mirror as I bring my cock to her ass.

"Oh..." She shakes her head, understanding what's going to happen. "Please... Not there."

"I'm going to make sure you come. And you'll come hard. But first, a little punishment. Because what else did I tell you? What did I say about my brother?"

I push against her tight hole, and she squeezes her eyes shut panting, muscles tensing to keep me out.

"This is happening. It'll be easier for you if you don't resist," I tell her.

"Please, Jericho. What do you want?"

"Isn't it obvious? I want your ass."

"No. I mean...please."

"What did I say about my brother?" I ask as she whimpers when her tight opening stretches enough to take the head of my cock.

"To stay away," she says, her voice barely a whisper. "It hurts. Please, it hurts."

"And you're zero for two. You're not a very good listener, are you?"

She shakes her head as I grip her hips, sliding one hand down to her clit to rub, pushing deeper into her tight passage. She closes her eyes, her mouth falling open, strands of hair sticking to the sweat on her forehead.

"I'll listen," she says as I rub her wet clit. "I'll do better."

"I know you will," I tell her. "Because having your ass fucked for punishment is very different to having it fucked for pleasure," I tell her, moving slowly to seat myself fully inside her. I don't want to hurt her. Just warn her. I hold still and rub her clit and watch her face as her body stretches and she stops resisting. "Good, Isabelle. That's good. Now look at me," I say, leaning over her to kiss the spot between her shoulder blades.

She nods, looks up to meet my gaze in the mirror.

"Does that feel good?"

She blinks, nods.

"Do you want me to fuck your ass as punishment or do you want me to fuck your ass for pleasure?"

"Pleasure," she pants as I begin to move inside her.

"Like this?"

She nods. "Yes. Yes. Like that. Please."

I smile. "Good girl. This doesn't have to be bad for you."

She nods but I'm not sure she's following because she's arching her back, pussy dripping. "Are you going to do better?"

"Yes."

"You'll say anything to come now, won't you?"

She nods wanting to please. Wanting to come.

I chuckle.

"Tell me how much you love my cock inside you."

"I love... I love you..." She stops, shakes her head. "I love your..."

Her words have me stop mid-thrust but when I look at her face in the mirror, she's not looking at me. She's lost.

She didn't mean what she said. She was repeating what I told her. That's all. Just distracted by sensation.

I look down at her, at my cock inside her, at her stretched to take me and when I move again, she moans, bringing her legs together and dropping her head as her walls pulse around me.

She comes and when she does, I thrust like I want to. Like I need to. Digging my fingers into her hips to keep her upright when her knees buckle. She pants, calling out my name over and over again, no need to ask her to do it. Her ass is tight around me, and she stumbles from orgasm to orgasm until she's begging me to stop. Until she can't take anymore. And only then do I let myself truly take her. Only then do I give in to my baser instincts and fuck her hard and deep and draw one last screaming orgasm from her.

I empty inside her, filling her, knowing even if she did mean those words, she will hate me soon. In just a matter of days when she learns what I've done, she will hate me.

44

JERICHO

I step off the elevator of 2500 St. Charles Ave. to the surprised sound of a gasp from the elderly receptionist.

"Good morning, Nora," I say. She's been here since I was a kid.

"Jericho... Mr. St. James. We... Your brother didn't mention—"

"Is he in his office?" I only pause briefly as I glance down the hall to the corner office Zeke claimed when I left.

"Yes, sir. I believe he's..." She clears her throat. "Meeting with his secretary but I can call him."

I smile. I can imagine what that meeting entails. "That's all right," I say, heading down the hall toward Zeke's office.

The building has been in our family for the last thirty years. A newer acquisition. From this floor

Zeke runs the investment firm. If I hadn't left, I'd be running things, but he's better suited for this job and I'm happy to have him handle it.

I reach the heavy oak door and don't bother with a courtesy knock. Instead, I open it and enter.

"Brother," I say.

Zeke glances up from the task at hand. He must be administering some form of discipline to his secretary who is bent over his desk, skirt raised, panties down around her knees. I hear the whoosh of the cane and she gasps just as it lands, instantly trying to rise when she sees me. He places his hand at her back to keep her down and smiles.

"Morning, brother. Early for you, isn't it?" he asks, unperturbed by my interruption as he casually checks her ass for the mark I'm sure is blooming as we speak.

"It is," I say and walk over to the side table where I pick up the silver carafe of coffee and pour myself a cup while he wraps up with the woman.

"We'll finish this after lunch, Selene. What do you have? Six to go?"

"Yes, sir."

"You're dismissed."

"Thank you," the woman says.

I turn to watch her awkwardly bend to pull her panties up and adjust her pencil skirt. Her cheeks blaze as red as her ass I got a glimpse of. She clumsily picks up the folders on Zeke's desk and rushes out the door.

"Didn't mean to interrupt that," I tell Zeke who tucks a long, thin cane under his desk and takes his seat.

"Nothing I can't finish later," he says, rolling back and crossing his ankle over the opposite knee. "Selene would probably thank you for the reprieve. Her spelling is atrocious."

"But she's good looking enough to keep her employed."

"I don't trust her with the actual work."

"Of course not." I sit down on the couch and look out over the bustling street realizing how much I've missed New Orleans.

"What brings you here?" he asks.

"Your conversation with my wife."

"Ah."

"What exactly did you tell her about Kimberly?"

"Only the truth."

"How much of it?"

"Enough to leave her wanting more."

"Is this payback?"

"I'm sorry?"

"For Kimberly. For what happened with her?"

"You fell in love. She fell in love." He shrugs a shoulder, but I see there's more in his eyes. "What sort of payback are you expecting?"

"I took her from you. Now you want to take Isabelle from me."

"I offered Isabelle my protection."

"She doesn't need your protection. She has mine."

"But I believe her question is who will protect her from you."

"Not your problem. Stay away from her."

"Isabelle came to me. Not the other way around. And she had questions."

"Which you happily answered."

"Don't you wonder where she got the information? That's what would trouble me if I were you, brother."

"What do you mean?"

"You have her locked away. She didn't know you existed, either of us existed, until you took her. How would she know anything about Kimberly? More specifically, about Kimberly and me?"

I must look confused because he continues.

"That's what she wanted to know. If you stole Kimberly from me."

I wince at the wording. It's true though to some extent. They were together. Then we shared her. Then I took her.

"I think your little wife may not be as isolated as you think. She's getting her information somewhere. I wonder what else she knows. Wonder who is feeding her the information. And, of course, what she's giving away about us."

I stand up. "It doesn't matter. None of it matters anymore."

"What do you mean?"

"I think she's pregnant."

He doesn't say anything, just watches me.

"I'll know for sure in a few days."

"Is she aware?"

I shake my head. "As far as she knows she's been taking her daily birth control."

"But she hasn't."

"I swapped the pills out."

"Jesus." He just looks at me like he can't believe it and I turn away from his accusatory gaze. "She'll hate you, you know that, don't you?"

My chest tightens. "It doesn't matter," I say, my voice robotic. It wasn't supposed to matter. Not in the beginning.

"Because you'll have what you need to move to the next step of your plan."

"Taking the Bishop inheritance."

He snorts, shakes his head like he can't believe this.

I walk to the desk, grip the edges of it. "He killed her."

"Do you see what you're doing?" he asks, tilting his head to the side. "Do you see that you're destroying a life? And not just one."

I draw in a tight breath.

He stands up. "So what's your plan, big brother? You've taken the girl. Married her. Put your child inside her. What now? What happens after she gives birth?"

I grit my teeth, turn, and walk to the window.

"Take the child and bury Isabelle beside Nellie Bishop?" he asks.

That was the plan. Originally. When Isabelle Bishop was just a name.

"Find some flimsy explanation for Angelique who has grown to love Isabelle by the way."

Love.

"Let me ask you one more question because if there's one thing I don't want it's a repeat of the past."

Recycle an ugly past. Carlton Bishop's words.

I turn to my brother. "What do you mean?"

"I mean when Carlton Bishop finds out, given what he's tried to do, what he's succeeded in doing, how can you think he won't try to hurt her again? Or worse?"

45

ISABELLE

I'm getting sick in Jericho's bathroom the next afternoon when there's a knock on the door. Someone rattles the handle and I thank goodness for the lock.

"Isabelle?" It's Leontine.

"I'll be right there," I say, reaching up to flush the toilet and sitting back against the tub, the tiles cool beneath my bare thighs.

"Are you all right?" she asks. "Open the door. I brought you up some toast and ginger ale."

"I'm not hungry." How can she think I want to eat?

I push the hair off my forehead. It's sticking. Do most people break a sweat when they throw up? It's been so long since I've had a bug I can't remember.

I drag myself to my feet and run the tap to wash my face with icy water then stand back to look at my reflection. I look terrible. Exhausted and gaunt. I haven't been able to eat much the last few days. Maybe week. It shows and not in a good way.

"Isabelle. I'm calling a doctor."

"I'm fine," I say, hurrying to dry my hands and unlock the door. I open it to find Leontine looking more worried than I've ever seen her. She stands back when she sees me, looks me over. I'm wearing one of Jericho's T-shirts but am naked otherwise. Thankfully the shirt comes to about mid-thigh. It was the closest thing to me when I woke up and felt the vomit coming so I grabbed it and put it on. It still smells like him.

"You're not well."

"Just a bug. I'm sure it'll be over in a day or two." I look at the unmade bed just beyond her and want nothing more than to crawl back into it. I feel so tired and just wrung out.

"Come on," she says and takes my arm. "Just eat some toast. You'll feel better."

I look at the toast and sit on the edge of the bed.

"I'm fine, really. I need to shower. I promised Angelique I'd help her fix her book and I overslept." I've been sleeping longer than usual. It's not like me.

"She'll understand. Eat. I'll call a doctor."

"If I eat it, you'll leave me alone?"

She sighs but nods.

"I'm fine. Really. It's nothing." I pick up the toast and bite into it, managing two bites. "See. Fine." I take another bite. "Just please tell Angelique I'll be there as soon as I can." It takes all my strength to hurry across the room and go into my own bedroom through the adjoining door. I lean against the closed door once I'm alone, my hand on my stomach, waiting until the wave of nausea passes to move.

I walk across the room to the bathroom where once I'm inside, I lock the door. I switch on the shower and strip off Jericho's shirt, inhaling the scent of him as I pull it over my head. Wondering what the fuck I'm thinking when I catch myself.

Last night was strange. All of it. From Angelique considering me her mom now that I'm married to her dad, to Jericho losing his shit when he overheard her saying it. To that pillory and to what happened there.

I really think his intention was to punish me for Angelique's comment. As if I can control that. I understand his jealousy of my relationship with his daughter. She trusts me. And although she's only known me for a little while, I'm here, a constant in her life. Her father is still unreliable. One swimming lesson isn't going to change five years of history.

But when we got home. Wait. No. Not home. When we got back and I said I was hungry, he made me a sandwich. He wouldn't let me do it myself. Okay, don't go overboard. It was buttered bread. He probably just didn't want me passing out in that pillory. That would ruin his fun.

My mind wanders to the night I had the nightmare. To how he held me. Anchored me to him. But I shake my head, shake off the memory.

The memory of what happened with the pillory sends heat coursing through me and this time when my stomach flips, it's not nausea.

I smear toothpaste on my toothbrush and brush my teeth as I step into the shower.

What we did last night was different than I ever would have expected. The thought of how he took me and how I liked it, how much I liked it, I don't know. I should be humiliated, right? He locked me in that pillory and then took me the way he did. How debasing is that?

I came hard, though.

Although I have no doubt he can make that an unpleasant experience, too.

But that's the thing. This is where I'm stuck. It's like the sandwich. Like him whipping his own thigh with the belt rather than hurting me. Like him getting me a glass of water and holding me after my nightmare.

He may want to be a devil to me but he's struggling to keep up the façade. He takes care not to hurt me. More care than I've felt in the last three years living in the house where, according to at least half of my blood, I belong. Not Julia, not Carlton, no one since Christian died has made me feel like they would put my needs above theirs. And Jericho has.

And I remember what I said last night.

I remember the moment the words were out. I don't think he heard me. Or maybe he thought, like I did myself, that it was just a mix up. Me losing control of my thoughts in the heat of the moment. Me panting for him to make me come like only he can make me come.

I don't know. I don't know what's going on in this house or in my head.

I don't know what I want.

Thirsty, I turn my face up to the flow of the shower and drink but it's a mistake. The nausea that's now becoming familiar overwhelms me and I quickly switch off the water and grab a towel, dropping to my knees and raising the toilet seat at once. I throw up the little bit of water I just drank along with the toast. From beneath the cabinet, I hear my phone buzz. I'd moved it there from behind the bed a few days ago. I heave once, twice, and although nothing comes, I feel sick.

The phone buzzes again, stops, starts again. It's not like Julia to keep calling if I don't pick up. I have been calling her back when I see I've missed a call. She knows he could be in here anytime and if he caught me with the phone, I'm sure he'd take it away. So, after the next round of dry-heaving, I crawl toward the cabinet, open it and rummage for the phone. I sit back against the tub. The phone starts up again and I swipe to answer.

"Hey," I say to Julia. "I was sick, I'm sorry—"

"I've been calling for hours. Isabelle there's a problem." She sounds strange. Like she's upset. Very upset.

"What is it? Is it Matty?"

Someone enters the bedroom and a moment later tries the door but it's locked.

"Isabelle?" It's Jericho.

"Just a minute!" I call out in a panic. "I have to go," I say into the phone.

"Isabelle wait."

Nausea turns my stomach again as Jericho knocks and tries the handle again. "Doctor's here."

"I'm going to be sick," I tell Julia.

Just before I pull the phone away and turn my attention to the toilet, I hear her say something. "I have them! I found them. You're not—"

Again, I heave. More toast. I only ate a few bites how can there be more? My mouth tastes awful. I feel drained and empty.

"Isabelle. Open this door."

I puke in response. I put the phone back to my ear at the next break. "I have to go. I'll call you as soon as I can."

"Listen to me. Listen. The pills. I found them. They're here. Almost three months' worth. They're all here."

"What are you talking about?"

"Birth control, Isabelle."

"I'm coming in," Jericho calls out.

"No. I have them. I'm taking them. Oh god." I grip the edge of the toilet and lean over it and I swear my stomach feels like it's been turned inside out and as I heave, I hear what she's saying. Hear the panic in her voice. I remember taking the little packet of pills from inside their hot pink plastic case and popping them out. I remember thinking they looked different, just a little different. And I remember the few drops of blood I bled during the week I usually get my period. I thought it was stress.

I sit back down, and I count. And I barely register the popping of the lock. The opening of the door. Because this can't be.

No. God. No.

"Julia?" I say, just as a large hand closes over mine and I look up at the blur of him. The vomiting has tears streaming from my eyes.

The vomiting and the betrayal.

Jericho St. James stares down at me, hard and angry, his forehead furrowed, eyes blazing as he slips the phone from my hand, looks at the screen before he disconnects it, cutting Julia off mid-sentence and pocketing the phone.

"What did you do?" I ask him, crawling away from him those few feet until my back is against the tub. I'm still naked and freezing now, shivering even as sweat runs down my spine. "What did you do!" I scream and it's not a question. It's an accusation.

And I know with the next wave of nausea that has me doubling over the toilet what this is. Why I've felt sick. Why I haven't been able to keep anything down and why my favorite foods have me retching.

I'm pregnant.

I'm pregnant with Jericho St. James's baby.

THANK YOU

Thank you for reading *Devil's Pawn*. I hope you love Isabelle and Jericho's story.

Their story concludes in *Devil's Redemption* which is available now.

ALSO BY NATASHA KNIGHT

The Sacrifice Duet

The Tithing

The Penitent

The Augustine Brothers

Forgive Me My Sins

Deliver Me From Evil

Ruined Kingdom Duet

Ruined Kingdom

Broken Queen

The Devil's Pawn Duet

Devil's Pawn

Devil's Redemption

To Have and To Hold

With This Ring

I Thee Take

Stolen: Dante's Vow

The Society Trilogy

Requiem of the Soul

Reparation of Sin

Resurrection of the Heart

The Rite Trilogy

His Rule

Her Rebellion

Their Reign

Dark Legacy Trilogy

Taken (Dark Legacy, Book 1)

Torn (Dark Legacy, Book 2)

Twisted (Dark Legacy, Book 3)

Unholy Union Duet

Unholy Union

Unholy Intent

Collateral Damage Duet

Collateral: an Arranged Marriage Mafia Romance

Damage: an Arranged Marriage Mafia Romance

Ties that Bind Duet

Mine

His

MacLeod Brothers

Devil's Bargain

Benedetti Mafia World

Salvatore: a Dark Mafia Romance

Dominic: a Dark Mafia Romance

Sergio: a Dark Mafia Romance

The Benedetti Brothers Box Set (Contains Salvatore, Dominic and Sergio)

Killian: a Dark Mafia Romance

Giovanni: a Dark Mafia Romance

The Amado Brothers

Dishonorable

Disgraced

Unhinged

Standalone Dark Romance

Descent

Deviant

Beautiful Liar

Retribution

Theirs To Take

Captive, Mine

Alpha

Given to the Savage

Taken by the Beast

Claimed by the Beast

Captive's Desire

Protective Custody

Amy's Strict Doctor

Taming Emma

Taming Megan

Taming Naia

Reclaiming Sophie

The Firefighter's Girl

Dangerous Defiance

Her Rogue Knight

Taught To Kneel

Tamed: the Roark Brothers Trilogy

ABOUT THE AUTHOR

Natasha Knight is the *USA Today* Bestselling author of Romantic Suspense and Dark Romance Novels. She has sold over half a million books and is translated into six languages. She currently lives in The Netherlands with her husband and two daughters and when she's not writing, she's walking in the woods listening to a book, sitting in a corner reading or off exploring the world as often as she can get away.

Write Natasha here: natasha@natasha-knight.com

www.natasha-knight.com

Made in the USA
Las Vegas, NV
02 December 2023

81991804R00249